BEN'S BEA
BY
RICHARD F JONES

Also by Richard F Jones
A Flight Home
Dancing with the Devil
Time On Their Hands
Mountain Intrigue
Gabriella
A Highland Life
A Highland Affair
To the Top and Back Again
Doing It My Way
The Road to Freedom
Escape to Scotland
Explosive Voyage

©2024 Second Edition. Richard F Jones. All rights reserved. Without limiting the rights under copyright reserved above, no part of this book maybe reproduced, stored in or introduced into a retrieval system, or transmitted, in any form, or by any means (electrical, mechanical, photocopying, recording, or otherwise) without the written permission of both the copyright owner and the above publisher of this book.

This is a work of fiction. Names, characters, places brands, media and incidents are either the product of the author's imagination or are used fictitiously. The author acknowledges the trademarked status and trademark owners of various products referenced in this work of fiction, which have been used without permission. The publication/use of these trademarks is not authorised, associated with, or sponsored by the trademark owners.

To my dear wife Meg, without whose help the publication of this book would not have been possible.

PROLOGUE

You imagine when a bullet hits you that the pain will be searing. I was anticipating mind numbing misery, teeth grinding agony, but in my case it didn't happen, mainly I suppose because I passed out almost instantly. Fortunately the bullet in question travelled through my right shoulder and came out on the other side, thereby causing little permanent physical damage. In fact the healing process of the wound was far more painful than the event, as I was in constant discomfort and bound up with stitches, plasters and bandages and taking antibiotics for weeks.

I do remember coming round and looking up at the paramedics who were attending to me. I could also just about make out in the background police officers standing around my prone body. My wound required a trip in a siren wailing ambulance to the local hospital. Of the incident itself my recollections are almost as sparse. I had driven into the country near my home in Spain to embark on one of my favourite walks. At the top of a narrow twisting lane there is a small car park leading to a wooded track. It was a mild day, the sun was out. I recall getting out of my car, then bending into the back seat for my anorak. As I did so I heard the noisy roar of a car's revved up engine coming up the lane. I shut and locked my car's doors then began to set off into the wood. My back was to the oncoming vehicle but I heard it slew into the car park. The next sound was the bang of the gun going off and that was it. Afterwards they kept me in hospital for a couple of nights, while a policeman sat outside the door of my single bed ward.

To relate the whole story we have to go back some time before the incident.

CHAPTER ONE

It all began one clear Andalucian night. A southerly from Africa had blown away the rain. Wood smoke from my neighbours' fires scented the damp air. I was on my veranda watching the lights of the fishing boats out at sea when a strong beam, like a spotlight, searched across the water about a mile out.

That night a gale had raged. While I was asleep it kept rattling my bedroom window, keeping me awake. I needed to get up to close it. The road alongside my villa runs down to the beach. While I was at the window I saw a vehicle's headlights heading that way. My bedside clock showed ten past three, I thought it strange. In the height of the summer we did get courting couples and sometimes campers making their way to the beach at that time of night, but very rarely at that time of year.

I thought nothing more about it until the following morning. I was on my dawn walk with Ben; the southerly was still behind the breakers. He had gone ahead, to explore, see what he could find from last night's tide. I heard him bark. At that moment he was out of sight beyond the rocky point. When I caught up I saw an open wooden boat, about fifteen feet long, beached on the shoreline.

'What have we got here old boy,' I said. The boat had either been abandoned or become adrift in the previous day's storm. I doubted the latter, there was no mooring rope trailing loose; an outboard motor was still clamped to its stern and there was no name on its bow.

The section of coastline I live on is notorious for the trafficking of illegal immigrants from Africa. At night their assorted craft linger out amongst the fishing boats, then drift in ashore before dawn.

I spotted the girl later on in the morning when I was shopping. A rampant bougainvillea covers the archway into the square; moisture from the previous day's rain dripped from its foliage when we both walked underneath. An hourglass figure forced me to stare. Long legs, straight jet black hair hanging down her back to her waist, she certainly wasn't Spanish. Moroccan perhaps? A dusky complexion though couldn't conceal a shining black eye.

I completed my shopping and made my way to the bar. In the corner three men were sitting huddled together by themselves. They had rugged features and unkempt clothes and like the girl, North African colouring. While sipping at my cognac I tried to listen in but it was a language I didn't understand. They appeared to be arguing; their hands wildly gesticulating all the time.

Later, when Ben and I were on the beach I saw the girl again, idly kicking her feet at the incoming waves. His bounding activity caught her eye. She stopped to stroke him.

'The sea looks inviting,' I said. She was wearing shorts. Without shoes her legs looked even longer.

'It's nice to swim when the tide comes in over the warm sand,' she replied. Her broken English was quite good.

'Are you on holiday?' I asked. Our eyes met, the black eye was recent, there were also bruises on both arms.

'No we're just passing through,' she said and turned her head away.

For a while we walked together. She played with Ben; her movements were lithe and supple. Eventually we parted and I headed for home. At the top of the dunes I looked back. She was making for the old derelict bungalow at the end of the bay.

That evening I couldn't relax, I kept thinking about the girl. Unable to stand it anymore, I put on my shoes and called Ben. Outside it was dark, although the gale had eased. I strode out purposefully across the beach for the old bungalow. Ben was puffing behind me, trying to keep up.

When I got near I slowed down, there was a light on inside, and I could hear music, gypsy-type music. A swirling violin and a guitar produced a compelling rhythm. I crept closer and peered in through a cracked windowpane. A fire inside created dancing shadows on the crusted walls. Then I saw the girl's body hurtle past the window. Salt spray had left a film of grime on the glass. Straining to get a better look I rubbed on the cracked pane. The glass was weak, my hand broke through and protruded into the room.

The music stopped, loud voices echoed from inside, Ben barked. In panic I dragged my hand back through the aperture, slashing my wrist on the fractured glass. Blood gushed out, preventing any thought of running away.

A huge rough looking man came out and said to me.' What do you want Señor?' He was one of the men in the bar; tall and thickset with wild black hair, just like the girl. His shirt was open to the waist, a dangling medallion hovered in a chest of curly dark hair.

'I was worried about the girl,' I replied. 'I saw her today. She had such bruises, now you seem to be throwing her around.'

'Señor she is my daughter.'

'But that's no way to treat her.'

He stared at me.

'Iolanthe,' he called inside. She emerged looking amazing in a white halter top and black tights.

'Iolanthe this man thinks we are treating you badly.'

She looked at me knowingly. 'Señor, they are not harming me,' she said awkwardly. 'We are acrobats, from a circus in northern Spain. I am injured.' She pointed to her face. 'I misjudged one of my turns and crashed into the bandstand.'

'We had better see to your wrist my friend,' the big one said. They took me inside. The girl bathed my cut, smiling at me all the time. I felt foolish.

'We have come south to find a little warmth, to help with my injuries,' she said while dabbing iodine. It hurt, I jumped, and she laughed. 'You see my shoulder is strained too but I have to keep my legs in training. This cut is going to need stitching.'

The big man drove me to the hospital in a battered camper van. I needed six stitches, they kept me in for the night. Ben remained with the girl in the bungalow on the beach.

* * * * *

Next morning I was discharged and took the local bus back to my villa. After I had washed and shaved I got out my old Mercedes and drove down the pot-holed track to the old derelict bungalow at the end of the bay. The car's aged springs moaned all the way. The camper van that had taken me to hospital wasn't parked outside. I was concerned about Ben. Maybe they had taken flight and gone off with him. His barking response when I rapped my fist on the rotting wooden door quickly dispelled my worry. The girl opened it and Ben came bounding out leaping up at me with affection, nearly bowling me over. The girl shrieked with delight. Again she looked stunning. That day she wore a tight fitting red polo neck pullover and clinging blue jeans. Her hair had been pinned up at the back in a bun.

'I was getting worried about you,' she said. 'Ben was also beginning to fret.'

We'd moved inside the bungalow. The conditions in there were, to say the least, basic. There was a rickety wooden table and some dilapidated chairs, but not much else. Sleeping bags were rolled up against the walls and there were a few oil lamps spread about. She enquired about the cut.

'Oh it's nothing,' I said, trying to make light of it. 'Have the men folk gone away?' I asked.

'Every day they have to go out to try and find work,' she replied. 'We are self employed. If we don't work we can't eat.'

'How long do you intend to stay here?'

'Probably until my shoulder gets well enough for me to resume full time training. Then we will go back to the circus, but it is cold up north.'

We talked some more, then when it was time to leave I said I would take her into town if she liked and buy her some breakfast, to which she agreed. Ben had come to no harm and remained relaxed in her company as we drove. Having her long legs next to me in the passenger seat was certainly stimulating. I took her to a café I knew where we would get a decent breakfast. We sat outside in the sun and tucked into croissants, bacon, coffee and brandy. She certainly possessed a healthy appetite.

Our conversation roamed over many things, and I was able to find out a bit more about her background. She told me her family had always been a circus act. Her mother, who had died in her middle age, had also been a trapeze artist. The three men travelling with her were her father and her two brothers. She and the brothers were now the major element of the act, but she was the star attraction since her mother's death, as well the chief cook and housewife to the men. 'Sometimes I get very tired,' she confessed. 'I think that's how I missed my turn. I was just over-tired.'

I watched at her tucking into her food. Her nubile body was beautifully formed in athletic maturity. Her face betrayed a youthfulness that suggested she would only have been in her late twenties. 'What sort of work do the men do when they go off for the day?' I asked her.

'I don't really know and I don't think they would tell me if I asked,' she replied. 'As long as they bring back some money for me to buy food I don't care. At certain times of year they do fruit picking but I don't know if they do that here.'

She told me her family was from Morocco, but she had lived most of her life in Northern Spain. Because they travelled so much she'd only occasionally attended school and admitted that her education was therefore incomplete. 'As soon as my body was developed enough I became part of the act,' she added.

When we'd finished eating I offered her a lift back to the bungalow but she declined.

'I'm not used to eating such rich food,' she responded. 'I need to walk it off or I'll be putting on weight. Then, I'll be in real trouble.' She made a fuss of Ben, thanked me for the breakfast and I watched in furtive desire as she walked away from the café with a fashion model's strut. Afterwards I did some shopping at the supermarket and then returned to my villa with Ben. After the trauma of the previous day I was glad to get on my veranda and lie back to bask in the sun.

That night I was again disturbed in the early hours by the sound of a vehicle heading down the road towards the beach. This time I was sufficiently motivated to get out of bed and take a proper look. Grabbing my binoculars I made my way out to the veranda and in doing so managed to disturb Ben, who followed me outside. I was only wearing a dressing gown and sandshoes.

'You must be quiet,' I whispered to him as we crept along the veranda. The night remained warm and moonlit. At that moment the only sound was the incoming swish of the waves.

Near the beach I could just make out the whiteness of a van. I trained my binoculars on it, but it was partially hidden amongst the trees so I couldn't get a proper look, although I would have sworn it was the camper van that had driven me to hospital the previous evening.

I pulled over a chair to sit and watch. Ben slumped down at my feet. For some time nothing much happened. There was no movement around the van or on the beach. Eventually Ben got fed up and went back to his bed. I was about to do the same when suddenly, out at sea, I again saw a spotlight flash across the water. That produced activity around the van, three or maybe four men got out. The trees still partially blocked my view making it difficult to be accurate. I did, however, clearly see the headlights of the van flash on and off three times, pointing out to sea. Then in the stillness of the night I could hear a man talking on what I presumed was a mobile phone. He was speaking in Spanish. A couple of the other men went to stand on the shore line. It wasn't long afterwards when I spotted a small craft heading for the shore. As it got nearer I could see it was a tiny rowing boat with what looked like four people on board. The larger boat with the searchlight had by then disappeared around the cliff at the end of the bay, and, I presumed, back out to sea. Gradually I began to hear the swish of oars cutting through the water.

When the rowing boat was near to the beach one of the men jumped into the sea and ran ashore with a rope. The two men on the beach waded out to meet him. Between the three of them they pulled the rowing boat ashore. The other three men eventually disembarked carrying kit bags and small parcels. It was difficult to describe them as they all wore hooded anoraks and what appeared to be jeans. Collectively they all pushed the boat back out into deeper water and slowly it began to drift disconsolately further down the bay away from them.

I heard the van's engine start up. All the men who'd been on the shore ran to it and jumped in. I dashed back into my villa, grabbed my mobile phone, dialled the number of the Guardia and was just in time to see the van belonging to my Moroccan friends disappear up the adjacent road.

Needless to say by the time the Guardia arrived the van had long gone and the beach was silent and empty again. One of the officers called in on me, while his colleague and another police car drove down to the beach. By then I had changed into my daytime attire. Ben barked when he heard the policeman's voice in the hall. After explaining the details of the incident I accompanied him down to the shoreline. The other policemen were on the beach flashing torch lights out to sea. Eventually we caught sight of the rowing boat some distance away, still drifting in the water. Two of the policemen headed that way. The other two took a statement from me, while I sat in the back of their car. I did explain to them my suspicions about the group of Moroccans, my recognition of the van and their occupation of the old derelict bungalow at the end of the bay. Afterwards I walked back to my villa and in time they all drove away.

* * * * *

Next morning I took Ben down to the beach for his morning walk. We headed again in the direction of the bungalow at the end of the bay. I could see the rowing boat which by then had been washed ashore some distance away. Then, to my surprise, Iolanthe was walking towards me on the beach, wading through the shallow water of the incoming tide. She was dressed in a pair of shorts and a dark blue t-shirt. Her hair was tied up in a bun again. I waved and called a greeting as we got near.

'Adam I'm glad to see you, I've been so worried,' she said and explained to me that her men folk had not returned last night from their previous days work. 'And then, very early this morning the police were knocking on my door. My Spanish is not that good and I couldn't understand much of what they said. From what I could gather though they were looking for the men and the camper van. They also said I could not stay in the bungalow any longer as it is a private property.'

I walked with her back to the bungalow, while Ben played alongside in the sea. As we strolled I told her what I'd seen the previous night. She was shocked. 'I can't believe they would get involved in something like that. That's terrible,' she said.

'I'm pretty sure it was their van,' I responded.

As we got closer to the bungalow I could see the van had not returned. 'I had better go in and wait there for them,' she said. 'If they don't come back I don't know what I am going to do.' She ran her hand over the top of her head and looked a forlorn, if rather beautiful figure.

'I'll take Ben back to my place,' I said. 'We'll have our breakfast then I'll come down to the bungalow in my car and see if your men have returned. If they haven't I'll take you to the police station and we'll see what they have to say. My Spanish is quite good and I know one or two of the blokes there.'

So that's what we did. Unfortunately on my way back across the beach I ran into Colin Wright, my neighbour and his two noisy dogs. One is a big Lurcher type and the other is what I would call a horrible little yapper. As soon as they saw us they started barking and running in stupid circles around Ben, something he hates.

'The early bird catches the worm eh?' Wright said with a supercilious grin on his face. I feigned ignorance. 'Couldn't help but see you talking to that glamorous piece of feminine pulchritude,' he added.

'Oh her,' I replied succinctly, not wishing to elucidate any more.

I had to tolerate Colin Wright, not only because he was my nearest neighbour, but also because I acted as his financial adviser, which was my main income earning employment in Spain. I worked under the umbrella of a larger set up but I did it on a self employed basis. My other occupation consisted of being a writer of fictional novels, which didn't make me much money at all. Colin is an ex-pat who moved out to Spain when he retired. According to him, at the time, his house in south London was worth 'a bomb.' It was at the height of the property boom and from the proceeds he had more than enough to buy the villa in Spain. To begin with his wife joined him in the venture, but she couldn't stand the life here and went back to London to live with her sister. As far as I know they still remain married. 'How is my money doing?' Wright enquired when my response to his questions about the girl dried up.

'It's a quiet time at the moment,' I said. 'The markets are a bit flat. But as you know they go up and down all the time.'

'I hope you are looking after it for me Adam. I'm relying on you.'

I confirmed that I was indeed looking after it then finally managed to extract myself from his presence, much to Ben's satisfaction.

Later that morning I drove to the old bungalow. There was still no sign of the camper van outside when I drew up. Iolanthe must have heard my car as she came outside to greet me. Her face still bore a worried look.

'There's still no sign of them,' she said as I got out of the car.

'Have you a mobile phone?' I asked.

She shook her head in a negative response. 'They all have, but I don't.'

'Do you know any of the numbers?'

She shook her head again. 'I'm afraid I'm not very technically minded.'

I looked at my watch. It was after eleven o'clock. 'We'd better go up to the police station and see what they have to say then,' I said. 'Do you have your papers?'

She went inside the bungalow to fetch them, change into a skirt and collect a jacket. Afterwards I helped her to try and secure the dilapidated door. All their goods were still scattered about inside. It looked as though she had made an attempt to tidy and pack some of them together. No way would the door lock properly, but we did the best we could.

At the police station we were ushered into a back room. I knew one of the men in there and the other one was one of those who'd called at my place on their way to the beach the previous night. Thankfully Iolanthe's papers were in order. 'You cannot continue to stay at the bungalow on the beach,' the one I knew said to her. 'I know it is in disrepair but the property is still privately owned, which means you are trespassing. You will have to move out today.' She looked across at me with big, wide, scared brown eyes.

'Do you know the make and registration number of your family's camper van?' he then asked her.

She hadn't a clue about the number plate, but between her and me we managed to cobble together a rough guess at the description of the type of van. 'Acting on what Señor Adam has told us and what we have seen for ourselves we have put out an alert for it's apprehension,' the police officer said. 'We have classed it as a suspected case of assisting illegal immigrants,' he continued. Again Iolanthe's eyes met mine. He then questioned her about her family's background, the circus where they worked in Northern Spain and what she knew about their activities since they'd been in the south of the country. She confessed she knew very little about the men's recent work.

'But what does the lady do if her family do not return for her?' I asked.

The policeman thought for a few moments. He was a tall, unshaven, dark haired man in his early thirties. 'We would have to take her into custody and maybe eventually hand her over to the Social Security. It could be deemed that she had been aiding and assisting criminal activities,' he said.

Iolanthe and I again stared at each other. 'We'll have to talk about it,' I responded quickly to the policeman. 'I'll let you know what conclusions we come to before the day is out.'

That's how we left it for the interim. They withheld Iolanthe's passport and papers, then insisted that she did not leave town in the immediate future. We left the police station together and walked to a restaurant for lunch. I ordered a bottle of Rioja which I badly needed.

While we ate we discussed the alternatives open to her. It transpired she had very little money. Enough euros to buy some food and bits of housekeeping, but certainly not enough to pay for hotel accommodation. Even the bus fare back to the circus in the North of Spain would be impossible on the amount of cash she had. Eventually I said that she had better come and stay with me for a couple of nights to see if her men folk returned. If they didn't and if the police agreed I would lend her the bus fare to travel back north. The only other alternative would have been for her to go into police custody.

With the benefit of hindsight I don't know why I had agreed to be so generous. I wasn't exactly flush with money myself. That this girl had made a hit with me was not in doubt. And she and her family had acted kindly towards me on the night when I slashed my wrist, so in some respect I felt I owed her something for that, but except for her gorgeous looks and what she'd told me and the police about her background, I really knew nothing else about her. And at that moment I did know that her family appeared to be involved in criminal activities but, I suppose all of us men are suckers for a pretty girl at some time or another.

* * * * *

When we had finished eating we returned to the police station and told them of our immediate plans, to which they agreed, on the condition that I informed them of any change in the circumstances, and that she reported in to the police station every two days. 'We will rely on you to do that Señor Adam,' the policeman I knew said to me sternly. They still retained her passport and papers. So all of a sudden I had voluntarily implicated myself into the machinations of her life.

I drove her back to the old bungalow and for an hour or two she packed together the items which she would need or were of any value; all that we could get into my car anyway. The rest we had to leave at the bungalow for a later time. Her men folk did not return that afternoon, so after a suitable time lapse, she wrote out a note for them about where she would be staying, which we pinned to the front door, before driving back to my place with the Mercedes fully laden with her belongings.

To my horror Colin Wright was passing my front gate with his two stupid dogs when we were unloading the car. The dogs began to bark, then needless to say Wright found it necessary to approach us to make some sarcastic comment. 'You're entertaining a visitor?' he said while leering at Iolanthe. 'Lucky man,' he added, nodding in her direction.

'Yes, just for a couple of days,' I replied, while continuing to busy myself with the unpacking. 'A family friend,' I said and carried the box at hand into the house while keeping my back to him.

'Of course,' I heard him say as I disappeared inside. By the time I next came outside, he and his yappers had gone.

'I wish I had a lovely home like this,' Iolanthe said as we moved around inside. My villa is not that spacious. There is a large open plan living/dining room, with a kitchen, half portioned off by a breakfast bar. There are two bedrooms. One en-suite and another separate bathroom off the small hallway. The accommodation is therefore suitable for two people. At the front is a balcony veranda with a marvellous view out to sea. The roof consists of another terrace on which there is a chimney barbecue. From there on a clear day you can see a view across the Mediterranean to the Atlas Mountains of Africa. 'Great,' was Iolanthe's added response on completion of the tour. I began to carry her things into the spare bedroom, while indicating that it was to be her accommodation. Ben followed us around, sniffing every bag and box.

When all the sorting out was done Iolanthe and I were left standing in the middle of my lounge looking at each other, both wondering what to do or say. At the back of my mind I had a good idea of what I wanted to do with her, but caution remained my watchword. I still knew so little about her, yet somehow I had got myself into a situation where I was sharing my home with her, which in effect also meant I was sharing my life with her as well. I decided at that moment that the safest thing to do was to make us both a cup of coffee.

'You have so many books,' she said to me, pointing at my bookshelves, while I was waiting for the kettle to boil. Ben had settled at her feet on the lounge rug.

'I'm a writer,' I replied. 'Those in that corner,' I said pointing to the spot when I returned from the kitchen area with the coffee, 'are all mine.' She turned to look. Then I had a full view of her long shiny black hair, her pert rear and long legs. I wanted to reach out and touch it all. Regrettably the coffee cups were still in my hands.

'Seriously,' she responded, then added after I nodded my confirmation of her question. 'How clever. Oh I wish I could write,' she said.

'Well you can read them if you like. It might inspire you to begin.' I picked one of my books out of the shelf and passed it to her.

She took it in her hands and caressed the cover. 'H'm,' she said. 'There's only one problem with that,' she added.

'What's that?' I asked.

'I can't read, or write.'

* * * * *

We settled down to drink the coffee and talk. As time passed I became more and more conscious of the dilemma I had put myself in. I was completely unused to sharing my home with anybody except Ben. Years ago there had been a live-in girlfriend but since then nothing resembling that sort of relationship had reappeared. There had been a few casual affairs and one night stands which had involved sharing a bed for a night or so, but nothing more than that. I suggested I take her out for a meal that evening.

'Adam I can't have you buying me meals all the time. I'm imposing on you enough already by staying here. I can cook you know. At least let me be of some use by helping to cook our meals.'

So that's what we did. Between us we managed to cook spaghetti bolognese for our supper. I enjoyed her company in the kitchen and she produced a different flavour to my usual concoction of that recipe. Alas, there was still this enormous temptation to put my hands about her, but somehow I resisted, mainly I guess because Ben kept getting under both our feet. Like me he was also unused to company around the house.

The evening proved to be difficult. After we had eaten we strolled together along the beach with Ben. The rolling foamy white waves stood out in the darkness. Afterwards in the bungalow she asked me to read to her some passages from my novels. She stretched out on the settee while I sat upright in the armchair and read the stories aloud. I needed to concentrate hard on the page in front of me to stop my eyes from wandering in her direction.

'That's marvellous,' she kept repeating when I finished each reading. 'You are so very clever. I wish I could do that.' The flattery was invigorating.

When it was time to go to bed we both became fidgety and slightly embarrassed. I was able to overcome my edginess by taking Ben out for his final visit of the night. While we were strolling around the garden, he woofed. Only once. An agitated stifled woof. Something had disturbed him or caught his attention. He possessed a sniffer dog's nose and at that moment it was working overtime. 'What is it?' I said. His head kept roaming the air like a periscope. I walked him around the edge of the garden. He sniffed here and there but there was nothing. When we got back inside Iolanthe had gone to her bedroom. I called out, 'Good night.' She repeated the phrase and I retired to my room.

The incident outside preyed on my mind and so what with that and thoughts of this nubile young body lying only a few feet away from me made sleep difficult. Eventually I must have drifted off. However it wasn't long before I was reawakened by Ben barking. I got up, put on a dressing gown and tiptoed to the lounge area. He was standing at the patio window still clearly alert and on guard. He wagged his tail when he saw me. 'What is it old chap?' I said. He whimpered, jumped at me and put his paws on my chest. Something had clearly disturbed him. I looked out through the patio window. There was a full moon, but I saw nothing move. As quietly as I could I crept back into my bedroom and looked out of the window there. Ben followed me. Suddenly I saw the shadow of a figure move on the road outside. I couldn't see the actual body but the shadow was of human form. I opened the window to try and get a better look, but it had gone, there was nothing in that spot anymore.

Our movements must have roused Iolanthe. I heard her bedroom door open. Next moment she was standing, framed in my bedroom doorway, wearing only a nightdress. Her long hair cascaded down over her shoulders into her bosom. Ben ran towards her affectionately.

'Is everything all right?' she said, while stroking him.

'Don't know,' I responded. 'Something out there disturbed Ben. I think I saw somebody moving around.'

'Oh Lord,' she replied. 'I hope it isn't anything bad.'

'You never know in these parts. Most of the time it's Ok, but we do get bouts of crime.' She looked at me with a worried expression. The tension in her face made her look even more beautiful. 'Perhaps they won't bother if they know there's a dog here,' I added.

'Let's hope so,' she said.

I took Ben back to his bed and tried to settle him down again. When I turned back for my room Iolanthe was still standing in the doorway.

'I was having trouble sleeping,' she said to me. At that moment standing in front of me was everything any normal red blooded man could possibly desire. Large areas of dark skinned naked flesh were visible around the edges of the nightdress. What was underneath appeared even more inviting. Her lips were slightly pouted. Even in the semi darkness her eyes looked vibrantly excited. I guess I allowed my resolution to weaken. I claim any other heterosexual man would have reacted in a similar manner.

Without saying anything I pulled her into my arms. Her response was welcoming. Our lips met, firstly into a soft sweet kiss, which prolonged into a deeper more searching exploration. My hands met no resistance as they wandered over her partly covered body. When we came out of that first passionate embrace I lifted the night dress off and over her head, then turned her around and into my bedroom. Neither of us said anything. I shut the door and we both climbed onto the bed completely naked.

CHAPTER TWO

Looking back on it now I suppose that was the beginning of the real trouble for me. With the benefit of hindsight I realise I had been gullible. I had weakened in the face of temptation. Without doubt our night of sex together was the highlight of my sparse sexual career. The curves of her body, the soft sensuous texture of her skin and lips provided a wanderlust for me to utilise. She also used her lips and tongue expertly to evoke erotic pleasures in me I had not experienced before. Large breasts and sumptuous nipples provided a playground for me to indulge myself on. How many times we did it I couldn't count. In between there were various bouts of sleep, but each time I was reawakened by the roaming actions of her hands, tongue and lips on me.

Eventually when dawn came the birds singing outside awoke me. At that moment I felt so satisfied that I was tempted to join in with their dawn chorus. I turned over and discovered that the space alongside me on the bed was empty. She's gone, was my initial thought. Done a runner? She wouldn't have been the first. Or had I perhaps dreamt it all. When I leant over and detected the fragrance of her perfume on the sheets I knew I hadn't dreamt it. Stiffly I got out of bed, put on my dressing gown and padded out into the living area. Ben came to greet me. There was no sign of Iolanthe. 'Where is she, old boy?' I said to him. He whimpered an unintelligible reply. Quickly I moved towards her bedroom. I was somewhat relieved to see that all her things were still in there. My other assumption though was partly true. After I'd put on some clothes I began to organise to take Ben out. As I was putting on his lead I spotted her on the beach, jogging, wearing only a t-shirt and shorts. Her long hair was flowing decoratively in the breeze. She looked fantastic. I felt another stirring in my loins.

By the time Ben and I made it to the beach gate she had also reached it. 'I was getting concerned,' I said.

'I'm sorry. I didn't mean to worry you. It's a beautiful morning and I still have to train my legs.' Her glistening white toothed smile lightened up my soul. 'If it's all right with you I'll take a shower and then I'll make us some breakfast,' she said. I nodded in agreement. 'Is there anything you would like?' she asked.

'Oh just some toast and coffee,' I responded, then headed off towards the beach with Ben.

As we walked I again conjectured on my situation. A part of me was obviously ecstatic with excitement, but deep down I still wondered what I had got myself into. I really knew no more about this girl and her family than I did after our initial conversations. Yet I had still given her the freedom of my home. At that moment she could be rifling through all my personal possessions with an intent to steal or misuse them at some time. Since her arrival I hadn't particularly locked anything away or even put important things out of sight. I considered I had been foolish in that respect and made a mental note to make amends when I got back.

My fears appeared unfounded when Ben and I returned to the villa. She was in the kitchen area preparing the breakfast. I attended to Ben's food needs and headed for the bathroom to wash and then the bedroom to change my shirt. From what I could see nothing had been tampered with. No cupboards or drawers appeared to have been opened. Even the unmade bed looked untouched. Glancing through the open door into her room I could see that she had made her bed and tidied up somewhat.

'What do you want to do with me today?' she asked when I was back in the kitchen area.

I resisted the obvious sexual response and said, 'I think we'd better go to the supermarket and stock up on some food.'

'I'm sorry,' she said. 'I'm being such a nuisance,' she said.

I shook my head. 'And while we are in town we should also go back to the police station to find out the latest developments.' She pulled a face. While we dallied over breakfast I made complementary comments about our night together in bed.

'Well I'm pleased I'm of some use to you,' she said, with a grin.

At the police station there was no more news of her family. However, they agreed to allow her to stay at my place for another seven days, as long as she continued to report in every two. They still kept her passport and papers. We went home and ate baguettes for lunch. Afterwards we ended up in bed together. Again I fell asleep and again when I awoke she had gone from the bed. When I padded outside she was lying out on the balcony on a li-lo. There was this terrific temptation to gather her in my arms again and take her back to bed, but I resisted the urge.

For the next couple of days our lives proceeded in much the same manner. One afternoon she wanted to go back to the old derelict bungalow and pick up a few more of her things. More pertinently her guitar, she said. That evening she surprisingly entertained me with a selection of folk songs; some Spanish, some Moroccan and a few more traditional American ones. I was mightily impressed. She had a deep, clear, resonant voice and a certain degree of professionalism.

* * * * *

Big problems began, however, a few days later. That day I had to go out to see one of my financial clients. I couldn't take Iolanthe with me for obvious reasons and as I didn't know how long the appointment would last it would have been impossible for her to wait in the car in the heat. So while I journeyed off she remained with Ben at the villa. I did wonder if I was being foolish to trust her so.

My appointment took longer than I had bargained for. During those months it was becoming increasingly difficult to find any competitive forms of investments for the clients. The recession had taken hold and times were hard for everybody. When I pulled up outside my front gate, on my return, Colin Wright was waiting for me.

'You've had visitors then,' he said as I got out of the Mercedes.

I tended to take everything Colin said with a pinch of salt so I muttered something like 'Oh yes.'

'Although I guess they were actually visitors of the young lady,' he continued. Once more I hesitated over my reply. He was always fishing for gossip or scandal, so I just looked at him with a questioning face. 'Yes, three very Moroccan looking men,' he confirmed. 'Stayed about half an hour,' he added with a condescending nod of his head.

'Oh them,' I responded succinctly and made haste to get inside the villa, leaving him standing in his driveway with a lot of unanswered questions remaining in his head.

Ben leapt up at me with his usual enthusiastic welcome when I entered the door. Iolanthe was out on the balcony sun bathing on the li-lo. I called out 'Hello,' to her as I switched on the kettle. She came inside.

'Everything OK?' I asked. She was wearing a skimpy blue swimsuit.

'Fine. It's hot out there,' she said. 'You were gone a long time?'

While I brewed a cup of tea I explained to her some of the difficulties of being a financial advisor in the recent economic climate. She listened patiently but said nothing about her visitors. When I had downed my tea I made moves to take Ben out for his beach walk. I still made no mention of it and neither did she. She made some excuse about wanting to practise on her guitar so Ben and I went out alone. I was glad of the time and space to think clearly by myself. Colin Wright had no reason to lie to me or concoct anything on a matter like that. He clearly thought he was showing neighbourly concern.

I decided to make for the old derelict bungalow to see if anything had happened there. Iolanthe had been right, the sun was hot. Ben romped in and out of the incoming waves. When I reached the bungalow there was evidence of tyre marks near the front door. The note we'd left on it was gone. I pushed against it and it opened with a laboured squeak. Inside the remains of the Moroccan's possessions had also gone. I looked around the nooks and spaces and inside the cupboards, but everything that would have been theirs had disappeared. The door emitted another creaking squeak as I closed it on my way out. I removed my shoes and padded slowly in and out of the water on my way back across the beach to my villa. What was this girl really up to, I thought? If she didn't want to hide the fact, why had she not told me about her visitors? Was she really setting me up for something nasty?

All these thoughts rotated in my head as I approached the villa. I was no nearer to any answers when I got inside.

* * * * *

She was still out on the balcony, plucking away at the guitar. I prepared Ben's food, then poured myself a large whisky and soda before I joined her.

'Why didn't you tell me about your visitors?' I asked as I sat down on an adjacent chair and supped on the whisky. She stopped strumming on the guitar and looked at me with a questioning expression.

'They weren't here very long,' she said defensively. 'It wasn't my family,' she added quickly.

'Who was it then?'

She hesitated before replying. 'Some friends of ours from up North. They had come down to visit us and seen the note on the bungalow door.'

'Your stuff has gone from the bungalow.'

She put the guitar down on the floor alongside her. 'I know,' she said. 'I told them to take it. The longer it remained at the bungalow the more chance there was of it being stolen or damaged. And I didn't want to burden you with it all. I'm causing you enough trouble already.'

There was no way I could verify anything she said. Colin Wright didn't know what the members of her family looked like. To him they would all be just people from Africa. If I questioned him further on the matter his face would probably bear that 'I told you it would be trouble,' expression.

'But I'm surprised you didn't tell me that you entertained visitors in my house.' I said and took another gulp on the whisky.

Again she hesitated before replying. 'Adam I am sorry. Of course I was going to tell you later on, but you'd rushed in to take Ben out and your head was still full of your work problems. I was going to tell you when we sat down together. I repeat they weren't here very long and most of the time we were outside on the balcony. They didn't really stay much in the house. I had to let them in as they'd travelled such a long way to see me.'

I still didn't know whether to believe her or not. I took another sip on the whisky. 'Have they been in touch with your men folk?' I asked.

She shook her head in a negative response. 'They knew where we were staying at the bungalow and they thought we were still all there. Then when they saw the note on the door they came over here. While they were here they tried phoning my family on their mobiles but there was no response. If the police hadn't have insisted that I remain here with you I maybe would have gone on with them to save you any more trouble. They were heading for Gibraltar.'

My mind was in a turmoil. I really didn't know what to believe. She had said it all so plausibly, but I'd already realised that she was a clever girl. Whatever, I had work to do, preparing quotes and such like after my afternoons meeting, so I retired to my bedroom to get on with it while she cooked the agreed supper.

Our meal was interspersed with edgy dialogue. The honeymoon was definitely over. To ease matters we decided to go out that evening to a local bar, The Cactus, for a drink. That visit, in a way, added another complication to our relationship. The bar itself was quite small, situated in the centre of a local shopping complex. I had been there before and it usually attracted a lively crowd. On certain nights of the week there was also some entertainment. A solo singer, or sometimes a small group would perform. There was a Karaoke evening as well, which I didn't attend. On all those occasions it was usually packed. The bar could only accommodate seventy or eighty people, which made it intimate, interesting and hot. There was a tiny stage in the corner which the performers had to squeeze onto with their equipment. That night there was a solo singer/guitarist who performed folk and classic rock tunes. He was quite good. We both enjoyed the evening and it had eased the tension between us.

While walking back to the villa Iolanthe said to me, 'I can do that.'

'What do you mean, sing and play on the stage?'

'Yes. I used to do it for the circus troupe.' We were walking side by side on the sodium lamp lit streets. 'Some nights, after the audience had gone home, for a special occasion, we would put on our own show, just for the troupe and their families,' she continued. 'I used to do quite a good singing turn, accompanying myself on the guitar. I'd show off a bit but usually it went down well. If I could do it here it would help me to pay you some rent. I can't go on sponging off you like this.' She had stunned me into silence. 'And it would be a bit of fun,' she added quickly.

'Well, OK' I replied. 'If you think you can manage it. You'd have to audition though.'

That conversation changed the whole atmosphere of our evening and we ended up going to bed together in my room.

* * * * *

Next day, while Iolanthe honed up on her singing and guitar playing I headed off to the police station. I still wasn't happy about the events of the previous day. Despite our romantic and sexual attraction I continued to wonder, and have doubts, about her intrusion into my life and where it was leading me.

One of the officers we'd seen before was on duty that day. He confessed that there had been no progress in sighting Iolanthe's men folk. 'I was only asking,' I continued, 'because someone I met in a bar the other night thought he had seen them around the town. He'd recognised them from when he used to see them at a bar in the square.'

The officer wrote a note about it on a piece of paper in front of him. 'I will tell the chief and we will increase our search locally,' he said to me.

'What about the potential illegal immigrants?'

'Nobody has been picked up in this area on that suspicion,' he replied.

I felt somewhat disillusioned by his responses. I knew that in Spain things do take longer to achieve than in the UK. I asked him how long they wanted to keep Iolanthe under house arrest.

'I will speak to the chief on that as well and let you know next time you bring her in,' he said to me.

CHAPTER THREE

When I got back to the villa she was still rehearsing on her guitar. I enjoyed listening to her sing, but I was beginning to think a whole morning of it would have been too much for me to bear. Over the next few days, she practiced her singing, while I took Ben for long walks and then later pursued my financial advisory work as best as I could. Once a day she would accompany Ben and me for her jogging exercise. There was not much progress on my writing.

In Spain, the luncheon break can occur anytime between noon and four o'clock, so one day, around noon, we went to the Cactus bar for some midday tapas. Iolanthe took her guitar with her. As I'd hoped there weren't many people there at that time of the day. The ex-pats were hardly out of bed by then and the Spanish tended to eat nearer three o'clock. I knew the owner of the bar, Sylvia, a battle hardened, well built blonde woman, spouting a harsh East End of London accent. She was not really to my taste, although she was a good cook and kept a decent pint of beer.

We ordered some drinks and something to eat, then I told her about Iolanthe's wish to sing there. She was initially unresponsive to the idea. 'Oh they all want to come and sing here,' she replied discouragingly. 'It's a tough audience in this bar and all the acts don't all go down very well, but I still have to pay them.'

I looked around, there were only two other men in there at that time. 'Perhaps she could sing a song or two for you now,' I said, 'then you can judge for yourself?'

At first I thought she was going to refuse, then she said, 'Oh all right. But make it snappy. I've got meals to cook.'

Iolanthe settled herself and the guitar onto a bar stool, strummed a couple of practise chords, then went straight into one of her American folk songs. Sitting with her long legs crossed in front of her, supporting the guitar, made her look seductively provocative.

She sang very well. Her voice resonated around the bar. The song only lasted a couple of minutes. When she finished the two men at the back of the bar both clapped.

'Oh, OK, not bad.' Sylvia said, while puffing on a cigarette.

'I'll do one more. A faster one this time,' Iolanthe cut in quickly, then went straight into a more upbeat tune. Again it didn't last very long and once more, when she finished singing, the guys clapped enthusiastically.

'All right, I'll give you a go,' Sylvia said to her. 'But I can't pay you much first time out. I can only manage twenty euros. Times are hard. If it works out OK I'll consider paying you more next time.' She consulted her diary booklet. 'I've got a spot free next Thursday,' she said. 'You can go on for half an hour before one of the more well known bands.'

When we had finished eating we left with a promise to call in again before the following Thursday. On our way out the two men at the back of the bar made complimentary remarks to Iolanthe about her singing. Their eyes though betrayed a belly full of lust about her looks. 'We'll try and come and see you next Thursday,' one of them said.

Later in the afternoon I took Iolanthe to the police station. I had phoned ahead to make sure the chief was going to be there. Once we were sat in front of his desk with a large, cooling overhead fan twirling above us, I asked him if there had been any developments on either aspects of the case. He confessed there hadn't. He told us he had contacted the regional crime squad who dealt with illegal immigrants, but there had been no sightings or contacts with anybody who could have possibly been the men I had seen on the beach. He went on to say that Iolanthe's family may have switched vehicles, which would make tracking them even more difficult. He questioned her at length about any possible location they might have gone to. She stressed that there was none she could think of. She had already contacted the circus up north in my presence and on my phone, but the men were not there, which she and I confirmed to the chief.

'How long is Miss Moussaoui going to have to remain in house custody?' I asked him.

He hesitated before replying. 'I am going to have to speak with the Civil Prosecutor,' he said. We were speaking to each other in Spanish. 'If we can't come up with any charges to bring against the young lady within a week, we will have to free her from her current constraints.' We left it at that with an agreement to go back to see him again within a week.

Then one night, sometime in the midnight hours I awoke to see her standing at the bedroom window. She was completely naked, just as she had been when I'd fallen asleep. The moonlight outside silhouetted the curves in her body. When I looked towards the window I could swear I saw the flash of a torchlight beam somewhere outside.

'What's the matter?' I said to her.

'Don't know,' she replied. 'I thought I heard something out there,' she continued, then moved away from the window and back towards the bed.

I got up and stood by the window for a few moments, staring and listening, but there was nothing. Iolanthe had remained standing by the bed, away from the window. After a while we both went back to bed.

'It couldn't have been much,' I said to her, 'or Ben would have barked.'

Another bout of sex intervened on my thoughts. Whether she had contrived the sex to take my mind off the incident or not I don't know, but next day I did wonder about it.

* * * * *

The Thursday evening singing date at the Cactus bar was soon upon us. In the late afternoon, after the lunchtime diners had gone, we went over there to try out the tiny stage and the microphone. As the evening time got closer Iolanthe began to get nervous. 'I'm always like this before a show,' she said and spent a certain amount of time in the second bedroom strumming away on the guitar by herself.

We arrived at the bar sometime before she was due to go on. Firstly we sat at the back with a couple of drinks and watched the punters arrive. While we sat there she received many flirtatious glances from the men.

When most of the seats were taken Sylvia came over to our table. 'I'll announce you now if you're ready,' she said in her shrill cockney dialect. Iolanthe nodded in agreement. Sylvia went to the microphone, made the announcement, pointed to Iolanthe, who got out of her seat and headed for the stage. Earlier in the week she had managed to purchase a reasonably priced, white, figure hugging, short dress, from one of the local dress shops, which set off her jet black hair perfectly. Her walk to the stage produced a lecherous, hollering and wolf whistled response from the men in the audience. Each of the songs she sang ended in a crescendo of enthusiastic applause. Called back from her seat next to me for two encores, she duly obliged. Afterwards our table was besieged by admirers, mostly male, wanting to know when they could see her perform again. To escape their attentions we eventually had to make for the back kitchen, where Sylvia paid her the twenty euros and said. 'You were very good. You'd better come and see me tomorrow and we'll arrange another date.' We escaped through the back kitchen door. When we got back to my villa she gave me the twenty euros.

CHAPTER FOUR

The euphoria of that night lived with us through the next few days. Then I had to go out again on one my financial visits, which kept me away from the villa for about three hours. Everything appeared normal when I got back home. I guessed Iolanthe had been rehearsing most of the time while I was out. Another date at Sylvia's bar had been agreed for the following week, so she was trying to learn some new tunes. I took Ben out for his afternoon walk whilst she continued to practice. On my way back along the sand I again saw Colin Wright heading in my direction with his errant dogs. Ben cowered behind my legs in anticipation of their onslaught. 'Oh Lord,' I thought.

'You've had more foreign visitors then,' he said to me as soon I was within earshot. His two animals began to chase around Ben like mad dervishes.

'Oh, when was this?' I asked

'Not long after you went out,' he replied.

'Friends of Iolanthe,' I said defensively.

'You want to be careful with that lot around your villa,' he continued. His dogs were still being a nuisance. I tried to shoo them away, to little avail. He did nothing to control them. 'There's been lots of trouble around here involving that lot. All sorts of crimes. Burglaries, drugs, illegal immigrants, everything.'

'I'll speak to Iolanthe about it,' I said and made moves get away from his stupid dogs.

Before I could get too far he said to me, 'I think we need to talk about my investments soon. They're going downhill fast.'

I had to do something to placate him. 'I'll call in on you this evening if that's all right with you,' I said. He agreed to that and we parted.

Iolanthe was still practising on her guitar when I got back inside the villa. I gave Ben his food and then confronted her. 'I'm told you had visitors again this afternoon?' I said sternly.

She stopped strumming. 'Oh yes. It was the same friends who came before. They were on their way back from Gibraltar and wanted to know if I'd heard anything about my family. They're heading back up north.'

'But why didn't you tell me.'

She hesitated. 'I suppose I didn't think it that important. They only stopped by for a few minutes,' she said slightly petulantly.

'Iolanthe I hope you're not playing games with me. It would only take the right or maybe the wrong word from me to the chief of police and they'd lock you up.'

'I'm well aware of that,' she replied. 'Adam, why would I want to take advantage of you. You're the only person who's helped me. I'm sorry about this afternoon. I just didn't think it was important. You'd been busy all day and like last time you wanted to get outside with Ben.' We left it at that but I wasn't sure anymore.

That evening, after dinner, I called around to see Colin Wright as we'd agreed. His dogs greeted me noisily and aggressively at his front door. We sat in his living room and went over his investment portfolio. I had to be honest and admit that his current balances didn't make pretty reading.

'Trouble is Colin, if we move it to try and get a better return we'll have to put the money into something more risky, and if we do that the money could go down the pan completely. As you know at the moment the markets all over the world are way down. You can read about it every day in the newspapers. What you are currently invested in is relatively safe, reliable companies, which will come back up again once the markets pick up. It's a matter of being patient.'

He threw some more queries at me which I tried to counter. Eventually he agreed to think on it for a few days. 'It's your money,' I said. 'I'll do with it whatever you tell me to do,' to which I received a few more caustic remarks.

To change the subject I said, 'The people you saw at my house this afternoon. Were they the same lot as you saw before?'

'Oh those guys all look alike to me,' he said, then thought for a few moments, before adding. 'Yes, I guess they were.'

'Were there three of them?'

He thought again. 'That's all I could see, but there may have been others in the car.'

'What sort of car was it?'

'Oh, I don't know. One of those people carrier sort of things. Ugly looking brute.'

'The colour?'

'Dark blue, yes definitely dark blue. Why has there been trouble? I told you there'd be trouble with that lot.'

'No, not specifically, but they may have something to do with another matter. Thanks,' I said.

Quickly I reverted our conversation back to the financial matters to avoid him giving me a further grilling on Iolanthe's visitors. After we'd exhausted the subject I left.

The events of that afternoon preyed on my mind for sometime afterwards. Iolanthe and I went to bed together that night, but in the early hours, while listening to her breathing alongside me, I went over and over the dire possibilities of the situation I had got myself into. My immediate relationship with Iolanthe as a companion was fine. She was interesting and fun to be with and relatively tidy around the house. She was definitely interested in my novels and I spent many hours reading them to her. Her singing and guitar playing had brought a new diversity into our relationship and obviously the sexual attraction, on my part anyway, remained intense. But there were a lot of unanswered questions that continued to swirl in my brain.

The following morning I decided to visit the police station by myself. The chief was in. 'I have come to ask how long you intend to keep this woman under house arrest?' I said to him bluntly, referring to Iolanthe. I was still aware of how long police matters take in Spain, so I continued by adding, 'I'm only trying to help her out as a favour. I've got other things I want to get on with in my life and I can't do them whilst she is around my house.'

He had a fair rotund head, thinning to baldness, a stocky body and wore small framed glasses perched on the end of his nose. He looked at me over the top of them and sighed. 'I feel we may have to release her from that soon,' he said. 'We were hoping that we may have acquired some leads on her family before doing so, but that hasn't happened.'

I told him about a possible sighting of them locally in a dark blue vehicle as described by Colin. I wasn't too specific about anything, I just said it was somebody I knew locally who had seen them before in a bar. He made a note of it on a piece of paper on his desk.

'I think we'd better have her in for questioning one more time before we agree to her release,' he said. He looked at a diary on his desk and gave me a time and date on which I agreed to bring her to the police station. I told Iolanthe about it when I got home.

'Want to get rid of me now, do you?' she responded caustically to the information. I smiled at her remark and left it at that.

For Iolanthe's next appearance at the Cactus bar, it had been agreed to raise her fee to thirty euros. This time it was a midweek, quieter night, but as such Iolanthe 'topped the bill.' Another male solo singer went on first, then Iolanthe started at about nine thirty. This time the bar wasn't as full as on the previous occasion but again it would be fair to say that she went down well. Enthusiastic applause and wolf whistles followed on after the end of each song. This time her set lasted about an hour, including a couple of encores. Once again many of the men gathered around our table afterwards and we had difficulty getting away. Another date was arranged with Sylvia before we left.

The following day I accompanied her to the police station for our agreed appointment. Firstly they wanted to interview her alone. I made the excuse of having some shopping to do, then returned in half an hour. When I got back she was still being questioned. For another twenty minutes I sat in the reception area tapping my feet and twiddling my fingers. Eventually I was called into the interview room. Iolanthe was sitting on one side of a table, with a police officer I hadn't seen before and the chief on the other side. She looked rather shell-shocked and distressed. Clearly it had been a difficult time for her. The chief offered me one of the spare chairs and said, 'We have decided to release Miss Moussaoui. Whether she remains at your house or not is between the two of you. We will return her papers. We have told her however that we still wish to interview the three male members of her family and if they get in contact with her, she is to let us know immediately, and I ask the same of you.'

I nodded in agreement. There were various documents for her to sign and other matters to deal with. It was the best part of another half hour before I was able drive her home. By then she looked and sounded worried. 'That was horrible,' she said to me as we drove.

A couple of days later I had to go out again to see one of my financial clients. Once more I was gone for the whole of the afternoon. When I got back inside the villa everything appeared eerily quiet. No Ben bounding towards me as I came through the door. That was unusual. At first I thought Iolanthe may have taken him out for a walk. I looked around the villa. There was no sign of either of them. When I went into her bedroom I realised she had left me. All her clothes and belongings had gone. As I walked through the villa I gradually realised that wasn't all that had gone. My TV had gone. My video player had gone. My laptop, camera, bedside phone, binoculars, microwave and cam recorder had also gone. What about Ben?

I dashed around frantically calling his name, he was not inside the villa. I went out onto the patio, ran up to the roof terrace and called out his name. I was panic stricken. Then I heard him bark in response to my call. I traced him to the garage. They'd locked him in there while they were engaged in their scurrilous activities. Thank the Lord, he's safe, I thought.

CHAPTER FIVE

While Ben was engaged with eating his food I toured the villa making an inventory of everything they'd taken. I found that none of my private documents, credit cards, passport or savings accounts had been touched. What little cash I possessed was with me when I was out. From what I could detect they had only taken consumer items which they could quickly dispose of. I sat down in my lounge to think. I concluded that all of the items were covered under my home insurance policy. But that wasn't the point. I had trusted this girl. Given her shelter in my home when she needed it. This was no way to repay me, I thought. I couldn't be sure of course that she had been a willing participant in the crime, but I was still mad angry. I went to the sideboard and poured myself a stiff whisky. While I sipped on it I could still envisage her sitting in the lounge strumming on her guitar. Despite everything, a vision of her lying back on the settee listening to me reading to her, was also still in my head. I needed fresh air to think.

With Ben I tramped off across the beach to work off my frustrations. He was having trouble keeping up. We made the bungalow at the end of the beach in what must have been record time. Behind me he was puffing profusely, with moisture dripping off his tongue by the time we got there. Outside the bungalow there were no vehicles or any other sign of life. When I tried the wooden door it stuck a bit. In my anger I kicked it open, resulting in another piece of timber falling off it. Inside it was deserted, just as it had been on my last visit. All traces of their possessions had been removed. I walked back along the beach, more slowly, trying to think of what to do next.

Once I had deposited Ben inside the villa I decided to call in on Colin Wright.

'I'm still thinking about it,' was his response when he opened his door and saw me standing outside. He was of course referring to his investments.

'No, no,' I retorted quickly. 'It's not that. Have you got a minute?'

'Of course. You look a bit upset,' he said. 'You'd better come in.'

Immediately his dogs bounded in my direction, I told him what had happened, after he had shut them in the spare room.

'Oh my dear chap,' he said, 'How awful for you. I did try to warn you. You just never know where you are with those people. I wouldn't trust them further than I could throw them.' He went to his drinks cabinet and poured me a large scotch.

'Did you see anything going on over there this afternoon?' I asked after thanking him for the whisky.

'No, I was out playing golf,' he said. 'But when I was driving back the blue vehicle I saw before came hurtling up our road. Nearly drove into me. It was going too fast for me to see anything much, but it did make me wonder. What are you going to do?'

I supped on the whisky and said, 'I suppose I'd better tell the police. If I'm going to claim on my insurance that's what I'll have to do anyway.'

For the next ten minutes while I downed the rest of the whisky I had to listen to a tirade of his prejudices against African people in general. In the end I was glad to get out of there.

The two policemen who'd been to my villa before were soon knocking again on my front door. The one who could speak some English took notes while I related the details. The other one wandered around the lounge looking at the situations where the goods had been. Regularly the walkie-talkie on his waist noisily interrupted.

'You wouldn't credit it,' I said to the one taking notes. 'All I ever did was try to help that girl.' He shook his head in mutual agreement.

'We see a lot of this sort of thing now,' he responded. 'It's the recession. These people are so desperate for money, they'll sometimes do anything. You're lucky they didn't attack you.' When he finished his note taking he said, 'We'll put another search out for the van.' I had given him an updated description and told him about Colin Wright's sighting. 'It's very doubtful you will ever see your goods again,' he said. 'They'll have sold them on by now. If you want to make a claim for insurance you'd better come to the station tomorrow and I'll type out a statement for you.' With that they were gone, leaving me to nurse my sore pride.

Sitting in my lounge afterwards with only Ben again for company I tried to think about what I should do. I could take the easy way out, claim on my insurance, leave the rest to the police, then try to forget the whole episode. Write it off as a learning experience. Put it all down to being duped again by a woman. It wasn't the first time and I didn't expect it would be the last. I had plenty of work to get on with. My book was way behind schedule and with the misfortunes in the financial sector there was going to be plenty of activity there, as Colin Wright had already proved. I really didn't need any more hassle.

But my pride had been hurt. I considered I'd been taken for a ride, and that stuck in my craw more than anything. The local police didn't appear to me to be actually busting their guts to get to the bottom of the matter. I guessed that in a few weeks the incident would be written off as just another crime statistic. Which would mean that the Moroccans would have got away with it. I envisaged them at that moment, all sitting together in a bar somewhere, laughing their heads off at my ineptitude. Well I wasn't going to tolerate that. I had to do something myself to get even.

How, where and when though were the questions I asked myself over and over as I continued to brood in my lounge with Ben at my feet. It would be pointless just driving off into infinity looking for a blue people carrier vehicle. The police had tried that and weren't having much success. The Moroccans could be anywhere in Spain, or for that matter, in Morocco. I wouldn't have a hope of finding them by myself.

The only person I knew who could perhaps help me was Antonio Silva. A client and a friend, of a sort. Antonio had his base in Marbella, further down the coast. He was into everything, night clubs, bars, discos, casinos and a hundred other things, which as his financial advisor I didn't want to know about. It was well known he sailed close to the wind in most of his dealings. My job was to keep his up front investments and pensions on a legal track. The rest of his business I kept well clear of. But I knew he also had many connections and contacts in the criminal underworld.

Next day I phoned and made an appointment to see him at his office. Marbella is a brash, larger than life Mediterranean metropolis. The women are glamorous and brazen; the cars are big, powerful and flashy; the villas and properties are glossily over the top and luxurious. Antonio's office is no exception. He employs the most alluring female staff you have ever seen. Most of them have been his mistress at some time or another. His office accommodation occupies the top floor of a ten storey building. All the rooms have expansive windows which command views over the harbour and out to sea. His office, the largest of all, is dominated by a huge half circular desk. Around the sides are expensive leather settees with accompanying tables.

I am delivered to his room by an immaculate looking blonde, whose hair hung down to a point at her waist. She has on a white shirt, a smart dark two piece suit and the most gorgeous legs imaginable. It was wonderful to brush past in front of her as she held open the door to Antonio's room.

'There you are man,' he says on seeing me. He's sitting at his enormous desk. Alongside him stands a tall elegant brunette. Her long hair is curled into ringlets. She's wearing a white figure hugging t-shirt top and a sleek dark skirt. As I walk towards his desk it looks as though Antonio's right hand had just been somewhere up the back of her legs. He makes an action to remove it as I get close.

He gets up out of his chair to greet me. His appearance never ceases to amaze. He is Spanish, through and through, although he speaks almost perfect English. With all the accompanying razzmatazz of his features, he looks fortyish, but in reality he is in his late fifties. The pock marks on his tanned face give away a certain history. His jet black hair, obviously dyed, is combed back in a frontal quiff. He is wearing a jazzy floral shirt with the collar turned up and white slacks. He comes around the front of the desk to shake my hand, firmly. There are two gold wrist bracelets, a Rolex watch hangs loosely from his left wrist.

He dismisses Maria, the brunette, and beckons me over to one of the settees. 'On the phone you sounded worried,' he said as we walked towards them.'That's not like you. I'm the one who usually does the worrying.'

When we'd both sat down I told him of my problems. He listened attentively. 'Man that's a bad business,' he said when I'd finished. 'We can't have someone doing that to you,' he continued, got up, moved to a drinks cabinet, and poured us both two large gin and tonics, with ice. 'What do you want me to do?' he asked when he was back at the settee with the drinks.

I took a badly needed sup of the gin. It was a warm day. 'Well, you know people,' I responded. 'I believe the local police are just going to give up on this eventually.'

'Ay, lazy buggers,' he interjected. 'Everything's got to be easy for them. They prefer to sit in their offices and fiddle about on their computers all day than catch the real criminals.'

I had already described to him about the four Moroccans and my relationship with the girl. He said nothing about that, just raised his eyebrows and gave out a faint smile when I told him. I'd also described the blue people carrier vehicle, 'I was wondering if you could put the word out to the right people,' I said. 'I'd like to track them down as I'm convinced they're involved with illegal immigrants.'

'What do you want, retribution?' he retorted. His brown eyes lit up.

'No, for God's sake, nothing like that. Please promise me you won't do anything like that. No, I want to bring them to justice. I mean the girl may be completely innocent.'

He chuckled. 'From what you tell me I doubt that. It seems to me that you are the one who is innocent. In you she found a perfect sucker. Women are like that. Didn't you know?' He laughed some more, shaking his head from side to side in bewilderment. 'Ok, you'd better leave it with me. I'll make some enquiries.'

We talked a bit more, then I made moves to leave. 'I think we'd better also have a look at my investments soon,' he said as we got out of our seats. 'They appear to be going downhill rapidly.'

'Don't I know it,' I responded.

'Give me a call at the end of next week and we'll have another meeting then,' he said as he accompanied me to his office door. 'By then I might have come up with something on what you've told me.'

* * * * *

For the first time in a while I was able to spend the bulk of my days concentrating on my financial work and my novel. Getting back to some normality on those matters was a relief. On the financial side there was plenty to do. The reaction to the financial crisis from many of my clients was the same as it had been from Colin Wright and Antonio Silva. One of the clients who I visited during that period was a man called Desmond Bloomfield. There was an investment of over half a million pounds to deal with which had been left to him in his father's will. I was given to understand by Desmond that there was a bit of a family dispute over the matter. But that was none of my business. My job was to invest the money. However, some time afterwards I received a rather nasty e-mail about it from a Terry Bloomfield, Desmond's brother, claiming that he was entitled to a portion of the money. I spoke to Desmond about it. He had already shown me a copy of the will and the money was in his bank account, so he told me to ignore the e-mail, which I did.

At that time I was quite glad to have peace and tranquillity back again around the villa, but I would be lying to say I didn't miss Iolanthe and the sex. During those days I regularly visited the police station to see if there had been any developments, but there weren't. I'd already filed a claim on my insurance policy for the stolen possessions. I also had another meeting with Colin Wright about his investments. I had managed to find some alternative schemes for some of his money, although I did emphasise the inherent risk involved. He told me he'd think about it for a couple of days. By his front door on the way out he said to me, 'Oh by the way, the other day, I think I saw the van your Moroccan friends were driving.'

'Where was that?' I responded excitedly.

'On the motorway, just out of town,' he replied. 'I couldn't be sure because it was going in the other direction, but it was the same colour, same make, everything.' I thanked him then rang the police with the news. They didn't sound particularly interested.

The following week I met up again with Antonio Silva. We sat on the same settees with another couple of gin and tonics. He had all his investment paperwork spread out on the glass top table in front of us and I had brought along his file which was too big to fit into a briefcase.

'The more I look at this,' he said pointing down at the mound of paper on the table, 'the more worried and confused I get. When I look at the projections on the bottom of the page from a year or so back, they bear no resemblance to the balance I have now.' He extracted the relevant statements from the pile and pointed out the differences. It took me a good quarter of an hour to explain about the ups and downs of the financial markets all over the world. At that point in time most of my new clients had only ever experienced the ups, so it took some explaining. Afterwards he shook his head and moved off to pour us both two more gin and tonics.

'I've brought with me some alternatives you might like to consider,' I said as he made his way back to the settees with the drinks.

He interrupted. 'Before we go into all that and while I remember to tell you, I may have some news on your Moroccans,' he said. I rested his file on the table and sipped at the drink. He continued. 'It seems there is a gang of them involved in the illegal immigrant trade. Whether your pals are part of it or not, I don't know, but the gang involved is definitely Moroccan.' I sat up and listened more attentively. 'Someone I know, who knows someone else, says that person knows where they all live. I'm going to tell you at the outset that if you do get involved it could be very dangerous for you. These people don't mess about. If they got caught they'd be shipped back to Morocco and put in jail for ever, probably in a dungeon or something worse, so you must be very careful.' He paused for a slurp on the gin. 'I can give you my pal's telephone number and he will either give you the other guys number or take you to meet him. I warn you though all these people are criminals and if you or anybody else gets on the wrong side of them, there could be violence. That's how they survive.'

I shuddered at the thought, took another large slug of the gin, before we got back down to financial matters. When I was about to leave him he gave me the telephone number of his pal and another warning to 'be very, very careful.'

*****

I thought about the situation for a couple of days. Did I really want a load of hassle involving an incident which was already history. The insurance company appeared to be processing my claim. There was plenty of my regular work, writing and financial, to get on with. I hadn't heard any more from the local police. My guess about the matter becoming just another statistic, was, I thought, beginning to materialise. Occasionally I took Ben on beach walks as far as the old bungalow. Nothing there had changed, the place was still deserted. But images of Iolanthe still rattled around in my head. The physicality between us had become lodged within me and I couldn't shift it. In that sense, to me anyway, she was still very close and very special. And then at the back of my mind I continued to wonder if she had really wanted to be a party to the robbery of my belongings. Perhaps her family had abducted her to carry out their deed, I conjectured. She had nowhere else to go, other than with them, or stay with me.

One morning after dealing with my writing and mail I decided to give Antonio Silva's friend a telephone call. His name was Cesario Alvardo. He spoke good English. At that moment I had no idea of what his work was, or if he was a criminal or not.

As succinctly as I could, without relating too many details about myself, except for my name, I explained to him the problems I'd had and emphasised my long standing connection with Antonio.

He guffawed slightly after I had finished outlining brief details of my relationship with Iolanthe and the outcome. It sounded as though he had a smoker's cough. 'That happens a lot nowadays,' he said, repeating the same analogy the police had applied. 'It's the recession. What do you want to do?'

'I'd like to try and find her.'

'You won't get your stuff back,' he retorted quickly. 'That'll have been moved on a long time ago.'

'I realise that,' I said. 'It's just that there were a few good things between me and the girl. In a way I can't believe she was a willing party.'

'Women can be like that,' he said, 'blood's thicker than water.'

'I know, but I would just like to try and find out.'

'OK' he said. 'It will cost you some money though. Not with me, but with my connections. And you could be putting yourself in danger. Illegal immigration can be a profitable business. If outsiders start to mess about in it, the people who run it could probably get nasty. It's not likely that they'll report you to the police. They'll have their own way of dealing with you.'

'I understand all of that as well,' I said.

We arranged to meet a couple of days later at a service station on the motorway. He provided me with a description of his car and it's number and was waiting in his white Seat Ibiza when I arrived in the car park. Cesario was a short muscular man with a good head of dark hair, swept back at the front. Wearing a blue t-shirt and cotton trousers of the same colour he looked as though either he or his family were of South American origin. He was smoking a cigarette as he got out of his car when he saw me approach. We shook hands, then he stubbed out the cigarette with his toe.

'Let's go and have a coffee,' he said to me and led the way to the cafeteria.

While we sat at a window seat and supped on the brew he made me explain again all the relevant incidents of my problem, but this time in more detail.

'H'm,' he said when I'd finished my tale. 'And are you absolutely sure that you want to go on with this. I repeat it could get dangerous and unpleasant for you,' he paused for a sup on the coffee. Sunshine streaming in through the window flashed on the four gold rings he wore on his fingers. 'This sort of thing happens all the time with the women around here,' he continued. 'It's that sort of place,' he added with a chuckle. 'You tell me the insurance company look like they are going to pay up. Why don't you just take the money and put the rest down to experience?' he said.

I paused before replying, I knew he was right.

'Because I still have a certain regard and concern for the girl,' I said eventually.

'Phew,' he snorted, sounding slightly exasperated. 'Ok. I have known Antonio Silva for many years and in that time he has sent me lots of business.' He didn't exemplify what sort of business. 'So I will do what I can for any friend of his. I will not charge you for my services, but the people I am going to put you in touch with will. I'll find out how much.'

He went on to say that the people he knew, who might be able to help me, lived up in the hills near the mountain town of Ronda. They run a farm up there, he said. I would have to go up there to see them as they never came down to the coast. The Moroccans also lived somewhere in that region. That's why his contacts were aware of their activities. 'Everybody knows everything about everybody else up there. They'll be able to ascertain for you if this girl you mention is with them. But as I said before, they will expect to be paid for their services and I would advise you that they do operate outside the law. I repeat it's entirely your decision.'

After a few more brief words we finished our conversation and made for our cars. When we were outside he lit up another cigarette. I gave him my telephone number. He promised to phone me in a couple of days. We shook hands and then without saying any more he got in his car and drove away. I really didn't know what to make of him as he was unlike anybody else I'd ever met before.

While I awaited his call I had a further somewhat acrimonious meeting with Colin Wright about his investments. The man was such a know-all. It was almost impossible to tell him anything. Before coming to Spain he'd been a policeman in the UK for twenty years. After that he'd been able to take early retirement on full pension. However, he still retained the policeman's habit of making notes. During our conversations on financial matters he would always have in his hands a notebook and in it he wrote down, in pencil, everything I said as though he was interviewing someone at the scene of a crime. Prior to his police career, after leaving university he'd been a teacher for about ten years, which I expect explains a lot about his attitudes. During our meeting he claimed to know people, 'who were still making big money out of their investments.' I asked him to give me specific examples of what they had invested their money in, but he couldn't. We parted with him saying that he 'might have to take my money elsewhere if things don't improve. It's all I've got you know Adam,' he repeated for the third time that day.

CHAPTER SIX

A few days later I received a telephone call from Cesario Alvardo. In his gruff, cigarette infected voice, he told me he had made contact with his pals in the Ronda region. They would want five hundred euros up front from me to suss out if Iolanthe and her family were living in the area. I blinked when he said the amount. For that money, assuming they found her, they would also keep a check on her movements for a while, 'if that's what I required,' he said. Firstly though they would want to meet up with me and the money, and I would have to go up to their home to see them. 'I repeat it's entirely up to you,' Alvardo said impatiently. 'You must remember though what I told you about it all.'

I had to make a quick decision. I had already discovered that he was not a man I could mess about with, but this was my only opportunity to make any inroads on the matter. If I prevaricated any more he'd lose patience, and that would be the end of it, so on the spur of the moment I said, 'Ok. I'll go ahead.'

He then gave me the telephone number and directions of how to get to the farmhouse of the people I needed to see. Their family name was Villaverde. The head man was called Jacob. Cesario told me that there were eight of them, father, sons and brothers. He said the best time to phone them and to see them would be in the evening as they worked out on the farm all day. 'I will leave the rest to you,' he said, adding that, 'If you have any problems you must phone me.' He ended the call by repeating the warning that it could all 'lead to big trouble.' How right he was to be.

*****

To get to Ronda I had to travel from the coast up a long, twisting and steeply rising road which passes through Coin. Geographically,

Ronda is situated north west of Marbella. I began my trip in mid afternoon so I could at least find this desolate farmhouse in daylight. Once you get away from the coast you enter a different world, a rugged mountainous world. Suddenly there are no expensive villas or glamorously manicured people. In fact there are not many people at all. Pretty quickly, even the cars you pass on the road are in marked contrast to the pristine motors you see on the coast. It takes the best part of an hour of concentrated driving to reach Ronda. Then you have to cross a big viaduct over a striking one hundred metre deep ravine before you get into the town itself. Therein it's actively bustling and quite large. The buildings are mostly old, a mixture of classic Spanish and Moorish in style, but architecturally interesting. I parked in the main square. Attractive trees line the streets. The town is also the home of one of the oldest and most famous bull rings in Spain, situated just off the square, it dominates the surroundings. I walked about to get a feel of the place. There are tourists, but even they look different from those at the coast. The local inhabitants appear to be mostly country orientated. Some are riding about on large horses, who stamp the ground and toss their heads vigorously as they move along. I spend about an hour there; have a coffee in a bar, then I drive on while the daylight holds. The farmhouse I'm looking for is still quite a few kilometres further on. I had rung the previous evening to fix a time with them. My Spanish held out just enough for one of the sons to give me another myriad description of road and junctions on how to get there. Cesario had forewarned him that I might call. I had also organised the five hundred euros and had it with me.

Armed with the directions I still managed to get lost, twice in fact. However, after about a forty minute drive from the Ronda I did manage to reach the arched structure of the main entrance. The accompanying wrought iron metal gates appeared to be rusty and looked permanently stuck open. Dusk was coming in. There was still a narrow dusty track, about half a mile long, to follow, through a desolate valley before I reached the farmhouse, set in the middle of nowhere.

The structure of the building was immense; four stories in all; like something from a bygone era. All the upstairs windows had closed shutters. In the area around the front of the house animals of various types wandered freely around the untidy concourse. Chickens, goats, a couple of sheep, small ponies, far too many to itemise. When I got out of my car a vicious looking pack of six dogs began barking ferociously, leaping up menacingly and baring their teeth at me. Fortunately they were all restricted by metal tethers.

The noise they all made must have alerted the people inside, as an ageing man, wearing a dilapidated straw hat was waiting for me when I got to the front door. The door he held onto was part of a pair, constructed of solid oak and at least twelve feet in height. He was wearing an earth stained working shirt and torn jeans. His skin was tanned dark, like old leather. The face was dominated by a large hooked nose and partly camouflaged by various out-growings of hair of indiscriminate length around his chin, jaws and mouth. He held out his hand for a handshake and announced in Spanish that he was Jacob.

I was guided through two passageways to a kitchen as big as most people's houses. The other members of the family were in there, including three women, half a dozen children, and four smaller dogs, who yapped on my arrival; also many cats, the number of which I was unable to count, in all it was a total menagerie. Most of the men folk were sat around an enormous kitchen table, with beers or goblets of wine in front of them. They all wore farming clothes encrusted with earth dirt like Jacob. All their hair and facial stubble was in various stages of dishevelment. When I stood in front of them every being in there, including the animals, looked at me as though I was something from another planet. However, each one of the men got up to shake my hand and greet me. I couldn't follow all the names. One, whose name was Nathan, who would have been in his early thirties, said he spoke a little English and would try to help me to translate if needed. I guessed he was the one who had answered my phone call. I was offered and accepted a goblet of dark, rich red wine which Jacob poured from a decanter. Some of them moved their chairs aside to allow me to sit between them.

When I'd settled Jacob said to me in Spanish, 'You are trying to find a girl?'

'Si,' I responded. I had brought with me a couple of pictures I had taken of Iolanthe on the digital camera, which I'd downloaded onto my computer before it had been stolen. Iolanthe was casually dressed to show off her best features. I passed the copies across the table to Jacob.

His bushy eyebrows lifted in surprise as he looked at them. 'I too would like to find a girl like this,' he said jocularly in Spanish, while pointing at the pictures, then passed the photos around the table to the other men, who made similar comments. It was perhaps a good job I didn't understand some of them. There was much sniggering and humour. All the while the children played with their toys and the animals. The women kept to themselves by the sink and busied themselves preparing the evening meal.

Slowly and with Nathan's help in translation, I related the major incidents in my relationship with Iolanthe, but emphasised the supposed illegal immigrant aspects and obviously their Moroccan background, as well as the apparent lack of interest shown by the local police. They all listened intently. Jacob sometimes shook his head and supped on his wine. 'As a result of my meeting with Cesario,' I concluded, in my pidgin Spanish, 'I understand that a gang of them may be holed up around here somewhere and that you could possibly help me find if Iolanthe is with them. I have no proof but I do wonder if she is being held under duress.'

Jacob looked at the other men. There was a degree of mumbling and communication between all them, most of which I didn't understand. After a few moments he said, 'Yes we will try to help, but we will require the five hundred euros first.' I fished into my pocket and drew out the wad of notes which I held up for them to see. He nodded in acknowledgement. 'There is a group of Moroccans who live in a farmhouse like this,' he continued, 'in the next valley. But we hardly ever see them. They keep very much to themselves. Only their women go into town shopping. The front gate is always heavily padlocked and the farm is surrounded by lots of wire fencing, so it might take some time before we could provide you with any information. I suppose we could make an excuse and visit them on a farming matter, but if they were holding the girl under duress and knew we were coming, they would probably hide her somewhere first.'

There followed an overall discussion between the men, again, little of which I could follow. Jacob eventually intervened. 'Yes we will try and help you,' he said pointing directly at me. 'But I can't guarantee you any success. This girl may not be there,' he emphasised with a shrug of his shoulders. 'But having taken your money we would not give it back. Times are hard,' he added.

'Ok, I understand that,' I replied. I gave them my telephone numbers and said I would keep in touch by phoning them, then I got up out of the chair and handed over the wad of notes. Jacob counted every one. We shook hands. 'Gracias,' I said looking at them all. They all replied in similar vein, then each one in turn came and shook my hand. Jacob escorted me to the front door.

* * * * *

As I drove away I wondered if I had become completely mad. As Jacob had said times were hard. Those years were difficult for everybody, including me, and yet I had just passed over five hundred euros I could ill afford to someone I didn't know, with no chance of getting it back. It was dark during the long drive home. I was tired and most of the way I referred to myself as a 'complete burke.' The only comfort was the magnificent sight of the millions of bright, twinkling stars, dancing in the sky as I drove back through the mountains. That was something else altogether.

When I got back to my villa I noticed something slightly out of kilter. The front gate wasn't closed properly. Not by much, but the latch wasn't clicked securely back into place. Somebody else may not have noticed it, but I made of habit of clicking it closed tight when I went out, because if there was a high wind it would blow it open. Then it would clang against the back wall and damage the wall and the gate. After I'd opened it and in the beam of my headlights I noticed tyre marks in the road. A largish vehicle had obviously been swung around there recently. My car wouldn't make tyre marks like that and I didn't drive in the manner that would cause them. I approached the front door warily.

I heard Ben bark when I turned the key in the lock. As soon as I was through the door he pounced on me with a little more energy than normal. It was a sign that something had occurred in my absence. Quickly I looked around the villa for any disturbance, but there wasn't any. Mind you, most of what was any use had already been stolen. Ben's whimpering though, as he followed me around, indicated that something had troubled him. When I took him outside his nose continually rotated around as though the residue of some smell was still in the air. That night I slept lightly, but nothing untoward happened.

To my surprise, the day after next I received a telephone call from Cesario Alvardo. He wanted to know if I was OK after my trip to the mountains. I confirmed that I was, but five hundred euros worse off. His catarrhal snigger reverberated in my ear. He went on to say that he had phoned Jacob to see how matters were proceeding. Jacob had told him that they were arranging to see the Moroccans on a farming matter. By all accounts some of their land abutted. A meeting had been organised to sort out a fencing problem.

For a couple of days thereafter I continued with my financial work, for which I had needed to go out and purchase another laptop, causing a further hole in my bank account. The insurance settlement cheque was due any day but I couldn't work without the proper equipment. Then, one evening, I received a telephone call from Nathan Villaverde. He said they'd met up with the Moroccans. He confirmed that there was a whole gaggle of Moroccan men around the farmhouse but he couldn't tell if any of them were Iolanthe's family. There was no sign though of anybody who looked like her. He did say that near the house they'd spotted a modern type caravan parked in the yard. Spread around the outside was some washing, the like of which could have belonged to a young woman like Iolanthe.

He said his family had come up with a plan. In a few days time they would begin the mutually agreed fencing work. Then at the end of the day they would leave some of the work uncompleted which under the cover of darkness would give them access to the Moroccan's land. Their plan was that a couple of them would then go back later and find their way to a spot near the farmhouse where they could observe the goings on. I asked if I could go with them. This resulted in a certain amount of discussion. I could hear agitated conversation with Jacob off the phone. I finalised matters by saying that 'it was my money that was paying for the trip,' so they agreed to my accompanying them on the search.

* * * * *

I wondered if they would get back to me, but Nathan did telephone me a few days later. He suggested I wore dark, lightweight clothes, a dark baseball cap and soft stout shoes. We were going to have to walk a few miles to get near the farmhouse, he said. I was instructed to be at their home just before ten o'clock the following evening.

 Driving up the long dark, twisting road again to Ronda, I continued to wonder if I was totally mad. Never before in my life had I attempted anything as reckless. Why I was actually doing it didn't make any real sense. Since the burglary my life had returned to its previously odd, but for me, normal format. So why was I risking my neck, and money, for something that was probably only a pipe dream? However, every day since she'd gone, this vision of Iolanthe refused to go from my mind. Constantly I visualised her sitting in my lounge or on my veranda strumming on her guitar. In the evenings when I read up on my days writings I still imagined she was stretched out on the settee listening to my readings.

* * * * *

All the Villaverde family were gathered around the kitchen table again when I arrived at their farmhouse. They'd obviously just finished eating. The women were washing up at the sink. When I joined them Jacob began to bark out orders to the other men. I understood little of it. It transpired that Nathan, and one of the other brothers, Eden, who would have been five or six years younger, were the two chosen to accompany me to the Moroccan's house. They were not going to take a torch in case the light was spotted. They were both dark haired and swarthy skinned, wearing dark clothes. Nathan had with him a high powered night vision sensitive set of binoculars. I was instructed that there was to be no talking, sound travels in the night they said. We would communicate by sign language only. I was also told to watch my feet, not the skyline when I walked, to ensure I didn't tread on twigs or bits of tree branches. Jacob said those sounds would be picked up by the Moroccan's dogs. He kept issuing instructions to the other men who seemed to ignore most of it, but they did occasionally nod in response.

Accompanied by a still nattering Jacob the four of us set off for the farmhouse boundary. Then, afterwards, it was just Nathan, Eden and me. Nathan instructed that there would be no talking from that moment onwards. The night was warm, clear and starlit with a half moon up.

I had trouble keeping up with the two of them and was quickly sweating profusely. Being twenty years older than them probably didn't help. In a short while we reached the fence they'd been repairing. There was a spot where they had just twisted together the adjoining strands of wire. Quickly the two lads unwound it to let us through. They then tied it together again. I was told later that they did this in case we had to find another escape route back.

I guess it must have been another two or three miles before the trees and the lights of the Moroccan's farmhouse came into view. As we got closer, using sign language, Nathan reminded me to keep looking down for twigs and branches. He also put his finger over his lips, to indicate complete silence.

Before we'd set off Nathan had mentioned that when they had visited the house, for the farming discussions, they had noticed a knoll, a short distance away. On the top of the knoll were some trees which he hoped would provide us with cover while we watched the house. It was the sort of spot where animals would shelter in the hot weather, he pointed the way. When we got to the knoll I could see that the farmhouse looked a bit of a wreck. Some chimneys had collapsed. Many slates were missing from the roof. Lots of the outbuildings doors were hanging off. We could by then hear sounds and movements from around the house, with voices, seemingly coming from the terrace. Nathan repeated the need for silence by replacing his index finger over his lips. I was having trouble avoiding the animal dung on the ground, the stench was overpowering. Somehow, we managed to take up a vantage point, behind the trees, from where we could see the outside terrace of the farmhouse. Some of the men were sitting out there drinking and smoking cigars. A light from the house illuminated them. I guess we were about a hundred yards away from them.

We remained there for the best part of an hour. Nathan and Eden occasionally trained the binoculars on the activity but not a lot happened. From time to time one or two of the women came out to talk to the men on the terrace, then went back inside, but even without the aid of the binoculars I could see none of them were Iolanthe. Nathan pointed out the caravan but there didn't appear to be any movement around there either.

I was beginning to wonder if it had all been a waste of time when, without warning, the caravan door opened. Eden spotted it first and pointed. We all watched closely as a figure emerged. Instantly I knew it was Iolanthe. Nathan had the binoculars trained on her. I gave a thumbs up and nodded my head in affirmation. He passed the binoculars to me. Iolanthe had her hair tied up in a bun. She was wearing a check pair of shorts and a white t-shirt. Again I issued a thumbs up and then focussed in closer with the bins. Like a voyeur I allowed the lenses to wander up and down her body. I felt like shouting out with glee but I knew I couldn't.

Then to my horror of horrors as I allowed the lenses to wander down her legs I spotted something awful around her ankle. It looked like a metal manacle. Adjusting the lenses I honed in further. It was indeed a shackle and leading away from it was a metal chain that led back into the caravan. The bastards had imprisoned her like a slave I thought. I felt like shouting out, but again I couldn't, so I shook my fist in anger in her direction. The other two wondered what I was about. I passed the bins back to Nathan and mimed by pointing down to my ankle and then to Iolanthe. He got the message and focussed in. After a while he nodded his head in acknowledgement and handed the bins to Eden. We sat there for some time taking turns at the binoculars, watching her. She remained sitting on the caravan steps smoking a cigarette for a short while. Then when she had finished it she went back inside the caravan and closed the door.

Nathan then made signs for us to leave. I was reluctant to go but I knew at that time there was nothing more we could do. On my way down the knoll in my anger and frustration I stepped in some more animal dung. I fought to control the urge to curse openly. We made it back to the fence in silence. I was still brooding. When Nathan had reconnected the wrylock he spoke for the first time.

'There was nothing we could do there,' he said in English.

I agreed. 'I have to formulate a plan to rescue her,' I said. 'I can't leave her like that.' They both looked at me warily.

'We'll discuss it back at the farmhouse with my father,' he said and we strode away. My feet still stank from the dung.

CHAPTER SEVEN

At the farmhouse we sat around the kitchen table with the other male members of the family, supping red wine and discussing possible ways of getting near to Iolanthe. I said I needed to talk to her, to try and establish what was going on. I was still confident she would respond to me. To achieve that was not going to be easy. According to the Villaverde family there were many people living in the farmhouse. To get all of them out of the way at the same time, to allow me even to talk to Iolanthe alone would be virtually impossible. Even then it would be unlikely that the women would leave the farmhouse. We agreed that the only way was to create some sort of diversion so that I could get near to the caravan unseen. By then it was well into the midnight hours and we were all tired. Constructive thought on the matter was therefore deferred to enable all of us to come up with ideas for a realistic plan.

Later on, at home, as I sat on my roof terrace, taking in the cool night air, admiring the stars above and sipping on a very large scotch I contemplated on my situation. For a while Ben sat at my feet, but as I had already disturbed his night time slumbers, he soon gave up and went back to his bed.

Methodically I went over the events of the night. Clearly I was venturing out on a dangerous limb. If I got into real trouble I would have nobody to blame but myself. The people I was involved with had all warned me of the possible consequences, but the sight of Iolanthe being shackled by a metal chain had reawakened my desire for her and reaffirmed my belief that she was being held under duress and maybe had not been a willing party to the burglary of my goods. In my thoughts that didn't alter the fact that she was probably more likely to have a commitment to her family rather than some itinerate British lover like me, with whom she had accidentally become involved. Eventually I retired to bed no wiser.

Ideas for a suitable plan of action rolled around in my head for most of the next day. Many of them, on reflection, I considered were farcical, I knew I was no James Bond. Trouble was I had no experience of this type of operation and also no real idea of what was feasible and what wasn't.

I therefore decided to put in a call to Cesario Alvardo. Surprisingly he agreed to meet up with me again at the same service station. After we had ordered coffees I related the experiences of my night with the Villaverde family and Iolanthe's apparent imprisonment.

He responded by saying. 'These people do have strange ways of dealing with their women. I mean your girlfriend could well be in the doghouse over some domestic dispute. You can't be sure. You could go to a bundle of trouble to get her out of there and then find she laughs in your face and tells you to get lost and mind your own business.'

'Well that's why I need to talk to her first. The problem is how to get near enough to do that without alerting the others. I can't just ring up and make an appointment.'

He issued one of his catarrhal sniggers, then thought for a moment. 'You'll have to get yourself in there under some sort of disguise,' he said. 'How? Is the big question,' he continued and I nodded in agreement.

He thought some more. 'You say that you know how to get to this farmhouse.'

'Yes, but there's a locked front gate. As I told you we went there over land, on foot.'

'But could you find the gate by road?'

'I expect so.'

'Well I think you need to stake out the front gate, probably over a few days. Watch the comings and goings. See what deliveries they have. You'll have to keep out of sight and hide your car. From what you've told me they'd recognise you and your car. You'll have to be totally inconspicuous.'

For a few moments I made no reply. I was trying to comprehend what I was continuing to let myself in for. 'Then what?' I said eventually.

'If you can come up with the names of a few delivery people who visit there, the type who are local and would be regular callers, then come back to me. I'll find out if we know any of them. But it would cost you more money. And, more importantly I can only reiterate the risk to yourself personally. It's entirely up to you.'

For some more minutes I asked further questions. When we parted I drove very slowly back to my villa with my mind still racked with doubt.

* * * * *

Over the next couple of days I tried hard to evaluate all the pros and cons of what I was contemplating. Really though I was getting nowhere. I seemed to reach a different conclusion at least three or four times a day. I suppose the arrival of a cheque from the insurance company, in full settlement of my claim, spurred me into some action. I needed to go out and replace the items that had been stolen.

After some intense research on the internet I set off for Marbella armed with a shoal of print-outs relating to each one. I had decided to combine a shopping expedition with another call on Antonio Silva. We needed another discussion on his investments but I also wanted his further advice on my problem. I phoned ahead to make an appointment.

Beforehand I spent a good two hours roaming the streets of the city, sussing out the cheapest offers on the equipment I needed. In the end I was fairly pleased with my purchases. Antonio then greeted me with his customary enthusiasm when I arrived in his office.

'What's the news on your troubles?' he asked when we shook hands. Then he guided me to the settees.

As briefly as I could I related the latest events. He listened patiently. Throughout my dialogue he guffawed and sniggered, 'Listen Adam,' he said when I'd finished. 'Why don't you just ask one of these attractive young women who work here to go out with you,' he said and spread his right arm out in a wide arc. 'I'm sure any of them would be delighted. At least you'd have some idea of their background and it would save you an awful lot of trouble.'

I laughed, he had a good point. 'What does this guy Alvardo do?' I asked. 'What's his work?'

'Nothing legal,' he replied with a chuckle. 'Nothing you would want to know anything about. Let's just say, to put it into a wide category, as something like import and export and leave it at that.'

I said nothing for a few moments. 'So you think I'm crazy to go on with this?'

He shrugged his shoulders, and said. 'A man's got to do what a man's got to do.' After that we settled down to concentrate on his investments.

When I got back to my villa I carefully unpacked and checked my purchases. After detailed inspection I considered that I possessed a good up-to-date selection of the products that had been stolen. How could I test them out? The TV, telephone and domestic appliances were easy as they could be played with in and around my villa at my convenience. The camera, camcorder and binoculars though would warrant a more out-of-doors location. What about a reconnaissance trip to the Moroccan's farmhouse I thought? So that evening I spent hours reading up the related manuals, while diligently testing each switch and button. I went to bed exhausted.

The following day I had no pressing appointments, so I rose at dawn, took Ben out across the beach, ate my breakfast, then prepared my gadgets for a trip back to Ronda and the valleys beyond. The excitement of being able to test out my new purchases, in field conditions, to some extent pushed the danger I was putting myself into to the back of my mind. It was a warm day, although not too hot. Before setting off I had managed to acquire an ancient Spanish road map, which I found didn't help a lot, so it took a little time to find the Moroccan's front gate. Because of my early start it was still only mid morning when I reached there.

Slowly I drove past. The gates were, as had been described, securely padlocked. I looked out for any evidence of a CCTV camera but couldn't see one. I then went about two hundred yards down the road, turned around and parked in a small lay-by. From there I duly applied my new Zeiss binoculars on the pillars and structure of the gates. They were metal, the pillars concrete. The performance of the binoculars was good. Still no sign of any CCTV, but I could see there was an intercom bell push. A pot-holed dirt track led back from the gates in what I presumed was the direction of the farmhouse, although from where I was I couldn't see it. On the other side of the road there was some open land which led to a ridge about another hundred yards away. With the bins I could see boulders and rocks which I figured I could hide behind, while still giving me a clear view of the gates. I sat there in the Mercedes for some minutes thinking. No way could I remain parked where I was for any length of time. If Iolanthe's family passed by they'd recognise my car. I turned the Mercedes around and drove down the road and away from the gates. A couple of hundred yards away I found an old track which led to a fruit tree orchard. My Mercedes creaked and groaned as it negotiated the pot-holes and humps. After a short while I was able to park under the shade of some trees, well hidden from the road. The track didn't look as though it was used much. Not by the Moroccan's anyway I hoped.

I had packed a 'survival kit' in a knapsack. As well as the camera, bins and camcorder I also included a good supply of water, some ham and cheese bocadillos and an anorak. I was wearing toned down, green, lightweight clothes and when I got out of the car I donned a peaked baseball cap of the same colour. I hoped I was adequately prepared for a long day.

It took me about twenty minutes to reach the ridge. By then I was sweating profusely. I gulped on some water and hoped I hadn't been spotted. Certainly no car, or person had travelled along the road in that time. I extracted my gadgets from the knapsack and tried to make myself comfortable behind a boulder. I didn't have to wait long for some action.

A dusty, rusty, pick-up truck soon approached the front gates from the inside track. I trained in with the bins. A man in a coloured shirt got out to unlock the padlocks. Although he wore a Stetson type hat I could see he was of Moroccan extraction. I was sure though that he wasn't one of Iolanthe's immediate family. Clumsily I exchanged the bins for the camera. There was a telephoto lens. My first attempt at trying to focus was pretty woeful, but I did manage to click some shots as the man pulled back the gates then drove the truck through. Another man of the same build got out of the passenger seat to close the gates afterwards. While he did so I completely failed to get the camcorder to film anything. When the pick-up had disappeared down the road, I spotted with the bins that although the gates had been shut, the padlocks had been left unlocked. I used the time until the next event to hone my skills on the intricacies of my new equipment.

A good half hour elapsed before I saw a blue off roader vehicle coming up the track towards the gates. To me this clearly looked like the one Colin Wright had described. The new Lumix camera was strapped around my neck and I focussed on the gates with the Zeiss bins. A man got out of the passenger seat, who I clearly recognised as one of Iolanthe's family. As he followed the vehicle through the gate he had opened, I clicked the camera into action and took several shots using the telephoto lens. While he shut the gates I powered up the camcorder and was able to film his walk back into the vehicle afterwards. He was definitely one of the men I had met with Iolanthe. The vehicle then drove off down the road towards Ronda.

A long time elapsed before anything further happened. I was getting hot, but the interval enabled me to check the camera and the camcorder for the images I had recorded. Overall I was reasonably pleased. For some of the shots I had obviously held both of the instruments at a crooked angle, but by and large they were recognisable of what I was attempting to capture.

It must have been getting close to midday before anything else happened. By then I was needing to towel myself down regularly to keep the perspiration from my eyes. Suddenly I spotted a white van approaching the gates from the Ronda direction. Spotting the word pescadores amongst other words, written in bold blue letters, on the van's side, I knew it was the travelling fish man. He got out of the van, talked into the intercom, then undid the gates and drove through and re-hooked them up afterwards. All the while I photographed and filmed him. It was half an hour or so before he came back and both he and I repeated the same process, before he drove off. Afterwards I ate my lunch and tried to cool off, downing much water, while I checked the images I had taken.

Again nothing stirred for a long time. By then the heat was getting to me. Then sometime in the early afternoon another van appeared, this time red, with the word Fontanero (plumber) on the side. He went through the same procedure at the gates as the fish man and I recorded it. When he eventually came back down the driveway and drove away, I decided I that I had become too hot and frazzled, so I packed up my gear and made for home. As I drove I considered I was quite pleased with myself. I had established that members of Iolanthe's family lived with the other Moroccans and I had also carried out Cesario's instructions.

After showering and taking Ben out I downloaded the images onto my laptop. They were certainly sufficient for what was required. With the zoom focus on the laptop I was clearly able to identify one of Iolanthe's brothers. Later in the evening I phoned Cesario. He gave me his e-mail address and asked me to download the images to him. He promised he'd get back to me.

* * * * *

It was a couple of days before I heard from him again. He said he wanted to take me to meet up with Herrera, the fish man who I had photographed a few days before. We met up at the same service station and he drove me in typical Spanish style into Marbella, in his Seat car. I had to cling on to my seatbelt. He smoked continuously, but he did keep his driver's window open, which in turn negated the effect of the air conditioning. During the journey he outlined a plan he had cobbled together with Herrera, to enable me to get near Iolanthe. It all sounded dubious to me, but I had come this far so I thought I may as well play along, for a while anyway. It was going to cost me more money though.

We were heading towards the harbour. A few blocks inland from there he parked outside a small warehouse type property, which I found to be a fish plant. The acrid stench instantly hit my nostrils. The noise inside was almost deafening. Fish were being transported on conveyer belts towards vats and tables for gutting, head or tailing, and a lot of other obnoxious processes. About five or six people appeared to work there. There was lots of ice and a lot of noise. Cesario guided me through it all to a small glassed office unit at the end, where he introduced me to Alejandro Herrera, who was wearing a blue and white striped apron over a stained t-shirt. On his head he had a small white cap, his face was swarthy and unshaven. We shook hands, after he had wiped his on his apron. Cesario had explained on the journey that Herrera only spoke a little English. He would translate where required, he said.

Herrera had to move fish boxes before he was able to offer us chairs. 'You want to check up on your girlfriend?' he said in Spanish when we had all sat down.

'Yes, I think she may be held under duress,' I replied in the same language. 'What do you make of the Moroccans who live there?' I continued.

He shook his right hand to mime as though things there were a bit odd. 'All that lot are a bit strange if you ask me,' he said. 'But they buy fish off me and they pay me in cash, so I cannot complain.'

I reiterated to him the plan that Cesario had outlined to me on our journey there. I mentioned about the caravan where I thought Iolanthe was being kept. Herrera said he had spotted it on his visits there and knew where it was located. The three of us talked some more about arrangements.

Herrera would require three hundred euros to get me in there. He would provide a lightweight overall type white coat to make me look like a fishmonger and the same type of cap as he wore. He said I should try and make the rest of my appearance as unrecognisable as possible and not speak at all while we were there. The best time for me to accompany him to the farmhouse would be a Friday, as most of the men went to an agricultural market further north on a Friday. Usually it was only the women left at the farmhouse on that day. He added that if things went wrong that he would disclaim all responsibility for me. I would be just a new employee who he was trying out, he told me. He added that he couldn't afford to lose a good client. If I wanted to go with him the following Friday I was to ring him on the number he pointed out on his business card, which he passed to me, and bring with me the three hundred euros. He would meet me at the service station at 7.00 am. He emphasised that it would be a long day as he would have to complete his round before he could take me back to my car.

For the next day or so I pondered on the matter. Did I really want to spend another three hundred euros? And this time I would be walking right into the lion's den, goodness knows what fate might befall me. Clearly there was no-one who would risk their neck to bail me out as Alejandro Herrera had clearly explained. There was also the possibility that Iolanthe would tell me to get lost and leave her alone. Everybody I knew had already told me I was completely bonkers to continue with the project, but this vision of Iolanthe attached to a metal chain continued to haunt me both day and night.

On the Thursday I went to my bank to draw out the three hundred euros. While I was there I noticed the balances on my accounts looked in a poor state. The payments for my new equipment had exceeded the cheque from the insurance company and as none of my clients were risking any new ventures there was little income coming in from my financial advisory business. I continued to ponder, but late on Thursday afternoon I did phone Herrera to say I would meet him at the service station the following morning.

We said little to each other on the journey up the mountain road to Ronda. Partly because of the language difficulties and partly because it was early in the morning and neither of us was in a particularly gregarious mood. For my part I was frightened stiff. I really had no past experience of this sort of thing and didn't have any idea of what to expect. I had donned the thin white coat and hat and hadn't shaved for a couple of days, which I hoped would give me the same sort of appearance as Alejandro. He had explained that there would be other calls to make before we reached the Moroccan's farmhouse. He felt it best if I remained in or around the van all the time and said nothing to anybody in case my accent gave me away. He added that he was used to doing this run by himself.

It was getting on for eleven o'clock by the time we reached the closed entrance gates of the Moroccan's farmhouse. The previous house calls had been interesting. I'd seen some wonderful out of the way places, but with every passing minute my levels of tension and anxiety increased. 'Let's hope the men have gone out,' Herrera said to me, in Spanish, before he got out to deal with the intercom and the gates. 'I'll drive up as near to the caravan as I can, without arousing too much suspicion,' he said when he got back in. 'Then I'll try to restrict the women to the kitchen. I'll take the fish and my knives in with me and keep them talking. But you won't have long with your girlfriend. Five minutes at the most.' I nodded, sensing the tension in my temples as we drove up the track.

There didn't appear to be a lot of activity around the immediate areas of the farmhouse. The animals and the vicious looking rottweilers, who barked fiercely when we drove up, were all wandering about the yard but there was no sign of any of the men folk. The dogs were all chained up. Herrera turned the van around and backed towards the caravan. 'In case we need a quick get away,' he said. 'Give me a few minutes to get inside and talk to them,' he added. 'If I'm not back in two minutes that'll be your time to move. Good luck.' With that he got himself out of the driver's seat and around to the back of the van. I could hear him fiddle with fish boxes and knives. Then he closed the back doors and walked off towards the kitchen door. The dogs all barked angrily. I watched him go inside, waited another two minutes, then carefully got out and looked around. All seemed quiet and clear so I headed for the caravan.

The dogs then all barked again at me. As I got closer to the caravan I could see that all of the windows had the shades drawn. Goodness knows how hot it must have been in there, I thought, I was already sweltering. As quietly and stealthily as I could I went around the back of the caravan away from the main house. When I was sure I was out of sight I took off my white cap and tapped on one of the windows where the blinds were drawn. Nothing happened, so I tapped again. Suddenly to my delight the blind was pulled across and there facing me through the window, was Iolanthe.

She shrieked with excitement. I put my index finger over my lips for her to be quiet.

Then she beckoned me to come round to the caravan door. I donned the hat, checked the main yard for people, then scurried around to the open door and jumped inside. Instantly she wrapped her arms around my neck and embraced me. I heard the chain attached to her ankle clank as she moved. 'How on earth did you find me,' she said as she continued to hug me. Again I raised my finger to my lips. It was indeed very, very hot in there.

'It's a long story,' I said in a whisper. 'There's no time to tell it now. I just wanted to find out if you are all right.'

She was beginning to cry, but continued to plant kisses on my cheeks. 'Adam they are keeping me prisoner here,' she said between sobs. 'My own family!'

'I can see that,' I replied pointing down at the chain. It was attached by a metal clamp to the floor of the caravan. I guess that meant it was screwed to the chassis. 'We've got to do something to get you out of here,' I said. We moved towards the settee and sat down, side by side. She had to move her guitar to make space for us both. 'We won't be able to do that today though. We'll have to devise some sort of rescue plan.'

'Look at you dressed like this,' she said and removed my hat. 'You are so brave. Adam I want you to know that I had nothing to do with the stealing of your things. I was vehemently against that. I tried to stop them, that's why they locked me up. I swear to you that's the truth.'

'I realise that,' I replied. 'If I can mount a rescue plan will you come with me?' I looked her straight in the eyes.

'Of course I will. I'll go anywhere with you, if you will have me.'

'That's it then. But you mustn't tell anybody, otherwise any plan will fail. Are your family away today?'

'Yes they've gone off with the other men somewhere. I don't know where. Please promise me that you will be careful. If anything was to happen to you I'd never forgive myself.'

'You're the important one now,' I said, 'but you must be patient. I'll have to go now, I'm out on a limb already.' I got up. She hugged and kissed me. I made for the door.

'You've forgotten this.' She was holding out my cap. I kissed her once more, then she opened the door and checked outside. There was no one about, so I headed quickly for the white van without looking back. The dogs barked at me again.

I was half way to the van when a tractor pulled into the yard. Aboard was one of the Moroccans. He wore a hat, but I could see enough to know that it wasn't one of Iolanthe's family. I hurried on with my head down towards the van. He switched off the tractors engine, jumped down and walked towards me. We met up by the door of the white van. I couldn't avoid him. 'What are you doing?' he said to me gruffly in Spanish. I had to think quickly.

'I needed to pee,' I replied as incoherently as I could in the same language, and made a gesture with my hands near my groin to that effect.

He grunted. 'Well just be careful around here,' he said, again in Spanish. 'This is private property.' I nodded and raised my hand in acknowledgement. He moved off towards the kitchen. Before I ducked my head into the van I looked back at the caravan. Iolanthe had been watching us through the caravan window. I didn't acknowledge her though.

A few minutes later Herrera returned. 'All right?' he asked me.

'Just about,' I replied. As we drove down the track I told him what had happened.

The rest of that day was very long and very tiring. Having seen Iolanthe all I wanted to do was get back to my villa, but as had been agreed, Herrera had to complete his round. As he drove we talked a little more about my problem. It was well into the afternoon before we re-entered the service station car park. I handed over the three hundred euros, thanked him for his help and said if I needed him again I would contact Alvardo. He wished me luck and then I drove home.

CHAPTER EIGHT

After that trip it took a long time for the tension in my body to unwind. The following day I felt exhausted. All the while though I had this burning anger at how Iolanthe was being treated. It was inhuman, I kept telling myself, and I had to do something about it.

But what? As I've said before I had no experience whatsoever of that sort of thing. My initial reaction was to go to the local police. They would probably go and interview the Moroccans about the aspects of illegal immigrants and my robbery, but both events were, by then, well in the past. My goods and any immigrants would have been passed on a long time ago and the Moroccans would, I expect, just deny all knowledge of it. Also if they did arrest them, they would also probably arrest Iolanthe as well and that would be the end of it as far as she and I were concerned. Whatever else, I did believe her when she had protested her innocence regarding my burglary and quite clearly she was being imprisoned in the caravan against her will. However, I was convinced that the police wouldn't take a blind bit of notice about that and would eventually lock all of them up. They were after all, extranjeros(foreigners).

So I pondered and pondered on the matter endlessly. Antonio Silva wouldn't want to get himself seriously involved with anything like that. I didn't know enough about Alvardo, the Villaverde family, or Herrera to trust them completely either. If I involved them further I would still remain virtually out on a limb, on my own, with no comebacks.

In a strange way I was shocked soon to discover that help may be at hand from an unlikely source. Late in the afternoon I had a telephone call from Colin Wright. He said he had made some decisions about some of his investments. 'Have you time to pop round and see me?' he asked. Internally I groaned. Seeing him was the last thing I needed at that moment, but on second thoughts I considered it would do me good to get something else positive for my mind to work on. I had brooded for long enough and I needed the money, so I agreed to call in on him.

His dogs greetings were tiresome as usual, but he soon herded them into the kitchen, then guided me onto the patio. Out there on a table, underneath a parasol, he had set out his papers and a large jug of gin, with tonics, ice and lemons. 'It's a hot day and I thought we could do with this,' he said while lifting the gin jug and offering me a slug. Willingly I acquiesced. For some time we talked about the decisions he had made regarding his money. Most of them I agreed with, but I suggested some amendments which eventually he went along with. Throughout our discussions he kept topping up the glasses and because of the heat I was happy to indulge. When we had just about concluded the business Colin said. 'We'll drink to that then,' and poured in another large slug. We sat back in our chairs. For the first time in a few days I felt almost relaxed. He then said. 'And what have you been doing with yourself recently. I haven't seen you out and about much on the beach and I've tried phoning you a couple of times on this,' he said pointing down to the papers on the table, 'but you've obviously been out.'

I suppose it must have been the gin that loosened my tongue. Well, maybe that coupled with my tiredness and anxiety. Normally I would never have related any of my troubles to Colin Wright, of all people. Anyway I began to tell him about my problems with Iolanthe.

The more I talked, the more he kept pouring the gin. Eventually, over about an hour I had related most of the details. Obviously I wasn't completely specific about the sex but I reckon he guessed most of that anyway. Throughout he kept shaking his head and uttering 'dear, dear,' and 'you poor man.' When I'd just about brought him up to date he concluded by saying. 'My dear chap, I must do something to help you.' To be fair to him, during that meeting, he never once said or even implied that he'd told me at the outset what trouble it would all be.

By then, in a way, I was glad to get it all off my chest, to someone who I could, at least in part, relate to. 'What to actually do next is my dilemma though Colin,' I said.

'Well my dear boy, you may have actually come to the right man. I do wish you had told me about this before.'

'What do you mean?' I said.

'I think I probably mentioned to you before,' he began, 'that for twenty years I worked for the Metropolitan police force.' I nodded. 'Well, like me, most of my old pals from there are retired now. And, also like me, many of them have retired out here to Spain. Some of them, because of their past experience have set up detective agencies and private security firms. We still keep in touch. They're the sort of people you need to help you with this.'

* * * * *

That night, after drinking so much of Colin's gin I was too zonked out to do anything more than crash out on my bed. For the first time in days I indulged in a proper sleep. It took Ben scratching on my bedroom door next morning to eventually awaken me. By the time I was up and about the realisation of what I had done the previous evening hit me. Of all the people in the world, the last one I would normally tell about my personal problems would be Colin Wright. I knew for sure he was an outright gossip, who not only prided himself on knowing everybody else's private business, but also took great delight in spreading what snippets of gossip he'd discovered around the whole region. From then on I guessed that my current dilemma would be exposed to all the gin swilling dons of the Costa del Sol ex-pat community. Wherever I went I'd be afraid to look any one of them in the eye for fear of them giving me advice I didn't want. And worse than that, Colin would have the perfect excuse for calling at my front door endlessly to badger me with matters relating to my troubles. I slumped in my lounge, still slightly hung over from the gin.

The expected avalanche though didn't actually begin until after that day's siesta. And even then he had the courtesy to phone me up first. 'I've been in touch with some of my pals,' he said. 'Would you like to come around or shall I come to you?' I invited him to my place. At least that way I could avoid his dogs and I felt I owed him some reciprocal hospitality.

Before he arrived I got out the gin bottle, tonics and some ice and set them out on the patio table. It wasn't long before I heard his ring on my doorbell. When I opened up he was standing outside with a self satisfied grin on his face. Ben chose to ignore him, as he always associated him with his stupid dogs. 'This looks nice,' Colin said noticing the bottles on the table as I guided him out onto the veranda. I poured us a slug each as we sat down, I was careful to heavily lace mine with lots of tonic. For five minutes or so we went over the investments we'd discussed previously. I confirmed that I had already set the ball rolling on the new ones via the computer.

'Anyway,' he said having finished off the first gin, 'that's not what we are here to talk about today.' I refilled his glass and let him help himself to the tonic. When he'd taken a sup, he said, 'I've spoken to some of my pals about your little problem.' I nodded and let him continue. 'All of them emphasise the need for care and caution on your behalf. This could turn out to be very dangerous work.' I nodded again, already knowing that.

He continued. 'Normally it would be expensive in view of the danger, but as I said all of them are old pals of mine and for me they would do it at a much reduced rate,' he said smugly and then downed another big slug of gin. He then said. 'Are you absolutely certain you want to go ahead with this?'

'As long as I don't end up getting killed or being bankrupt, yes,' I replied. He finished off the second gin. I pushed the bottle in his direction for him to help himself.

'Well, the person I had in mind would want to meet you first. Normally they'd charge for that but as it's me they'll do that for nothing.' I nodded. 'His advice is that it would probably be best to attempt this rescue under the cover of darkness. Sometime in the early hours of the morning.' I nodded again. 'I think you told me that there was access across a neighbouring farm and you know the people there?'

'That's correct,' I replied, 'but I'd have to check it out with them first.'

We talked quite a lot more about the possible scenarios. In conclusion I agreed to meet up with his pal and talk through the likely cost. By the time Colin got up to leave he had virtually polished off my bottle of gin by himself. 'I'll leave you that bit to finish off,' he said condescendingly, while pointing at the inch or so of gin left in the bottle, as he got out of his seat. He agreed to phone me when he had arranged an appointment date with his mate. Ben woofed at him as he went out through the door.

* * * * *

Two days later Colin drove me in his open topped BMW sports car to Malaga, to meet up with his pal, Charlie Wolfenden, who ran a security business. His villa residence was situated on the outskirts of the town. I whistled silently to myself in envy as we pulled up in front of an impressive pair of wrought iron gates which opened after Colin had spoken into the intercom. Driving alongside the manicured gardens and the infinity swimming pool on our way to the front door I thought this can't be bad on the pension of an ex-policeman.

Wolfenden was a big bluff, London Eastender who looked more like a bouncer than a policeman. He bore a number one haircut and a golden earring attached to his left lobe. He was wearing an expensive casual shirt, golf type shorts and sandshoes. He shook my hand with an iron-like grip. His lavish villa was kitted out like the home of a pop star, with glass and mirrors everywhere. I was also introduced to his trophy wife Daphne, a glamorous blonde, wearing lots of make-up, which made it difficult to tell her true age, yet she was definitely younger than Charlie. A leopard-skin swimsuit drew attention to her curvaceous figure.

She brought us some cool drinks and we all sat on the terrace, out of the sun, overlooking the swimming pool. Wolfenden made me go over the facts of my problem and the steps I had taken to date. It took some time but he listened intently. He shook his head when I'd finished. A reaction I was getting used to.

'Trying to do what you want could be very dangerous,' he said. Another comment I was becoming familiar with. 'If those Moroccans are involved in the illegal immigrant business it's quite likely they'll have guns of some description. Sometimes to save their necks they even get involved in gunfights with the police. So don't say I haven't warned you.' I shuddered somewhat on hearing his words. 'And I agree with Colin,' Wolfenden continued. 'With these Moroccan families you also never know for sure. They're very family orientated. It's quite likely that if we rescued her she'd turn round and say she wanted to go back to them. I'm telling you this now, because I don't want you to be upset later on.' Across the table Colin was nodding his head in agreement.

'What's it all going to cost me?' I asked.

'Depends what you want us to do. How much can you afford?'

'Just about nothing.' I replied with a chuckle. 'It's cost me eight hundred euros to get this far and I've still got nothing to show for it.'

'Well, if we were to mount a full rescue operation I'd have to kit all my boys out with everything. As I said we couldn't take any chances with that lot. You never know how these sort of situations are going to work out. We've had to use armoured vehicles before now.' I winced. What am I doing getting mixed up in all this I thought. 'That would cost thousands,' Wolfenden concluded.

'That's out of the question,' I replied and looked across at Colin Wright.

'What about if Adam did all the dangerous bits himself,' Wright said. 'I'd be prepared to help out, and if you provided the guidance and maybe some back up?' he said referring back to Wolfenden.

'Maybe that's possible, yes. You're an old friend, so I'd help you out of course, but I still have to make a living.' The thought of Colin Wright involving himself with me on an escapade to rescue Iolanthe made me shudder again. Out on the town he'd live off that for the rest of his life.

But I was stuck in a cleft stick. No way could I afford another big outlay of money. If I really wanted to get Iolanthe out of her 'jail' it seemed that I was going to have to take on the onerous parts myself. So for the next hour or so I described the various scenarios I'd found at the farmhouse and the help I'd received from the other people I'd employed. Wolfenden listened carefully, occasionally interrupting with pertinent questions, before he said. 'I think, like Colin that you're going to have to do it under the cover of darkness.'

Then for another half an hour or more he outlined possible ways of tackling the situation. To me, each one sounded as frightening as the other. All the while Colin Wright kept smiling and nodding his head with that 'I told you so expression' on his face. By the time Wolfenden had finished I was mentally worn out. It was agreed that I would telephone him when I had decided upon which plan to adopt. He said he would be happy to advise me further. All the way home Wright kept up a constant, excitable dialogue on everything that had been said, but I was too exhausted to do anything but occasionally say 'yes' and 'no.'

At home, for the next few days I racked my brain over what to do. All the plans Wolfenden had outlined for Iolanthe's rescue seemed to me to be not only fraught with real danger but way beyond my physical capabilities. To make matters worse two or three times each day I received a telephone call from Colin Wright with his additional suggestions for each plan. There was no doubt that by then he'd really got the bit between his teeth. Most of the time all I could summon up in reply was, 'I'm still thinking about it.'

To escape his calls one lunchtime, I took myself off to the Cactus bar, where Iolanthe had made her singing debut, for some tapas and a couple of cool beers. Sylvia greeted me like some long lost friend. 'Where've you been hiding yourself stranger? Haven't seen you in ages,' she said.

'I've had a busy period with work and a couple of other problems,' I replied, not wishing to expand much further. I ordered a beer and something to eat.

'What about that pretty girl you brought in here to sing?' Sylvia said as she drew the beer. 'Now she was good. Lots of the men keep asking me when she's coming back.'

I hesitated before replying. 'She's gone back to her family at the moment,' I said and left it at that.

'Well you tell her if she wants to sing here again, she's more than welcome. I'd have to sell tickets for that.'

I guess it was those words of Sylvia's that finally motivated me into action. She had been damn right. Yes, Iolanthe had been pretty good on her singing spots. And yes, she was indeed worth rescuing. And more to the point I missed her like hell. Our brief meeting at her caravan 'jail' had re-stirred my feelings on that matter. So without telling Colin in the evening I telephoned Charlie Wolfenden at his villa.

He sounded as though he had already partaken of a few 'sherbets' that evening, but by and large he was helpful. We went over a couple of the ideas he had outlined and elucidated some more on the intricacies of actually putting them into action. I was therefore grateful, yet I remained totally unsure of my ability to carry them out.

Before embarking on any plan I had to get in touch again with the Villaverde family and Alejandro Herrera. The plan Wolfenden had proposed, which I was hoping to implement, would not be possible without their help. A visit to the Villaverde's farmhouse for a discussion was therefore organised. At first they were reluctant to get involved further. The Moroccans were their nearest neighbours and they said they couldn't risk a permanent feud with them. I mentioned that their neighbours were involved in the illegal immigrant trade, amongst other things, and that seemed to soften their objections. In the end it was Nathan and Eden who spoke up for me. They both had, of course, seen Iolanthe and her predicament. They said they were prepared to help me. In the end the others agreed to co-operate. Jacob said they wouldn't charge me any more money, so I must have made some sort of hit with them. Also I needed to make sure, near the day I had planned to carry out the plan, that Iolanthe was actually still at the caravan. That required another visit to her place of captivity, courtesy of Herrera. I needed to tell her the date of the rescue and hopefully what would happen. This time I arranged to meet Herrera at the spot where I had hidden my car on my reconnaissance day there. He said he would bring with him the white coat and hat and he wouldn't charge me any more. While all this was going on Colin kept badgering me, but I wouldn't tell him what was going to happen.

On the next Friday I met up with Alejandro Herrera at the tree covered hiding spot near the gate entrance to the Moroccan's farmhouse. I donned the white coat and hat he'd brought. Again, I'd allowed a few days stubble to grow on my face. He told me he'd made one call at the farmhouse since our last visit. The caravan was still there with most of the blinds drawn, but whether Iolanthe was inside or not he couldn't tell.

'You must think a lot of this girl?' he said to me as we drove down the track towards the house.

'I guess I do,' I replied.

He smiled at me and said he would adopt the same procedure as before and take the fish and his equipment into the kitchen, then try to keep the women folk occupied. 'I can only string it out for five or six minutes though, so you must be quick,' he said.

This time when we arrived in the farmyard there were two or three other vehicles parked about the place. I couldn't spot Iolanthe's family's blue traveller, but the pick-up truck I had seen come out of the gate before was amongst them. This could be trouble, I thought.

We both sat in his van for a few moments checking out the surroundings. Except for the various animals moving about, all appeared quiet. The rottweilers at that moment were not around. 'Now remember you are just a part-time employee with me,' Herrera said. 'Good luck,' he added and got out of the van. Again I waited until he was inside the kitchen door. I checked around the yard then got out of the van, ran towards the caravan, went around the back and knocked on a rear window. As before Iolanthe was astonished to see me.

She squealed when I was in her arms inside the caravan. I put my index finger over her lips for silence. 'I have to be quick,' I said. 'There isn't a lot of time to explain so you must listen carefully. OK?' She nodded and again we sat down on the settee.

As rapidly as I could I described to her my intended plan. She listened in open mouthed horror. Then said somewhere in the middle of my dialogue, 'You can't do all that for me.'

'Yes I can, and I am, so shut up and listen.' Her jaw dropped open again, but I continued. I told her I hoped to carry out the operation on the following Tuesday night. She nodded. Then to her surprise I placed into her hands a small mobile phone I'd bought in town, for her to use on the Tuesday night.

'I don't know how to work these things,' she protested.

Three times I showed her how to turn it on and off, then made her do it three times herself. 'That's all you've got to do,' I said. 'I've set everything but you must not switch it on until you go to bed on Tuesday night. Then you must put it under your pillow. Until then you must hide it somewhere safe and definitely not use it.' I showed her again the button to press to answer my call. 'You must not touch it until Tuesday night though.' I repeated. 'Do you understand?' She nodded, yet she still looked a little dumbstruck. 'Now where are you going to hide it?' I asked. She pointed to a place under the mattress of the bed. I explained a few things more then said I would have to leave.

She hugged me when I got up. 'Adam you must promise that you will take care.' I promised to do that. She checked outside the caravan door. The metal chain on her ankle clanked when she moved. She nodded that all was clear. On the way past I kissed her on the cheek, then I was off in the direction of the white van.

Before I was half way there two of the Moroccan men came into the yard from the farmhouse followed by the rottweilers, who on seeing me, set up a cacophony of barking, then made a bee-line for me. I could see that the men were not part of Iolanthe's family. One was the man I had met on my previous excursion there with Herrera and the other one was, I think, the guy who I had photographed getting out of the pick-up truck at the front gate. The dogs, who were loose, raced at me baring their teeth menacingly. I was terrified. The two men tried to call them off, but one of the dogs kept on coming at me. I cringed. Desperately I tried to climb into the white van, but my effort was in in vain. The dog leapt up at me. His teeth dug deeply into my leg. I screamed out in pain. One of the Moroccans then grabbed hold of him.

'What are you doing?' he shouted at me in Spanish. The dog continued to snarl and bark threateningly. No way could I move from the spot I was rooted to.

In Spanish, I made the same excuse as before about needing to relieve myself. The man was not impressed. His dog continued to express himself in more vehement and vicious terms, snarling and straining his angry face and neck with eyes that indicated he wanted to devour me. The other man had collared the rest of the dogs and was attaching them to the chains. The one who was struggling to hold on to the dog that attacked me continued to verbally harangue me. He reiterated about the farmhouse being private property. They didn't want people wandering around he said forcefully. If I needed to go to the toilet I should use the one in the house, he told me in no uncertain terms. I apologised profusely. '*Si, siento,*'(Yes, I am sorry), I repeated many times but he continued to berate. The dog still struggled viciously to get at me.

'*Siento, estos sordo,*' (I am sorry, I am deaf,) I cried out, trying to placate the man, by admitting that I couldn't hear or understand them. However he continued to shout and wave his free arm, while the other arm struggled with the dog. At that moment I was convinced my number was up.

Fortunately for me Herrera came out of the farmhouse kitchen door and the dogs turned their anger and venom on him. By then though they were mainly under control. The moments respite had enabled me to dive into the white van. When I looked down blood was oozing from my thigh, staining my trousers. I used my handkerchief to try and stem the flow. Outside I could hear Herrera repeatedly telling the Moroccans that I was a new employee he was trying out and continued to apologise for my actions. The Moroccan man told him not to bring me back there again. Herrera kept apologising while putting his fish boxes and kit into the back of the van, still expressing his apologies, while the dogs continued to bark ferociously. When he eventually sat alongside me I pointed to the blood on my leg.

'Bloody hell,' he swore in Spanish. He got out of the van, causing another uproar from the dogs. From the rear compartment of the van he brought some ice and a relatively clean towel, handed them to me, then said. 'Let's get the hell out of here.' We sped away from the farmhouse. 'Seems like you won't be able to come back here again. Not with me anyway,' Herrera said as we travelled down the track.

While I attempted to press the ice wrapped towel onto the wound I related some of the details of my meeting with Iolanthe. He mentioned that when he had gone to the back of the van to fetch the ice, he had spotted her standing at the open caravan door watching what was going on.

We made it to my car where I carried out more repairs to my thigh. 'You shouldn't really drive back to your home with a wound like that,' Herrera said. 'It's not safe. You might pass out.' I brushed away his protests. He gave me some more ice. He said that he may not go back to the farmhouse again.

'I'm sorry about losing you a customer,' I replied.

'That's why I charged you the three hundred euros,' he said. 'If I was lucky that's what I might have earned from them in six months.' Shortly afterwards we both drove off, he in one direction to complete his round and me in the other, hopefully back to my villa.

CHAPTER NINE

Half way back to my home I was beginning to wish I had taken Herrera's advice. Blood was still oozing copiously from my leg and I was beginning to feel light headed. With every passing mile I felt worse. I could only drive with one hand on the wheel, as the other one was needed to be clamped on my thigh trying to stem the flow of blood. Sweat was constantly running from my brow into my eyes making my vision blurred. I felt it would be useless to attempt to make it to my home. If I got there I would probably collapse in a heap on the floor. So I decided to try and reach the local hospital, the one the Moroccan's had taken me to in their van.

Because of my injuries I parked my car at an eccentric angle in the hospital car park. From there I staggered towards the out-patients department clutching the towel against my leg while blood continued to liberally flow from the wound. My outrageous arrival managed to arouse instant activity from the nurses and doctors, mainly I guess because my trail of blood was making an awful mess on their nice clean polished floors. A wheelchair was quickly found and I was taken into a small casualty room. After I had explained the cause of the accident, two doctors and two nurses poured constant attention on me. The wound was cleansed and stitched. I was inoculated with three different needles, including one which I was told was for tetanus and given a hefty dose of painkillers.

'No way can you drive home,' the doctor said to me. 'Unless you have someone who can pick you up, you'll have to stay in here for the night, at least.'

What about Ben was my instant thought? Who would see to him? Reluctantly the only sensible answer I could think of was to telephone Colin Wright.

'Of course I'll come and pick you up my dear chap,' he responded to my call. 'What on earth have you been doing to yourself this time?' I told him I'd explain later.

Within half an hour he was at the hospital, bearing a Cheshire Cat like grin when he saw my predicament. The medics wheeled me out to his car in the wheelchair with instructions to return in forty eight hours. I got Colin to straighten out my improperly parked car, then he drove me home. Along the way I had no alternative but to explain to him the details of my recent assignment at the Moroccan's farmhouse and my intended plan there afterwards. Needless to say he was sceptically fascinated by the whole adventure. To him, I guess it sounded like a tale from a Boy's Own comic magazine, which resulted in him being even more anxious to get on board.

At my villa, much to Ben's disgust, he came inside with me. He suggested that he made me a meal but I pleaded that the injections had left me weary and with no appetite. 'Once I have seen to Ben and his food,' I said, 'all I want to do is get my head down.' So we left it at that, with his promise to call in and see how I was in the morning.

*****

The collective effect of the injections and tablets they'd given me at the hospital instantly cut in as soon as my head hit the pillow of my bed. I was knocked out for the best part of twelve hours. Again it took Ben scratching at my bedroom door to awaken me. When I tried to move I was as stiff as a board. I had to roll out of bed sideways. When I was upright the ache and pain intensified. It was a struggle to reach the bedroom door. Then I had to hold on to it for support. Ben's early morning affection nearly bowled me over.

After seeing to his breakfast I staggered to the bathroom, looked in the mirror and viewed an unpleasant sight. Suddenly I realised that I had planned to carry out Iolanthe's rescue on the coming Tuesday night and no way did I want to withdraw from that. Too many arrangements had been made, which meant I had three days to get myself into some sort of physical shape.

While eating breakfast I downed another fist full of pain killers and the antibiotics the hospital had prescribed. Like the proverbial bad penny though, Colin Wright was soon on the telephone, wanting to know how I was. I explained my circumstances.

'It's just that during the night I've had some more ideas about the rescue plan,' he said. That's what I'd been dreading. I restrained him by saying that because of the aches and pain I needed the morning to get my act together. He agreed and I said I would call in on him after I had taken Ben for a walk after the siesta.

Some time in the late afternoon I struggled to his front door. My walk with Ben along the beach had been painful and difficult. I discovered I had a pronounced limp. When Colin opened his front door I asked if he could keep his dogs off me. He obliged by shutting them in the kitchen.

'You look in a bad way old chap,' he said to me as he guided me onto his patio. 'Looks like you need one of these,' he continued pointing to the gin bottle on the table.

'Better hadn't,' I responded. 'The tablets they gave me are pretty lethal. I've got to try and keep a clear head, at least until Tuesday.'

He looked at me sternly. 'Are you absolutely sure you really want to go through with it? You've already seen how dangerous it's going to be. Whatever this girl means to you, surely it's not worth getting yourself killed over it. I doubt if they'll kill her,' he added.

I took a deep breath. 'I'm committed to getting her away from there Colin and that's that,' I said sternly.

For the next half hour or so he harangued me with various ideas relating to the rescue plan, some of which I thought were totally preposterous and others downright impossible. There were a couple that I was prepared to consider adopting. The first was that he would drive me there and back. Initially I rejected his suggestion, but after further thought I considered it a realistic proposition. In my state of health the physical exertion of getting Iolanthe out of the caravan unseen was going to be enough to cope with, without the added strain of me driving there and all the way home. Colin also owned a fearsome looking pair of metal cutters. 'How else were you going to release her from that chain?' he said as he showed them to me. 'She won't have a key handy you know,' he added, then instructed me how to use them. 'You must practise with them over the weekend,' he said.

The next couple of days were painful and difficult. The whole of my body ached as though I had fallen down a mine shaft. The gash on my right leg throbbed and the surrounding area of skin was beginning to turn into all the colours of the rainbow. Getting about wasn't easy and my legs felt stiff when I walked. All I could do was to keep downing the tablets and take light exercise. Colin called on me but I ensured that his visits were brief, claiming that I needed to rest. He continued to reveal new ideas which he thought would be suitable for the rescue plan. My standard reply became, 'I'll think about that one Colin.' In between I spent some time on the phone making arrangements with the other people who were going to assist me.

In the middle of Sunday night I was awoken by the telephone by my bed ringing. Wearily, in my semi-drugged state, I answered with a yawning response. Then for some moments there was nothing at the other end of the line. All I could hear was a scrabbling sound and what seemed like heavy breathing. Believing it was a hoax call I made movements to switch the phone off. I was stopped by a familiar voice, 'Adam is that you?' I instantly recognised the voice of Iolanthe.

'How did you get my number,' I replied in response. I looked at my clock, it showed it was two thirty.

'When my family came to your house to collect me they took your phone, but when they weren't looking I managed to write down the number on a piece of paper. Adam, I've been so worried about you. I saw what happened with the dog. I've been upset ever since. Are you all right?'

I said I was, just about. 'I thought you said you didn't know how to work a mobile phone.'

'I didn't, but then I had it under the bed and what else have I got to do all day, so I eventually worked it out. Then I remembered the piece of paper with your number on.'

'But you mustn't use it. If your people hear you speaking on it you'll blow the whole rescue attempt.'

'I know that. I only take it out from under the bed in the middle of the night when I can't sleep. But I was so worried after seeing that dog attack you. Are you still able to go ahead with everything on Tuesday?'

By then I was sitting upright in bed. 'Of course I'm going ahead with it. But you must promise me that you won't use the phone again. I repeat you could blow the whole thing if you do.'

She promised, then said. 'But you must also promise me that you will take care. If anything happened to you I'd never forgive myself.'

I made attempts to reassure her, then implored that she disconnected the call. Afterwards I found sleep difficult. Periodically I drifted off for an hour so, but each time I re-awoke thinking about her situation.

On the Tuesday morning I had to revisit the hospital to have my stitches removed. Colin drove me there in his car as I wanted to return with mine. When I arrived the staff peered ominously at my leg as though it was a poisonous specimen. At first they said they weren't going to remove the stitches until the swelling and bruising had gone down. I pleaded, by saying I had to go away on a family trip next day. There followed a lengthy period of head shaking and prevaricating on their part, but I persisted and reluctantly they agreed to extract the stitches. I have to confess that the whole process was extremely painful. 'Now you must ensure that you continue to rest this leg,' the doctor said to me sternly. 'You must not undertake any excessive physical activity until the swelling goes down and the bruising is gone, or you'll risk infecting it.' I nodded my head in response and said nothing, then drove my car home, with Colin following.

*****

On Tuesday afternoon I spent a lot of time on the phone making final preparations for that night with the people involved. I also attempted to bandage my leg with something that would stay on, whilst being flexible enough for me to walk and keep up with the others. I knew the limp would hamper me and the wound cause me pain, but there was nothing I could do about that. Through the afternoon and early evening I continued to down painkillers and the antibiotics and hoped they'd see me through. I rested as much as I could. Ben didn't get his customary afternoon walk, but I filled up his metal food bowl to the brim.

Afterwards I set my bedside alarm for nine o'clock and dozed off. When I awoke my body was again as stiff as hell. I did some gentle exercises to try and loosen up, took Ben out around the garden, then changed into the same dark clothes I had worn before. I had advised Colin to do the same.

We'd agreed that he would call around for me just before ten o'clock. He was early. I laughed when I noticed he'd blackened his face. He'd brought the relevant tin with him. 'You should put some of this on dear boy,' he said holding out the tin towards me. 'If there's a moon up, or there are lights on, with this, they won't reflect on your face.' To keep him quiet I duly obliged. He also had on dark clothes and had with him a black Basque type beret. I had to suppress a smile when I saw it, although I accepted he was more used to this sort of thing than me. During our intercourse on his ideas he had revealed some of the police raids he had taken part in.

We set off for the Ronda road with all the equipment we were going to need stowed in the boot of his car. I'd dosed up again on the pain killers. There wasn't much traffic. He jabbered incessantly all the way. I prayed that we didn't get stopped by the police for if they saw us with our blackened faces and his beret they'd have searched the car boot, and arrested us on the spot as criminals about to go on a job. Colin's driving was what you might call erratic. On the way I warned him that the Moroccan's didn't speak much English. 'Bloody Dagoes,' he responded. I made him promise to be on his best behaviour. We were soon through Ronda and heading for the Villaverde's farmhouse. When we were near their gates I phoned ahead to tell them of our imminent arrival. The gates were open and we drove up to the house. By then it was dark, and there was no moon. The sky above had become cloudy which suited us fine.

My limbs were still stiff and aching when I got out of the car. I hadn't travelled that far since the previous Friday and I needed to undertake some loosening exercises before I could walk properly. Jacob and Nathan were waiting for us outside the front door of their farmhouse. Their faces bore a slightly whimsical look at our appearance. I made the introductions. Everybody shook hands. 'Are you going to be all right?' Jacob said to me in Spanish when he saw me limping. I had already told them on the phone, about my altercation with the dog. 'You look in a bad way,' he added. I tried to reassure him. Nathan looked concerned. We all went inside.

As before most of the men were seated around the kitchen table. This time their faces all bore more serious expressions. Handshakes were exchanged. The women were again clearing up after the evening meal. We had planned to set off for the Moroccan's place about one in the morning, so there was time to kill. Colin and I sat at the table with the men and together we all went over our plan in detail. They sipped at some wine but Colin and I settled for water. It had been agreed that Nathan, Eden and I would be the only ones to venture onto the Moroccan's land. One or two of the other men brought up points which we discussed. Either Nathan or I had to translate for Colin but I have to admit that he behaved himself remarkably well.

As the hour of one approached everybody began to make preparations to move. We all set our watches to the same time. Colin and I retrieved our gear from the boot of his car. Nathan, Eden, Jacob and a couple of the other men went out to the farm sheds to gather what they needed. Eventually those of us who were going to be involved headed for the same spot in the fence, adjoining the Moroccan's land, we had used to enter last time. The sky outside remained cloudy. This time I wore a stouter pair of walking shoes and had advised Colin to do the same. I could feel my bad leg dragging as we strode out. When darkness had fallen, earlier that evening, a couple of the men had gone to the fence and loosened the wire that was nailed to the posts.

The plan was that Jacob and two of the other sons would wait at the gap in the fence, with Colin, for us to reappear, hopefully with Iolanthe. When we reached the fence line I used my own mobile to telephone her. I listened as it rang out. There was no reply. I let it ring and ring. Still nothing. I switched off and re-dialled. Again it rang with no response. 'Stupid girl, come on answer,' I said under my breath. I looked at the others. Concerned faces stared back at me. Was this the reality after all I thought. Perhaps she had been deceiving me all along. Maybe she had no intention of leaving with me. Had it all been a hoax I deliberated to myself.

Again I switched off the phone, shook the instrument and re-dialled once more. I let it ring and ring. It was more painful moments before I heard her say, 'Adam is that you.'

'Yes,' I said. 'Are you all right? Why didn't you answer the phone?'

'Because somehow I must have turned the sound off when I was fiddling with it. I didn't realise I had. I could see it ringing but I couldn't hear anything. I was panic stricken, but eventually I found the right button.'

'Bloody hell,' I said, expressing my exasperation. 'Well, we're on our way now. Is that all right?'

'Yes, but please take care.'

'Yes, yes,' I responded. 'You must turn off the phone now and wait for me to tap on your window. Do you understand?'

She said she did. I switched off my phone and glanced at the others. Their faces looked relieved.

'Time to go,' I said. By then the other men had undone the wire. Nathan, Eden and I walked through. The Spaniards exchanged words of encouragement amongst themselves and Colin said 'good luck,' to me. By then he was wearing his black beret.

The three of us strode off into the darkness. Soon I was struggling in their wake. After about a quarter of a mile we split up. The two of them went off to the left, making for the other side of the farmhouse, while I headed for the copse on the hill, with the animal dung, I had hidden in before. By the time I got there I was puffing like an old man and my leg was throbbing painfully. Sweat was pouring out profusely from under my baseball cap. I needed my shirt to wipe some of it away. If anything the stench of dung at the knoll was worse than before. I could feel myself wanting to retch, but I managed to fight the temptation. I had with me a kit bag in which I'd carried the cutters. Inside it there was also a bottle of water which I gulped on thirstily. Then I had to wait. We had agreed that nothing would happen until two fifteen exactly, to ensure we were all in the right positions and that the other two had enough time to do what they needed to do. The minute hand on my watch seemed to take for ever to tick round to the appointed time.

CHAPTER TEN

At the precise moment the minute hand on my watch hit the fifteen minute mark I heard the explosions, four in all. They echoed around the night sky like we were on the edge of a war zone. The effect was certainly dramatic. Nathan and Eden had taken with them four sticks of gelignite to the other side of the Moroccan's farmhouse. Over there was the remains of a small quarry, which the previous owners had probably used to extract rock from for their building projects on the farm. I was told by the Villaverdes that it was totally obsolete and well away from any land used. The spot though was ideally out of sight and an excellent place to sink in and explode a few dynamite charges without causing any real damage. The lads had also taken with them some flares which they let off at the same time. The intention was to cause a violent, noisy distraction, which we hoped would take the Moroccan men folk away from the farmhouse to investigate. Nathan and Eden would then have to hoof it back to the hole in the fence, via a round about route, away from the house. The four ear splitting booms were certainly loud enough to wake the dead. The dogs at the house responded instantly. Gradually the other animals joined in with their own vocal retorts. The flashing firelights of the flares remained in the sky for some time afterwards, adding to the animals furore. The two boys had done well, their work was done.

Then it became my turn. As soon as the explosions finished I trained my binoculars in on the farmhouse. Within a few moments lights started to come on all over the building. Human activity was evident. The animals continued with their noisy agitation. Before long I could see people coming out of the building in various forms of undress. Gradually the outside lights were switched on. At that time the flares were still alight in the sky. Eventually the men began to board their pick-up trucks and tractors and head in the direction of the commotion. I hoped Nathan and Eden had managed to get well out of sight. It was time I made a move.

Attempting to avoid the animal dung, I scurried down from the knoll as fast as my painful leg would carry me. It wasn't easy. The quicker I tried to go, the clumsier I got and half stumbled many times. I was also trying to work my way around to the back of the caravan and keep out of view from the farmhouse. Many of the inhabitants were still around the area near to the outside yard.

Somehow, goodness knows how, I reached the van. By then I was nearly choking with exhaustion and breathlessness, with the revolting taste of animal dung still tainting my mouth. I tapped on the back window. Iolanthe slid the blind across. She exclaimed in delight when she saw me. I let her open the door and check outside before I moved. She nodded to me that the coast was clear. I ran around and hustled in through the door.

'You poor man,' she said trying to grab hold of me.

'There's no time for that,' I said, brushing her aside. 'Have you got everything?' She had obviously taken in my previous instructions as she was wearing a dark outdoor jacket, jeans and trainers. On the floor by her side was a kit bag, which looked full. 'Let me have your leg,' I then said impatiently. She put her foot up on the settee. I extracted the cutters from my knapsack. She looked horrified. 'It's all right I'm only going to cut the chain,' I said.

She put her hands over her eyes. I attacked the last ring next to the bracelet with the cutters. My first attempt was pathetic. The chain was about twice as thick as anything I'd attempted in my garage. Gruffly I told her to get her leg up higher. She put her foot on the table, where I could get more of an angle on it with the cutters. Two more goes and she was complaining again. 'Mind my leg. I can't do anything without my legs.' Her hands went back to covering her eyes. A third try still didn't crack it. 'Shit,' I hollered quietly.

I took a deep breath, squeezed my eyes in concentration, then while holding the cutters tightly, I snapped my arms together as hard as I could. Instantly pain seared up from my hands to my elbows. I had to stem the outflow from my throat to stop the sound of my cry bellowing out. Miraculously though I heard the chain clunk down on to the floor. Again Iolanthe tried to hug me. 'Come on, we have to go,' I said brushing her away. I whispered for her to check outside the door. She looked then said it was OK. I told her to switch off the lights. By then my arms, legs, and shoulders were all aching with pain. 'We have to go round the back,' I said. 'Whatever you do just keep running for the knoll.' I pointed in its direction. 'Don't worry about me. I won't be able to go as fast as you, but I'll catch you up. Come on let's go. Run!'

Iolanthe could certainly run. I should have known that she could outstrip me from watching her jogging on the beach. Even with the shackle still on her ankle she was half way to the knoll before I had hardly got past the caravan. My backpack was weighing me down. She kept looking round at me. I kept waving at her to keep going. My stumbling, weaving pattern stride continued until I eventually caught up with her under the trees. By then I was already exhausted. I stumbled into a heap at her feet, trying desperately to suppress fits of choking and coughing. Having got that far I didn't want anybody from the house spotting us. When I looked back there were people still about the yard. By then the flares had fizzled out, but the dogs continued to bark. The stink of dung was all around us.

'You are such a brave man,' Iolanthe said bending down to try and attend to me. She produced a small bottle of water from her kit bag on which I supped. The first gulp made me almost choke again. 'Why are you doing all this for me?' she asked while I sipped.

That's a very good question I thought. 'I'll tell you later,' I replied and struggled to get up. 'Come on we've got to go before they set the dogs loose.' She helped me upright. I looked back at the caravan. The door was still closed, so I hoped that up to that point nobody had checked in there.

Then we were off again. Once we were out of sight of the farmhouse Iolanthe grabbed my hand and began to pull me along. She was going too fast for me, so regularly I stumbled and sometimes fell. Each time she picked me up and continued to drag me towards safety. Sweat emitted from every pore in my body. Half the time my eyes were blinded by it. The pain in my leg was like a searing fire. Regularly I cried out in anguish but we kept going.

It seemed to be taking us forever to reach the fence line. In my half blinded state I began to wonder if I had taken the wrong route. By then Iolanthe was now the one who was willing me along. Then in the distance I could just about make out the fence line. The sky was still shrouded in cloud but as we got nearer I could make out the huddle of bodies waiting for us. I had in fact taken us slightly off line and we needed to veer to the left to reach them. Like an exhausted couple completing a marathon race Iolanthe and I fell into the waiting arms for support and comfort. Colin grabbed hold of me. 'Well done lad,' he said. Nathan and Eden were already there.

Again though, there was no time to tarry. It was important we cleared the site before the Moroccans let their dogs out loose on their land. By that time I guessed they would surely have discovered that Iolanthe was missing. We could still hear the dogs barking in the distance. Carried along on each side by willing arms we were both conveyed back to the farmhouse, while the other men made the fence secure. I continued to cough, splutter and choke until we were inside.

There the women had made us drinks. I refused alcohol as before the night was out I was going to have to do more driving. I was given a towel and a bowl of water was put beside me on the kitchen table. To be able to towel myself down was heaven. One of the other men produced a change of shirt for me to wear.

Even then we couldn't stop for long. After quickly expressing my gratitude and shaking hands with all the Villaverde family, particularly Nathan and Eden, Colin and I had to move on. All the men seemed suitably impressed by Iolanthe. Each of them placed an enthusiastic kiss on both her cheeks. We had to get away from the area before the Moroccans could get out on the roads to check on us. After telling the Villaverdes that I would be in touch, the three of us bundled into Colin's car. We gave Iolanthe instructions to lie out on the back seat until we were well out of the area. Two of the men accompanied us in a truck to their main gate.

CHAPTER ELEVEN

Colin's erratic driving made the trip back to my villa around the hairpin bends hazardous. To him it still all seemed like some great schoolboy adventure. He attacked the twisting roads like a Formula One racing driver which only exasperated my pain and caused Iolanthe discomfort in her prone position on the back seat. Once we were well past Ronda and nearing the coast we did allow her to sit upright.

Our journey didn't end once we reached my home. My own car was parked in my driveway and packed for a getaway. No way could I let Iolanthe stay at my villa. That would be the first place her family would look for her. I needed to get her away from there instantly. I had therefore booked a holiday apartment for a two week period at another small town further down the coast.

The morning sun was beginning to peep over the horizon when we pulled up outside my front gate. I grabbed my possessions from Colin's car and ran into the house to fetch Ben. Within moments the three of us piled into my car and I reversed out of the driveway. While locking the gate I expressed my thanks to Colin and gave him a set of the house keys. It had been agreed that he would keep a close eye on the place in my absence. Knowing his enthusiasm for such matters I could at least be assured of that. He had instructions to call the police instantly if anything suspicious occurred. He also had my mobile phone number.

Whilst inside my villa I had been able to swallow another handful of pain killers. However the combined effect of my injury and the recent athletic activity, coupled with the tablets, was beginning to catch up on me. On route to the apartment the pain got worse and several times I felt quite dizzy. Occasionally I had to stop the car to regain the balance in my head. Iolanthe became concerned. She mopped my brow and neck with the water we had with us and made me drink copious amounts of it. I knew she couldn't drive so I was forced to carry on. Fortunately at that time of day there was very little traffic.

Heaven knows how, but we did eventually make it there. I pulled into a designated parking space and got Iolanthe to call in on the concierge for the relevant keys. If he had inspected my dishevelled appearance I'm sure he wouldn't have handed them over. I was still wearing the same clothes as I'd worn at the farmhouse, however, on my brief entry into my villa I had managed to wash my face.

There was a lift to take the three of us and our possessions up the four flights to the reasonably comfortable apartment. There was a balcony with a good view out to sea and two bedrooms. When I unpeeled my sweaty trousers the right leg underneath looked a ghastly mess. The thigh was swollen and the bruising colours were even more inflamed. Iolanthe gasped when she saw it. She made me sit down, fetched a towel and water then began to bathe it.

'This is all my fault,' she said.

'It was the rottweiler that bit me,' I responded, trying to make light of it. She hugged and kissed me, but all I really wanted to do was to lie down and crash out.

Once she had cleaned me up I staggered to the nearest bedroom and fell in a heap on the bed. Briefly I could feel her trying to straighten my body out, but almost instantly I was unconscious. She went off to sleep in the other bedroom.

I haven't a clue what time it was when I awoke next day. The latter part of my elongated sleep had been bedevilled by nightmarish dreams involving all the Moroccans, the Villaverde family and gun powdered explosions. Eventually I had to force myself to wake up to escape from the horror of the dream's reality. Outside there was bright sunshine. Inside the room it was stickily hot. When I tried to move I cried out in pain. Moving my right leg was almost impossible.

Looking down at it I could see the swelling had dramatically increased.

My cry brought Iolanthe and Ben into the room. 'Are you hurting badly?' she said moving in my direction. Ben jumped up to put his front paws on the bed.

'I can't move,' I replied. 'You're going to have to help me. Get down Ben!'

He moved away. Iolanthe attempted to hold onto my paining body. Every inch I moved brought forth further loud shouts and much grimacing. 'What time is it?' I asked when I was just about sitting upright.

'Coming up to two o'clock,' she said. 'Adam that leg looks awful. You're going to have to have it looked at.' Looking down on it again I could only agree with her. It had become a frightful sight.

Between us I somehow managed to get on my feet, but I had to hold onto the bedside table to stay that way. I made Iolanthe fetch one of the lightweight dining chairs and with its aid I made tentative steps to walk. Amidst more vocal outbursts of cursing I reached the lounge and slumped down on a more comfortable chair.

While I tried to unscramble my brain I learnt that Iolanthe had already taken Ben out and fed him. She had also been shopping for some food. I looked down at her ankle and noticed that she'd covered the metal shackle with what looked two or three pairs of longish socks. They made it look as though the leg had an injury, but they did cover, and to a degree, hide the shackle. 'Does that hurt?' I asked pointing at it.

'Not as badly as your leg must do,' she replied.

For the next hour or more, with her and the light chairs help, I made it to the bathroom. Again, with her assistance, I tried to clean myself up and put on some fresh clothes. Then she cooked scrambled eggs, toast and coffee, which we ate at the dining table. It was the first time I'd had an opportunity to talk to her properly since the rescue.

'What's the situation with you and your family?' I asked when we were settled.

'Difficult would be the polite word,' she replied. For the first time since our re-acquaintance she had let her hair down long and had applied make-up to her face. Despite my grogginess the sensations of attraction for her were beginning to stir again in my incapacitated body.

'Did they kidnap you?'

'Yes.'

'Why?'

'Because I said I wouldn't go with them. And because I vehemently objected to them stealing your possessions.'

'So what did they do?'

'They literally picked me up, bound my hands and feet, gagged me, then bundled me into the back of the car, after collecting all my possessions.'

'Did you know where they were taking you?'

She ran her fingers through her hair and tossed back her head. 'No,' she replied. 'I still don't actually know where it is.'

'Besides burgling my house did you find out any more about their other activities.'

'No, that's why they kept me in the caravan, so I couldn't hear what they were discussing. They came to visit me two or three times a day to bring me food and talk to me, but most of that time they had to listen to me berating them.' The fire I'd seen in her eyes before had returned.

'Did you meet any of the other people?'

'Not really. Sometimes when I was sitting on the caravan steps I would see them in the yard but they wouldn't speak to me. Even when I was rude to them.'

By then my leg was causing me much discomfort and I was having to squirm continuously in my seat as we talked. 'So what were your people going to do with you?' I asked.

'I don't exactly know. I have a feeling that we would all eventually go back to the circus and I would still be their prisoner, or slave if you prefer. Unfortunately that does happen in our country. You see I have no money. I have no home. Besides you, I have no real acquaintances. I am living in a foreign country and now they have my papers.' She shrugged her bare skinned shoulders. She was wearing a vest type black flimsy halter top.

'Well we're going to have to do something to get you sorted out,' I said.

'I don't think we can do anything until you've had that leg looked at,' she responded. She was right. So after we had finished talking and eating I sent her downstairs to enquire with the concierge if there was a local casualty hospital. I couldn't risk going back to the one at my town. If her family were searching the area they might spot us. They would definitely still remember my car.

While she was gone I put in a call to Colin Wright.

'How are you?' he enquired. As briefly as I could I updated him on my physical condition. When I'd finished he said, 'You were right!'

'About what?' I asked.

'You've had visitors. This morning. It's all right. Don't worry. I've been to check. There's no damage. They turned up in the blue vehicle, the same one as before and parked it outside your house at about eleven o'clock. One of them went to your front door, rang the bell a few times, then walked around the garden, but eventually he got back in the vehicle and they drove away. He even closed the front gate. Once they'd gone I went over there straight away, but as I said there's no damage. Should I ring the police and tell them I've seen the blue vehicle.'

I thought for a few moments recalling Iolanthe's words. 'If you could. The Moroccan's are obviously involved in criminal activities. The quicker they're apprehended the better. But don't say anything yet about me and Iolanthe, or where they were staying at the farmhouse. I have to get her secured somewhere first.' He agreed to do that and we rang off.

There was a small hospital unit in a nearby town. With the concierge's help we managed to arrange for a taxi at considerable expense, to take us there and back. As I struggled into the cab outside the apartment, I spotted him watching us from his front doorway. I could see the doubts etched on his face. We certainly didn't look like your average tourist couple.

I suffered a long uncomfortable wait, on a poorly designed plastic chair, at the casualty unit. This time there was no trail of blood on my arrival to facilitate any kind of emergency. However, when I was eventually inspected, the same expressions of despair and astonishment were shown when the medics looked at my leg. A doctor was sent for. Heads were shaken in amazement. Again they wanted to keep me in so I protested vehemently. If I had been Spanish they almost certainly would have insisted, but as I was a stupid extranjero, they probably thought, 'Oh well, if he wants to kill himself that's his business. It will be one less off our hands.'

The wound was cleansed, I endured more injections, given more tablets. I was told that the leg needed continual rest and needed to be propped up. I was not to walk more than necessary, even around the apartment. I definitely could not drive. I would be breaking the law if I did, they said. More helpfully I was given a set of metal crutches. When we eventually got back to the apartment I crashed out to sleep again.

It was the next morning before I awoke. The stiffness and the pain were still prevalent. Again I needed Iolanthe's help to get upright. The crutches though proved to be a boon. How to carry anything else when I held them in both my hands was a problem. We ate breakfast, then I said. 'We're going to have to do something about your shackle.' I got her to show me it again. On inspection, her ankle looked chaffed and bruised, no way could I saw it off. I would have been scared stiff of sawing through her leg.

While I'd been sitting in the hospital waiting room I had pondered on the ways of having it removed. I knew it would be impossible for her to get about much longer with that locked on her ankle. Before the medics saw me I'd had a brainwave. Later in the morning, from the apartment, I phoned Charlie Wolfenden and explained the situation.

Initially he was pleased to learn about the success of the rescue, although he had already received some bragging details from Colin Wright. He chuckled when I told him about the problem with the shackle.

'You do manage to get yourself into some scrapes,' he said.

'Don't tell me about it,' I responded.

Wolfenden said that if I gave him the address of the apartment he would send 'a little man to see me.'

'What does he do?' I stupidly asked.

'Well let's just say that as far as you're concerned he's a locksmith. Actually he is one of the criminals I put behind bars when I was a policeman. Since then he has almost gone straight and now he's living down here on the Costa. He'll undo the lock for you. He'll expect to be paid though.'

'How much?' I asked.

'Fifty euros should do it,' Wolfenden said. I swallowed hard and took a deep breath.

Later in the day, an almost dwarf of a man with a cockney accent appeared at the apartment door. Besides being extremely short he was completely bald, and sporting a straggling goatee beard. He was wearing a blue and white hooped t-shirt, like the convicts used to wear in old photographs, a scruffy pair of khaki shorts and opened toe sandals, encompassing bare feet. He was carrying what looked like an old doctor's bag, which I subsequently discovered was full of his tools.

'Which one is the the patient,' were his first words when Iolanthe let him into the apartment. He spotted me standing behind her on my crutches. I think he initially thought it was me. I pointed in the direction of Iolanthe. 'Oh yes, very nice,' he responded, looking her up and down. 'I can see I'm going to have to take this one home with me and work on it for a while.' Iolanthe's glorious smile lit up the room. He put his bag down on the tiled floor. 'Let's have a look at the damage then.'

She was wearing chequered cropped slacks, a couple of pairs of socks still covered the shackle. She removed the socks and lifted her leg up onto the settee for him to inspect. 'Oh dear. Even nicer,' he said. 'Are you sure you don't want to come home with me for treatment.' Iolanthe shook her head and smiled glowingly again. 'Am I allowed to touch,' he said. She nodded, then from his bag, he took out a pair of wire framed spectacles, which he perched at the end of his nose.

'M'm. One of those,' he said on inspection of the ankle he held in his hand and moved the shackle around gently. 'I won't ask how you got it.'

'Best not to,' I interjected.

From his bag he extracted a bunch of keys. Diligently he tried many of them in the lock but none of them would open it. 'M'm,' he repeated, then delved back into the bag. This time he brought out a twisted thread of metal wire. 'This won't hurt' he said, then inserted the wire into the lock and twisted it around inside various times. After a few moments, magically the shackle came apart and fell on the ground. 'Good lock that one,' he said. Iolanthe hugged him. Her leg was free. He wiped his brow and put his bits and pieces back in his bag.

'I think it was agreed that fifty euros would cover it,' he said next.

Reluctantly I went off to the bedroom to fetch it. He talked to Iolanthe. When I was back with the money he thanked me, shook hands with us both, said, 'Now if you want any further treatment, don't hesitate to contact me. Burgess is the name.' With that he turned on his heels and was gone. When the door was closed Iolanthe squealed and she rushed into my arms. Her enthusiasm nearly bowled me over.

* * * * *

I was still sidelined by the state of my leg, but with the help of the tablets, prolonged rest and sleep, I was gradually able to regain my mental faculties. Over the next couple of days Iolanthe continued to ask how she was 'ever going to repay me for what I had done for her. The money you are spending on me must be costing you a fortune,' she said often. My standard reply became 'don't worry I'm sure I'll think of something.'

My incapacity though did give me time to think and make telephone calls. Iolanthe was delegated to take Ben out and shop for our food. I told her to keep a low profile as I didn't want any chance of her being spotted. So most of the time she wore an extra large pair of sunglasses and a baseball cap with a large peak that shielded the majority of her face. From time to time I did notice, from the balcony, the concierge watching her come in and out. By then I was convinced he had severe doubts about us. In between she cooked our meals.

Phoning Colin Wright I learnt that there had been no further activity around my villa. He related that he visited my home three times a day with the dogs and that all was well. 'What are you going to do with her now?' he then asked me.

'I'm working on a plan. When it's finalised I'll let you know, as I could still be grateful for some further help.'

I heard him sigh at the end of the phone. 'Well I hope you know what you're doing. You're taking on an awful lot by yourself,' he said. When he'd rung off I asked myself the same question. Then I made several telephone calls in connection with the plan I had in mind. Also, by having my laptop with me I was able to do a certain amount of financial work over the internet. Somehow I had to try to keep my income stream flowing as with all the recent outlay my own financial circumstances were becoming desperate. By then my novel was totally on a backburner. I also knew we couldn't afford to remain at that apartment any longer than the booked two weeks. I doubted if the concierge would authorise it anyway. And I knew that there was no way that Iolanthe could come back with me to stay at my villa. Her family would be sure to catch up with her if she was there.

One evening, after dinner, when we were together in the apartment, I asked her, 'What would you think about singing for your living?'

A surprised expression filled her face. 'I don't know that I'm good enough to do that,' she responded.

'Sylvia at the Cactus bar said you were. She told me she could sell the place out if you went back there to sing.'

'But I couldn't go back there. My family would get to hear about it and then they'd surely find me.'

'I agree. I wasn't actually thinking of that, but would you be prepared to give the singing a go. It would help to pay for your keep.'

She paused for a moment to think, tossed her head in the air, then swept her hair back off her face with her hand. 'I guess so,' she eventually replied, 'but I'd have to practice hard again. I haven't sung since that night, and I haven't got a guitar. No way could I have brought that with me when I ran from the caravan.'

'We can buy another guitar,' I said 'A cheapish one anyway, to start off with. Would you be prepared to give it a go ?'

She thought for a short while then said. 'Of course I'll give it a go. I have to do something to pay my way. And it's time I stood on my own two feet.' When I looked up at her a steely look had spread across her face.

So I explained to her the plan I had in mind.

* * * * *

Gradually over the next few days my leg movements began to improve. The swelling started to go down and I was able to get about on one crutch, however, the attendant bruising colours remained just as vivid. I knew there wouldn't be a guitar shop in the little town where we were staying, so one day I sent Iolanthe on a reconnaissance bus trip to Torremolinos, a larger conurbation further down the coast, where I guessed there would be a music shop.

She was gone most of the day but she came back pumped up with excitement. There were, indeed, two such shops. One was a pucker music store and another was a second hand shop selling predominantly musical instruments. When she told me the related prices I knew we had to narrow our choices down to the second hand shop. However, for over half an hour she regaled me with descriptions of the various instruments. I know nothing whatsoever about guitars, but I listened avidly and let her enthusiasm carry her along.

By then we were well into the second week of our stay at the apartment and I was aware that I was going to have to start to make moves to get us out of there. Before I could do that I had to test out my leg.

With the aid of my laptop and Google, I got Iolanthe to show me where the second hand shop in Torremolinos was situated. By using the same internet procedure I was then able to find a suitable car park nearby. My idea was to test my leg by driving there. Most of the trip to Torremolinos was via the motorway, so there would only be a small amount of complicated in-town driving to manage. From the car park to the shop looked a short distance to cover on foot with my one crutch.

We duly set out next day. Parking my car in the multi-storey presented me with the biggest challenge. My body was still as stiff as a poker and the leg remained painful, so twisting round to reverse in to a parking space was difficult. From there I hobbled to the shop where a galaxy of instruments was on display for us to view. Iolanthe handled them all reverently. In time we settled on one which was within my budget, after she had confirmed that it 'would do the job.' My leg hadn't actually given out during the day but when we got home I was very tired. I dosed myself up again with pain killers, then crashed out once more on the bed.

After a day to recover we headed, in my Mercedes, to see Antonio Silva in Marbella.

CHAPTER TWELVE

To be back out and about amongst civilisation lifted my spirits enormously, almost banishing from my thoughts the continuing pain in my leg. Iolanthe was wearing a cheap figure hugging red dress which she had bought when we were in Torremolinos, and had with her the guitar we had purchased there. I had phoned Antonio beforehand, to briefly outline my ideas. Compared to the comparative peace of our quiet little seaside town, Marbella was all hustle, bustle and traffic.

We were escorted into his office by another leggy blonde. By my evaluation though the girl I had alongside me was better looking.

'There you both are,' Antonio said rising from his desk to greet us. He and I shook hands, then he moved across to kiss Iolanthe on both cheeks. 'So this is our problem,' he said. 'I can see now Adam, why you're taking such trouble.' Iolanthe gave him one of her best smiles. He guided us over to the side settees and offered cool drinks, for which I was grateful. The tablets I was taking continued to make my mouth feel as dry as sandpaper.

My plan was to try and get Iolanthe some singing work in a couple of Antonio's night clubs. Most of them had cabaret acts. I was sure she had the talent to make a living at it. I had suggested she should adopt a stage name and if necessary wear a different colour hair wig when she performed, to disguise herself. Beforehand, on the phone, I had also briefed him about the trouble we had at the farmhouse and since. And before setting out for Marbella I had also ensured that Iolanthe was completely in favour of my plan.

'All we have to establish now is that the little lady can sing,' Antonio said after we had aired most of the factors. 'I see you've brought your guitar with you,' he said pointing at Iolanthe. 'Shall we give it a go?'

While remaining seated on the settee she picked up the guitar, strummed a few cords, tuned one or two of the strings, hummed a few notes, then settled.

Although she had practised all the previous day I knew she was nervous. After singing three or four chords she sang a bum note. She stopped playing, said, 'sorry,' coughed, then started again. This time she sang the song perfectly right the way through. Antonio politely clapped at the end.

'Ok, very good,' he said. 'But I'm not the professional in all this. You'll have to convince one of the nightclub managers as they audition the acts.' Iolanthe and I nodded. 'I'll arrange an appointment,' Antonio added

The other part of my plan was to organise accommodation for Iolanthe in Marbella or nearby. Antonio owned numerous apartments there and many of his 'girls' and some of the cabaret acts, lived together in them and shared the rent. Antonio said that if the nightclub manager was prepared to take her on, he would lend her the first months rent, in lieu of wages, until she earned some money. 'I can always take it out of Adam's fees if you don't repay me,' he said with a chuckle. Again Iolanthe and I looked at each other then nodded our agreement in response.

He walked over to his desk and telephoned one of his club managers. An appointment was made for Iolanthe to go there the following day. Time was of the essence as we didn't have many days left in the holiday apartment. 'If you can convince him you're good,' Antonio said afterwards, 'you'll definitely be a star.' On our way out, when Iolanthe's back was turned, Antonio winked at me, gave me a thumbs up and nodded his head approvingly.

*****

For sometime as we drove back to the apartment she was very quiet. 'Are you happy to go through with all that?' I said eventually to break the silence.

She hesitated before replying. I had the top of the Mercedes down. Her hair was flying loose in the slipstream. 'I wouldn't exactly say I was happy, but what other choice do I have? I can't stay with you, I know that. And as I am now, I have no money to stay anywhere else.'

'You could go back to your family?'

'Phew,' she sniggered. 'I think I'd rather go to jail than that. I'd have more freedom there. At least this way I would have a certain amount of freedom and have an opportunity to do something for myself.'

'OK,' I said, 'we'll give it a try.'

There was more silence. Then she said. 'You know Adam I am grateful to you for doing all this for me. I'm sure I don't deserve half of it.' I made no reply and we journeyed on.

* * * * *

The next day we travelled again to the outskirts of Marbella, to the designated night club, where we were met by a gaunt looking Spanish young man, with dark receding hair, named Eusebio. He was wearing an open necked white shirt and black trousers. He spoke quite good English, but his manner was jumpy and brusque. The night club was empty and almost completely unlit. Iolanthe had her guitar with her. He put a stool on the bare stage, pointed to it and asked her to sing. He and I stood in front of the stage and watched.

She wore the same red dress as on the previous day, the only one she possessed at that time. She sang two songs perfectly. She also put on a bit of an act, swirling the guitar around her body as she sang. I was impressed, so was Eusebio, albeit that he wasn't exactly over enthusiastic, but I guess that was his manner.

'No bad,' he said, in poor English, when she had finished. 'Ok, we try you out next Wednesday night. The cabaret es in two halves. One act for about three quarters of an hour. Then we have dancing for the customers and after that the main act comes on. You will be first act, OK?'

By then Iolanthe had come down from the stage and was standing alongside us. She nodded her agreement.

'OK. See you at nine o'clock next Wednesday,' he said and started to move away.

'How much will she earn?' I asked before he had gone too far.

He turned to face us. 'Oh, I don't know,' he replied, shrugging his shoulders. 'We say forty euros for the first night. After that we review it and maybe pay some more. Eh?'

Iolanthe and I both looked at each other but before we could reply he was gone, leaving us to find our own way out. 'You're not going to be able to afford a luxury villa with an infinity swimming pool on those wages,' I said to her as we walked across the car park to my Mercedes.

From there I phoned Antonio Silva to tell him that Iolanthe had passed her audition. I asked about the apartment accommodation. He gave me the address of an apartment block four or five miles away from the nightclub. He said that was the one he had in mind for her. We could drive past it if we liked, but we wouldn't be able to go inside as most of the girls would be out. We discussed the rental. At forty euros a gig Iolanthe wasn't going to have much left to live on.

After getting lost a few times we managed to find it, a typical twelve storey out of town apartment block, where the working class Spaniards would live. There was nothing special or attractive about it, but it looked recently built and suitable for the purpose. Again there were a lot of silences on the way back to our seaside tenancy.

When we got inside we held each other tightly. She began to sob a bit. 'Hopefully it will only be for a short while,' I said.

'I know,' she replied. 'I know I have to do it.'

* * * * *

Over the weekend we made arrangements to leave 'our holiday home'. By that time the pain in my leg was easing, yet the swelling was taking a long time to go down. However, by then I was able to get about without the aid of the crutch. Consequently on the Saturday we ventured again into Torromolinos. Iolanthe needed to buy some more cheap dresses to wear for her stage act, as well as extra strings for her guitar, a supply of plectrums and a few other items to enable her to live by herself. We visited a Taberna, sat outside in the sunshine and enjoyed a couple of drinks and some tapas.

On the Saturday night, for the first time since we had been back together, I felt up for it enough to attempt to indulge with her in some sex. I guess it wasn't the best performance I have ever given. On my part there was more moaning and groaning from my aches and pains rather than actual sexual satisfaction. I was however relieved that I could still manage it. Afterwards I felt more relaxed, my spirits had been uplifted and I slept soundly.

The following day was to be our last day together for some time. Our union the previous night had brought us back close together again physically. We spent a certain amount of time huddled in each others arms. The day was warm and sunny. We walked the beach arm in arm, accompanied by Ben. I still insisted that she wore her dark glasses and baseball cap. We ate lunch out, then began packing up our belongings to leave on the Monday morning. That night we went to bed early. We were back together as an 'item.'

As had been arranged with Antonio Silva, on the Monday morning, we all travelled to his office in Marbella. In many ways we were sad to leave our holiday apartment. Despite my bodily troubles, it had been a sanctuary of peace and seclusion where we had been able to hide from the world and grow together as a couple. That

Monday morning we were heading back to the reality of our situation.

We didn't spend long with Antonio as he was busy. He had arranged for one of his 'girls', who worked in the office, to take us to the apartment Iolanthe was going to live in. It transpired that she also lived there. Tatiana was pleasant enough, in an offhand way. I drove the three of us there. Iolanthe had brought her goods and chattels, plus the guitar which was the sum of her total worldly possessions. Tatiana showed us around the accommodation. It was passable, if slightly untidy. There were three bedrooms, one living room, with kitchen dinette, two bathrooms and a balcony. She gave Iolanthe a key and said that she and the other girl usually got back there in the early evening, so it would be OK for Iolanthe to practice her guitar and singing in the day.

I had promised to take Tatiana back to Antonio's office so it wasn't long before I was forced to leave Iolanthe alone in her new home. The desolate expression on her face, when we hugged and kissed goodbye told me everything. But she did whisper to me that 'it is better than being in the caravan.' I made her promise to wear her dark glasses and cap when she went out. I had given her some extra money to buy food and said I would pick her up to take her to the nightclub on the Wednesday evening.

After depositing Tatiana outside the office I made my way back to my villa.

* * * * *

It wasn't long before Colin Wright was knocking on my door.

'How are you? Is everything all right?' he queried.

I had no alternative but to invite him in. Ben headed for his bed in the kitchen area. I confirmed to Colin that I was still in recovery mode from the dog bite. We sat in my lounge.

'And what happened to the girl?'

'She's Ok,' I said. 'I've found her a safe place.' I wasn't going to tell him where or anything else about it. Despite his good intentions Colin did gossip and the ex-pat community in the area was always incestuous with rumour and innuendo. I just couldn't risk it. Colin looked put out.

'Have I had anymore visitors?' I asked him trying to change the subject.

'Not since. I don't think so anyway.'

'Colin I am most grateful for your help in all this,' I said. 'Without your assistance I wouldn't have got half this far. At the moment the whole thing is on a knife edge. It's a delicate balancing act trying to keep us both safe.'

'Well I hope you know what you're doing. If you want help you only have to ask.'

'I know that Colin,' I said. With that we went on to talk about his investments, then he was gone.

When I had re-settled in my villa I sat on the balcony with Ben and a large whisky and pondered. By that date I had finished taking the antibiotics, occasionally resorting to a pain killer. When I actually stopped doing things the ache and pain in the leg would return quite badly. I also got very tired quickly so it wasn't long before I made for bed. For the first time ever, my villa seemed very empty and lonely. I was missing having Iolanthe around me.

Despite apparently having crashed out into a deep sleep as soon as I'd got into bed, I was awoken in the early hours by what I thought was a car engine. Then Ben barked. I sat up instantly. I still couldn't exactly hop out of bed but I did make it to the bedroom window. Somewhere up the road, out of direct sight, I could see a vehicle's headlights. I went into the kitchen and tried to settle Ben. When I looked out of the kitchen window I could see that I had left my car parked in the driveway, so if it had been Iolanthe's family in the vehicle they would know I was back home. I stroked Ben then went back to bed, but I didn't sleep very well from then on in.

* * * * *

For the following days, up to the Wednesday I was very much on edge. I had a constant feeling that I was being watched. I guess it was partly imagination but the incident of the other night had to some extent spooked me and I hadn't slept well since. I was glad I was going to Marbella to do something positive.

I arrived at Iolanthe's apartment around eight o'clock. The two Spanish girls were there but they were both taciturn in their response to me. Iolanthe greeted me with hugs and kisses. She took me into her bedroom. She was wearing one of the dresses she had purchased in Torromolinos, a blue one and new very high heeled shoes she had purchased locally. A lot of make up had been applied to her face and she was wearing a wig of shoulder length hair, tinted redder than her normal colour, which made her look more Spanish.

'How have you been?' I asked.

'Oh, OK. I'm missing you though.'

'Me too. Are the girls all right?'

She pulled a bit of a face. 'OK, I suppose. They don't bother me much. They're gone all day, so I have the place to myself and after they've eaten in the evening, most nights they go out. When they do come back in it's two in the morning. Then they wake me up because they talk so loud.'

I tried to say something about it not being for ever, then said, 'Are you up for tonight?'

'I'm very nervous, but I've been practising like mad. At least that's given me something to do.'

Soon afterwards we headed off for the night club. This time we entered through the stage door. Eusebio was inside wearing a black dinner jacket, tie and satin seamed trousers. His greeting was as brisk as before. 'The customers are beginning to arrive,' he said. 'We'll let them settle down then we'll put you on.'

As nine o'clock approached Iolanthe got ready in a tiny dressing room the size of a bathroom closet. Final touch ups were made to her make-up. She tuned the guitar constantly. I could tell she was nervous. 'You look fantastic.' I said. She gave me a weak smile.

When she moved to the wing of the stage I went out into the club proper and stood at the back, by the bar, and ordered a beer. There were lots of strobe and dancing lights floating around the arena. The stage was fully lit with more coloured lights and spotlights. I guess about a quarter of the tables were occupied. People were mainly ordering drinks from the waiters. It was still very early in the evening for a Spanish night club. A coloured man, on the edge of the stage, was playing a repertoire of tunes on a piano everybody knew but couldn't put a title to.

A further ten minutes elapsed before he finished to muted applause. Then Eusebio came out on stage carrying a microphone on a stand and the same stool Iolanthe had sat on for the audition. In Spanish, he said into the microphone, 'Now I want you to give a warm round of applause to someone who is making her debut here tonight. Please welcome Raquel Padillo.'

A spotlight was turned on and Iolanthe walked on stage looking glamorous. The applause wasn't exactly ecstatic but she did get a few wolf whistles. She only knew bits of Spanish but I had encouraged her to say 'Gracias' lots of times during her act. She said it before she began her first song, a ballad with a repetitive beat. She sang it well, she looked great, but most of the customers were disinterested. Many of them kept on talking and drinking while she sang. She finished to mild bouts of clapping. You couldn't really call it applause. '*Gracias,*' she said again into the microphone.

Another two numbers were sung to the same reaction. Then she swung into a much faster upbeat song and began to swirl the guitar around her body as she had done at the audition. That was better, the audience began to clap in tune with the beat. She seemed to begin to enjoy herself. The song ended to enthusiastic applause and more wolf whistles. She continued in that vein until the close of her act. At the end some of the audience were standing out of their seats to applaud her as she walked off the stage. I followed around the back way and greeted her as she came out of the wings. 'You were great,' I said and hugged and kissed her.

Eusebio came over to us. 'Not bad,' he said. There was almost a smile on his face. 'You'd better come back on Friday night at the same time. We put you on Friday, Saturday and Sunday nights. There will be a bigger audience.' He started to move away.

'What about the fee?' I said.

He turned and hesitated before he said, 'OK. We make it fifty euros from Friday night.'

I hugged her again then drove her back to the apartment. The other two girls were out so I went inside. It was great to spend an hour or so with her. We didn't indulge in sex as by then she was still living off the reaction and applause she'd received at the night club. We agreed that I would not go back there for a few days to see if she could manage by herself. She told me she could get a bus to the nightclub. It was only three stops away and she had tried it out in the day time. If she was really late finishing she could always get a taxi back from the night club, she said. Apparently they offered reduced rates for the staff.

It was late when I drove home, but I felt a lot better about everything. Next day I took Ben out for his early morning walk. I thought if I went early I could miss Colin Wright. Then I drove up into town as I needed some shopping. After my late night at the stuffy night club I remained in need of exercise and fresh air. I didn't want to meet up with Colin on the beach. Ben had had his walk so

I headed for a track I knew which led to a good walk through the forest.

CHAPTER THIRTEEN

The next thing I fully recall is waking in a hospital bed in a small private room. I had been anaesthetised while they dealt with the gunshot wound in my shoulder. I could see a Spanish policeman sitting outside the bedroom door talking to a pretty dark haired nurse. She must have seen me move, and came into the room.

'*¿Que tal?*' (How are you?) she said to me.

I replied in the same language that I wasn't sure. I asked where I was. She said that I was in a hospital in Malaga and that I was being treated for a gunshot wound. Suddenly I was aware of bandages on my right shoulder and my right arm being in an elastic sling attached to a rail above the bed. My left hand was attached to a drip feed. The nurse took my blood pressure, my temperature and my pulse. Whilst she did so, she told me that as soon as I felt up to it that the police wanted to talk to me. I didn't have to rush though she added. She had lovely brown eyes. She passed me a beaker of water with a straw, then said that in an hour or so I could have something to eat if I wanted. I asked her what time it was. She said, five o'clock in the afternoon. In a short while she left the room saying she would be back soon. She spoke to the policeman as she passed him, but he remained sitting on the chair.

Gradually I began to get my bearings. The nurse had propped the pillows up behind my head so I could look around. I could see out of the window to the city below. There were extensive bandages and padding on my right shoulder. At that moment it didn't hurt, but I guessed I'd been dosed up on painkillers. Some of my clothes were on a chair near the bed and my shoes on the floor beneath. I couldn't see my shirt. I guessed they'd had to cut it off. Apart from that, a jug of water and the medical equipment there was nothing else of any consequence in the room.

Within ten minutes the nurse was back. She repeated '*¿Que tal?*' I replied 'OK.' She asked if I felt up to talking to the policeman. I said '*Si.*' Then I remembered Ben. Somebody would have to see to him.

She went out of the room and fetched the policeman. Like most Spanish policemen he had a languid disinterested air about him. He was tall, wearing an open necked shirt and trousers in the Guardia green. He had short dark, almost crew cut hair and four or five days of stubble on his face.

'Hola, señor,' he said to me. I nodded and replied '*Hola*'. He asked me if it was all right to talk. I nodded again. He admitted that he only spoke a little English. In Spanish I asked him what had happened to me.

He went on, mainly in Spanish, to describe that they had received a call out from the man who'd found me lying on the pathway to the wood. A fellow walker, a Spaniard with a dog, by all accounts. On arrival the police called the ambulance when they saw the gunshot wound. They discovered that I had not been robbed. My wallet, phone and other bits and pieces were still on me when they got there. These were at the police station. My car, he said, also appeared untouched. That too had been taken to the police station for forensic tests. 'Did I have any idea who might have done it?' he asked me. He was still standing at the foot of the bed.

'I may have an idea,' I replied.

'Did I feel up to talking to the detectives?' he said next.

'I guess so,' I replied, then told him about Ben being on his own in my villa. I asked if somebody could visit Colin Wright and tell him about the predicament. He had a key I said and would go and deal with the dog.

He said he would go and phone. I asked him if the detectives could bring with them my phone. There was somebody I needed to contact urgently I added. He said he would see what could be done. He left the room and I saw him outside speaking on his mobile walkie-talkie. The nurse came back in the room and fussed around me. She told me that she would not let the detectives talk to me for too long as I needed rest. She gave me some more water and added that when they were gone she'd bring me some food.

It was about a quarter of an hour or so before I saw two detectives in the passageway outside my room. They were talking to the other policeman and the nurse. She appeared to be lecturing them, then the two plain clothes men came into the room. They introduced themselves but I instantly forgot their names. They were however carrying a plastic bag containing my possessions. They said I would have to sign for them. I lifted my right arm slowly to indicate my incapacity. They said they would leave the form with the uniformed man, for me to sign later. 'What about my dog?' I asked.

'We have sent someone to call on your neighbour,' the detective said.

Between them they went over, mostly in English, the details of what the uniformed man had already told me about finding me on the footpath. They revealed that they had found the offending bullet. It was standard issue for a lightweight shot gun, available in any gun shop. Then they re-asked if I knew who may be responsible. As best and as succinctly as I could I told them about Iolanthe's family and about the farmhouse where they were staying, as well her captivity there. I said I'd rescued her by traipsing across various fields in the middle of the night. I also said that the police in my town had an open file on the matter linking the Moroccans to the illegal immigrant trade. One of the detectives, a thin, tall, bald headed man made notes as I talked. 'And where is the girl now?' the other one asked. I hesitated before replying.

'At the moment, she is at a safe place under my protection,' I replied.

'But we will have to interview her,' the tall thin one said. 'This is a potential murder case.'

'Ok,' I said. 'But I would like to be present when you do that.'

'But you're not going to tell us now where she is?'

'No.' I said dogmatically. 'I am too ill to remember at the moment. I need to speak to her first. She is very frightened and scared that her family will abduct her again. If you see her first you will probably only arrest her as an accessory to the case and I'm not having that.' The detectives looked at me with a resigned expression on their faces. I continued. 'You can beat me up and torture me if you like but I will still not tell you and if you do that it will only prolong my stay in hospital.' I smiled at them and they both shook their heads. 'Find the family first, then I'll go with you to see the girl,' I added. 'I think they're the ones who did this,' I said, pointing to my right shoulder with my left hand.

The nurse came into the room. '*Vale. Es sufficiente*,' (Ok. That's enough), she said and began to shoo the men out of the room. They left saying that they would be back to see me next day. She then fussed with my bed and asked if I would like some food. '*Por favor*' (Yes please), I replied. She told me that once I had eaten she would give me another injection which would send me to sleep. She was quite pretty, short in height, with short dark hair curled around her ears and I think she had a soft spot for me.

What happened for the rest of that day is a blur. I guess I was zonked out most of the time. In the morning the doctor came to see me. The uniformed policeman was still sat outside my door. The doctor told me that I was a lucky man. The bullet had passed through my shoulder blade and out the other side, thereby causing little permanent damage. They would however need to keep me in for a few more days for observation and rest.

When he had gone and the nurse had finished with me I got her to pass me my mobile. I rang Iolanthe on the mobile I had given her. She was horrified to hear my news and wanted to come and visit me. I told her no. If she did that the police would probably put her in custody. I told her that the safest thing was for her to carry on with her singing and remain incognito. I said the police wanted to interview her, but that I wanted to be present at that. She continued to express her incredulity at the events, but I told her not to worry.

'Do you think it was my family?' she said.

'I don't know,' I replied.

Later on in the morning the two detectives came to see me again. They told me that officers had been up to the Moroccan's farmhouse. None of Iolanthe's family were there. The tall, bald one said that complaints had been made to them about dynamite being set off on their land on the night I rescued Iolanthe. 'What would you know about that?' he asked me.

'Not a lot,' I replied. 'It was a still night and I heard no dynamite. How would a simple Brit like me know how to set off dynamite? I think they're just making it up as an excuse to ward you off.' The two men again looked at me with resigned expressions on their faces.

'You can't take the law into your own hands,' the other one said. He was the shorter of the two and typically swarthily Spanish.

'Did they admit that they held the girl there as a captive?'

'They said she was part of the other family and what they did with her was their business. I haven't actually interviewed the officers who went there as it was only last night they visited. I've spoken to them on the phone but they're off shift at the moment.'

'What about the blue four by four vehicle?' I said next. 'The police in my town have the details of that?'

'There is another alert out for it,' the bald one said.

They then proceeded to question me further in more detail about my rescue of Iolanthe. I have to admit that I was very sparing with the truth, and made up a story about a solo rescue by me. In all honestly I don't think they believed a word I said. The nurse came to my aid. 'That's enough,' she said to them in Spanish. 'This man is under sedation and is supposed to be resting.'

On their way out of the room the shorter one said. 'Until we get further with our enquiries we don't think it would be safe for you to go back to your home. Is there anywhere else you could stay, somewhere out of the area?'

I hesitated before replying. 'I don't know. I'll have to think about that one.'

When they'd gone the nurse turned to face me. I gave her a wicked smile and a thumbs up. She flicked her right hand hair bang behind her ear and tossed her head in the air.

'How long am I going to have to stay here?' I asked her

'Another three or four days at least. Not until you've finished the antibiotics anyway. They won't let you go until they're sure there's no infection. Even then you will have to come back a couple of times for a check up.'

So there it was. I not only had a bad right leg, but by then I also a bad right shoulder. I was becoming an invalid I thought.

* * * * *

To try and cheer myself up later on I phoned Iolanthe. I wanted to know how her singing had gone the previous night. She, however, was more desperate to know about my condition. She still wanted to come and see me. She sounded worried and concerned. I continued to say 'No' to that. The show went well she eventually told me. There was a bigger crowd and the applause more rapturous. 'Two of the men even asked me out,' she said.

'Why don't you go?' I responded. 'You might get a free meal.'

'How could I do that knowing you're in that condition.'

We talked some more. Hearing her voice cheered me up. Then I phoned Colin Wright. He had been to take care of Ben, but expressed his shock on learning of my fate.

'Adam, I'm worried about you,' he said. 'You do seem to get yourself into some awful scrapes. Are you sure you're all right? Do you want me to come and see you?' That was the last thing I wanted.

'Thank you, no,' I replied as politely as I could. 'But I may be grateful for a lift out of here when the time comes. Can you manage with Ben until then?' He said he could and that he would take him out for walks with his dogs. I knew Ben would hate that but I thanked him.

'Do you think it was the Moroccan's who shot you?' he asked.

'I guess they have to be the favourites,' I said. 'I can't think of anybody else who'd want to bother, unless it was a case of mistaken identity.'

'H'm,' he responded. 'What will you do when you're fit enough to leave there?'

'Don't know at this juncture. The police say it might not be safe to go back to my villa. I might have to find a safe place for a time. You haven't any ideas have you?'

'Let me think about it. I'll get back to you.'

We spoke some more then ended the call.

CHAPTER FOURTEEN

Over the next few days my mobility improved. I was able to get out of bed and walk about, with the aid of a crutch and the kind nurse's assistance. I discovered that her name was Isabel. When she was around me I put on a bit of an act, so she had to help me walk and do other things for me. I was enjoying the attention. A uniformed policeman continued to remain outside my bedroom door and the detectives came back to see me a couple of times. There was still no progress in their search for the Moroccans, although the two of them had been to see the other family at the farmhouse, who still protested about the dynamite explosion on their land. The police had questioned them about where Iolanthe's people might be but their response had been that they had set off to try and find their daughter and they'd heard nothing since. The police in their area were, however, active in trying to establish if they were involved in the illegal immigrant trade, the detectives said. All of it was now part of the ongoing enquiry relating to my shooting. They still pressed me on Iolanthe's whereabouts, but I wouldn't budge on that. I told them that as soon as I could get out of the hospital I would take them to meet her. I confirmed that she was safe.

I spoke to Iolanthe regularly. Her singing activities were going well but she still wanted to visit me. I held my ground on that one and said I would come to see her soon, with the police. I was pressing the doctor to give me some indication of my likely release day. He confirmed that it wouldn't be until I had finished the course of antibiotics, which would be on the coming Thursday. Then one afternoon I had a telephone call from Colin Wright. He sounded excited. 'I may have some news on a safe place for you to stay,' he said. A subject that had been troubling my mind ever since the detectives had mentioned it.

When Colin was excited about something he tended to gabble a bit, so two or three times I had to get him to repeat what he was saying. 'I have a friend who has a small house up in the hills,' I managed to glean eventually. It transpired that the friend was another ex-policeman. 'They only use it in the summer. They reckon it's too cold for them up there in the winter months,' he gabbled on.

'How much will it cost?' I asked.

'As long as you pay the electricity and your own calor gas, they will let you stay there for nothing. You can think of it as a house sit,' he said. 'Graham is always worried about the place in the winter. Apparently they get a lot of snow, ice and gales up there and the property is sometimes broken into. Last winter he had most of his furniture stolen. It's miles from anywhere but if you kept it quiet nobody would think of looking for you there.' I liked the sound of the idea.

'Colin as soon as these people will let me out I'll have a look.'

Afterwards I kept pushing the doctor for a release date. By then I was up and about but my arm still remained in a sling, which meant I couldn't drive. Once the sling was removed he told me I would still need to have physiotherapy to get the arm moving. He knew of my circumstances regarding the shooting and I badgered him to let me have an afternoon off from the hospital to visit the property. Colin had by then told me of it's location. After a lot of arguing the doctor agreed that I could go on the Wednesday afternoon. Next time the detectives came to see me I broached the subject with them and they agreed to take me there. 'At least you'll be able to see if it's a safe enough place for me to stay,' I said to them. For the time being I didn't mention anything about it to Iolanthe. I wanted to see the place for myself first, so we kept our conversations to the state of my health and her singing performances, which she mentioned continued to go well. She was by then working four nights a week, which enabled her to pay her own rent. Her semi disguise seemed to be holding up and she reported no sightings of her family or any other bother.

After lunch on Wednesday Isabel fussed around me like a doting mother as she prepared me for my trip out. I was given a list of instructions of what to do and what not to do for my comfort, she provided me with a bottle of water and some cushions for the car journey. I was going to miss her when I was finally released. She wanted to take me down in the lift to the police car in a wheelchair, but I wouldn't have that, although she did accompany me to the exit door. Just after three o'clock in the afternoon I set off in the police car with the two detectives.

Once we were out of the town and on the twisting, bumpy road to the mountains I was glad of the cushions Isabel had provided. During the journey the two detectives described to me their most recent actions in my case. They had re-interviewed the man with the dog who had found me. It seems that no cars had passed him on his way up the road to the car park. Forensic checks had revealed nothing on inspection of my car. The detectives guess was that my assailant never actually got out of his vehicle. After firing the shot, which he would have seen had hit me, the police suggested that he, or they, drove straight back down the hill and away. An alert was out for the Moroccans at all ports and airports. Police had been sent to the circus in Northern Spain to try and get hold of a picture of them, but there were still no sightings.

After travelling about twenty miles we turned off the main road by a sign that indicated a water treatment plant was somewhere along a hardcore track. We passed the building relating to the plant, then the hardcore surface continued on upwards in a never ending spiral to a height of what must have been over fifteen hundred feet. The car's wheels constantly created a cloud of dust behind us as we journeyed. I wondered what on earth we were going to find. We negotiated a sharp bend around a big, old olive tree, then drove up an even steeper track full of pot holes that made my sore body hurt even more. The track ended in front of a three storey, recently modernised finca residence. The property was situated on a level plot which commanded the most fantastic views across the valley and the surrounding mountains. My body seared with pain as I struggled to get out of the car. After forcing myself to stand upright I took in a big, deep gulp of fresh mountain air. The hard core track finished outside the finca, but I spotted a footpath that led away from it into the surrounding mountains.

'Perfect,' I said loudly.

A short, curved tarmac driveway, guarded by a metal chain, which was padlocked, led to the front door. The building was faced with yellow sandstone brick, off which the bright sunlight reflected vibrantly. The three of us strolled, limped in my case, around the outside, peering in through the windows. We didn't have a key. There was a basement cellar, a middle floor where the main living rooms were situated and what looked like a bedroom in the dormer shaped roof. Through the windows we could see that the premises was sparsely furnished, no doubt due to the robberies. There was however, a sofa, a dining table and chairs and a TV. Outside, on the roof, was a satellite dish. To me it looked ideal.

'At least from here you will be able to see anybody coming up the track,' the bald detective said. 'You'll spot the dust cloud miles away.' We were by then standing on the front terrace admiring the view of three different mountains.

When I looked back at the house I spotted an outside security light pointing down the track we had come up. 'If it works could we have an alarm fitted to that?' I asked.

'*Es possible*.'(It is possible). You'd have to get the owners permission first,' the other detective replied. 'You may have to pay for it yourself, but we would organise a police car to come up here twice a day to check on you. And we'd give you a phone with a direct line to the police station.'

'Well what do you think?' I said to the two men.

They spoke to each other in Spanish, then the swarthy one said, 'It's probably as good as anything we could find. It might be a bit lonely though,' he added with a chuckle.

'That suits me fine,' I replied. 'I am a writer! And I've got a dog.'

We looked around some more. Behind the property, leading up to a steep rocky jagged peak, there were many old gnarled trees, mostly olive, some coppiced probably centuries ago. There was also good pile of split logs at the side of the driveway. After some more minutes we drove down the track and back to the hospital.

My outing had caused me discomfort and I was very tired when I arrived back in my hospital room. Isabel chided me for embarking on such a trip, but I was glad of her attentions. While she was fussing with me I told her about the finca and its wonderful views. 'It's the sort of place I'd like to take you to for the weekend.'

She playfully slapped me on my good wrist and went quickly out of the room.

* * * * *

The following day I spent a lot of time on my mobile, mainly to Colin Wright and eventually Iolanthe. It was confirmed that his friend would allow me to live in his property on the terms previously discussed. I was told the outside light came on automatically if something or somebody came up the drive in the dark and it was agreed that an alarm could be attached to it at my expense. By then it looked like I was going to be released from hospital on the Friday. Colin agreed to come and take me to my villa to collect Ben and my possessions for an elongated stay at the finca, then drive me back to Malaga police station. The police would then take me, under the cover of darkness, to my new abode. I suddenly realised I was going to be forever in Colin Wright's debt.

Dealing with Iolanthe was more problematical. When she heard of the latest developments she wanted to be with me the next day. I thought it more important for her to continue with her singing, particularly as she had made such a good start. In reality that was the only way she was going to make a future living for herself, I told her. 'To drop out now would be stupid,' I said.

'But how are you going to look after yourself in an isolated place like that in your current condition,' she replied.

'I'm going to have a policeman visit me twice a day,' I replied half jokingly.

She continued to argue.

'I will arrange for you to come there after your singing dates at the weekend,' I said. 'The police have to interview you. As yet I have not told them where you're living.' I could tell she wasn't happy but that's how it was left.

Throughout that day I had meetings with the doctor and the two detectives. There were more phone calls with Colin and a consensus was reached on what would follow. I would be discharged after lunch on the Friday when Colin would come to pick me up. The doctor wanted me back in there for a further check up on the following Tuesday. That I considered would be a suitable day for me to bring Iolanthe to Malaga.

That Friday as you can imagine was somewhat frenetic. Isabel, my nurse, fussed around me all morning, providing me with extra bandages and goodness knows what else to take with me for my stay at the finca. Before I left I needed to have physio treatment on the arm and shoulder. I was going to have to keep the sling on at least until the next Tuesday, although the movement of the arm was getting better. Isabel brought me lunch with what were obviously extra helpings. 'How are you going to cook at that place by yourself?' she asked me.

'Perhaps you could come and do it for me over the weekend?' I enquired.

'P'h,' she responded and went out of the room.

When Colin Wright arrived at my hospital room the real chaos began. The doctor was already in there giving me last minute instructions. Isabel was also talking to me at the same time telling me which of the tablets I had to keep taking, how many and how often, while stuffing bandages, plasters into a carrier bag for me to take with me. Colin made it a four way conversation, none of which I was able to absorb properly. My head began to spin, no doubt in part due to the tablets. In the end I shut up and ignored everybody. Isabel carried my meagre belongings down to Colin's car. I carried the crutches. My right arm was still in a loose sling. When everything but me was in the car I turned around to face Isabel.

'Thanks for everything,' I said to her in Spanish, then kissed her on both cheeks. 'Will I see you on Tuesday?'

'Probably not. You'll be an out-patient then.' She turned and headed back into the hospital. I made a mental note to buy her a present and visit the ward when I was next there.

'How is it you always get the pretty ones?' Colin said to me as he drove us out of the car park.

Awaiting me at my villa was an excitedly boisterous welcome from Ben. He had clearly missed me. Fending him off and keeping him at arms length from my injuries was a major task. While Colin took him outside to relieve himself I tried, in my still semi-invalid condition, to gather enough items of clothing and whatever else I would need. It didn't help that I had some difficulty in thinking straight. Colin had managed to get together Ben's bed and such like, together with a quantity of dog food he had purchased for him. Eventually, everything was loaded into his car and we set off on the return journey to Malaga. All the way, as he'd done on the outward journey, he quizzed me intensely about the shooting, my injuries and what the police were doing about it. I had still the impression that he thought of it all as some continuing schoolboy adventure. En route, Ben who was sitting on the back seat, amongst my possessions, intermittently licked the back of my ears.

This time Colin took me to the central police station, where he and a Guardia officer loaded my goods into an unmarked people carrier. It had been agreed that my car would remain at the police station. When the removal was done Colin and I shook hands and agreed to keep in touch, initially by telephone.

'I owe you big time,' I said to him.

'Good,' he said. Then he was gone and Ben and I were taken inside into what was like a rest room for the policemen. It also turned out to be a canteen and I was able to order some food and coffee. There was going to be no food awaiting me at the finca, but I was told that a policeman would visit me in the morning to check if I was all right. If I gave him a shopping list, they said, he would bring the necessaries back with him in the evening. My body was starting to feel sore again. I had to think hard to remember what tablets Isabel had told me to take.

* * * * *

Somewhere around ten o'clock that evening two uniformed Guardia officers, both wearing a belt load of armaments, came into the rest room to collect Ben and me for the journey. The back portion of the people carrier, where we were to sit, had tinted windows. We set off at some speed. The carrier was a more comfortable ride than the previous police car. The journey there took under an hour. Once we were on the hardcore track leading to the finca, the officers sitting up front began to speculate on the isolation of the dwelling. It was a clear night, the moon was up. Even through the tinted windows the surrounding mountains looked spectacular bathed in moonlight. They stopped the vehicle outside the chain barrier. The outside light came on. By then we had been provided with the house keys. They drove up the driveway and parked outside the front door. We all got out.

'*Estupendo!*' One of them said when he turned around and saw the view. They carried my goods inside, while I dealt with Ben. They checked that the lights worked and turned on the water supply, which I had been told was from a spring behind the property. Before long they were ready to leave. I thanked them, we shook hands, one of them said, 'Buena Suerte' (Good Luck). The other one reminded me that a local policeman would come up in the morning and that I was to give him a shopping list of anything I needed. Then they were gone.

With Ben sitting alongside me on the front the terrace, I watched their headlights all the way down the hardcore track until they went out of view. Then Ben and I were really on our own. Our chosen home was a complete wilderness. The nearest house would be at least three or four miles away in the next village. Silence prevailed. I drank in the air and the scenery. 'Well we've got some place here old boy,' I said to Ben. He licked my hand. Since we'd been reunited he'd hardly left my side. We remained on that spot together for some time.

Then a sound made me jump. For moment I couldn't make out what it was. I listened harder. 'Whoo!' it went again. Eventually I realised it was a tawny owl, hooting in the trees behind us. I turned around and listened some more, I couldn't spot him. So we were not completely alone after all.

He continued hooting until we went inside. By then my body was beginning to ache again. I fished around inside the bag Isabel had given me for my tablets. I had remembered to bring some bottled water with me from my villa. I gulped at it and swallowed what

I thought was the correct tablet and walked around the property. It was sparsely furnished with most of the things I would need. I checked that all the windows and doors were locked, then settled Ben in his bed. Afterwards, partially due to the effect of the tablets, I crashed out on the bed in the dormer bedroom fully clothed. I slept without moving or hearing a thing until dawn.

* * * * *

The view from the lounge window next morning was spectacular. The big dome of the sun was beginning to peep over the top of a distant easterly mountain. The rest of the sky was completely clear. With the aid of my binoculars, I could spot a herd of goats rambling around the nooks and crannies of a nearby jagged rock. I saw to Ben, brewed some coffee, then sat and nibbled at some biscuits, continuing to look at the scenery, while he ate his breakfast. Noticing the half finished packet of biscuits reminded me to begin to write a shopping list for the expected policeman. I had discovered that the basic requirements of human living were already available in the many cupboards, so it was primarily food and drink that I wrote on the list. That morning my body didn't feel in too bad a shape. I was able to get about without the crutch and the sling was mainly a prop. I guessed the tablets were beginning to have an effect.

As soon as we were able I took Ben out on a reconnaissance of the surrounds. I needed a jacket. It was damn cold out there at that time of the morning. We couldn't go far as I didn't know what time the policeman would arrive. The first thing that hit me was the silence, almost deafening in its intensity. As far as my eye could see, nothing moved, nothing stirred. The owl obviously had better things to do at that time of the day. I discovered that within half a mile or so, around and behind the property, were some of the grandest mountains I had ever seen. Ben was sniffing the air as though he wanted to set off for them at that moment. At the back of the house was a small shed. A pile of split logs alongside looked enough to see me out. I'd already discovered that there was a log burning stove in the lounge. The cooker range was powered by calor gas. The basement was full of junk, plus a calor gas boiler, which I had been told heated the water and three radiators in the house. There was also an immersion heater.

As one does in Spain, I had to wait a long time for the policeman to arrive. His name was Cruzado, he lived in a house in the village, which also served as the local police station, with his wife. He didn't apologise for being late but said that he had been organising an alarm man to call later in the day. He wanted to know if everything was *'vale'* (OK). I confirmed it was and gave him my shopping list. He said he'd get his wife onto it as soon as he got back to the station. We both laughed. I made him some coffee and we talked about the locality. As a youngster he'd walked in all those mountains, he told me, waving his arms in their direction. It was agreed that he would in future get there about nine thirty in the morning and five in the evening. If he was going to be late he'd phone me on the special phone they'd given me. Much later that morning the alarm man arrived. When he set it off the noise it made pierced the surrounding silence, I guessed you could have heard it thirty miles away. It made Ben bark anyway.

When they'd all gone I got on the phone to Iolanthe. That evening, she said, she was performing at the night club. She wanted to know full details of the house and the surroundings, then added that she wanted to come there next day. I advised patience and made out a case for the following Tuesday to meet up in Marbella. Afterwards I called Colin Wright. It seems he had previously visited the property when his friend had been staying there. He said he wanted to come and see me next day. In view of his help and involvement I could hardly refuse. Afterwards I consumed the rest of the biscuits then took Ben on a more lengthy walk along the footpaths that led to the mountains. When we got back I considered that I no longer had any excuse not to get on with my book.

CHAPTER FIFTEEN

Colin Wright duly arrived at the finca mid-morning next day. By then my policeman caller had long gone. The previous evening he'd brought with him shopping bags full of the goods his wife had acquired for me. That morning I gave him another list of the items I had forgotten on the first one. We remained on cordial terms though. I always gave him a cup of coffee and I think he enjoyed the trip into the mountains. 'Incredible,' he would always say when he sat down at the dining table to look at the view.

Colin, of course, knew of the property and the view. Ben scurried under the dining room table as soon as he arrived.

'How are you getting on?' he enquired. I had no gin to offer, but I made him a cup of coffee.

I told him I was doing OK. He wanted to know about the injury and I described how that was progressing. We talked about the hospital visit on the following Tuesday. I had yet another favour to ask of him regarding that.

'I am going to try and get Iolanthe to meet up with me and the police on that day,' I said. 'If she gets the bus to your place would you bring her to the hospital?'

His eyes lit up. 'Would you like her to stay the previous night at my place?' he added with a smile on his face. 'Save her the bus trip?'

'Thanks, but no, the car trip would be enough, please,' I responded with a chuckle.

He did ask if I wanted him to go to Marbella to pick her up, but I didn't want that. I still preferred to keep her hideaway there a secret. He did, however, agree to do what I asked.

Then he revealed the real purpose of his visit to me. 'I'm worried about you out here, in a place like this, on your own,' he said. 'You've already had one pot shot taken at you.' I listened attentively. 'Would you like me to arrange for Charlie Wolfenden to provide you with some proper security? That's his business as you know.'

'But I already have the police for that,' I protested.

'I know, but Charlie could give you round the clock protection. The police can't do that. You don't know what to expect from the people you're up against.'

'No way,' I replied. 'I could never afford it anyway.'

'You could pay him back over a period of time,' he said. 'You've only got one life.'

I argued vehemently enough to convince Colin that I had no wish for anything like that.

'All right, have it your own way,' he said eventually with a shrug of his shoulders. 'But I insist you have this,' he added, then from the pocket of his jacket, which had been draped over the back of his chair he produced a terrifying looking Luger pistol. He laid it on the table then added a packet of bullets. I was taken aback, astounded.

'I wouldn't know how to use one of those,' I said.

'I'll show you now, in the back yard. It's all right, it is mine. I've had it for years.' He demonstrated how the bullets loaded into the handle.

I coughed, I protested, but he'd obviously made up his mind about it. He took me out onto the back terrace and aimed at a distant tree. The one shot he fired hit the tree trunk bang smack in the middle. I was impressed. The echo of the gunfire echoed all around the valley. From inside the house I heard Ben bark. Then for half an hour he gave me a comprehensive lesson on how to use the gun. He told me that he'd been taught how to use firearms during his time with the police. By then I was able to take my arm out of the sling to do simple things. With it I aimed three bullets at the same tree and never hit it once.

'You have to practice,' he said.

After more instruction he thankfully took his leave. Afterwards my whole body was shaking. I sat at the dining table looking at that fearsome gun and the packet of bullets and wondered. What the hell am I going to do with this damn thing I thought? Ben was sitting at my feet whimpering. Later I spent time telephoning Iolanthe about the arrangements for Tuesday. Until that day arrived Ben and I walked some of the nearby easier hills. I made attempts to restart on my book and received the policeman twice a day. I'd hidden the pistol in a cupboard. Once, as an experiment I fired it at the same tree and still missed the tree altogether. My owl pal in the upper reaches of the trees behind us continued to echo out his plaintive cry at night. I knew how he felt. With the aid of my Zeiss bins and my camcorder I did manage to capture some long distant, hazy images of him.

* * * * *

On the Tuesday morning I dosed myself up with pain killers and awaited Cruzado, who was going to take me down to Malaga. By then my arm was feeling looser and less sore. Ben was to remain at the finca as I hoped to be back some time in the afternoon, hopefully with Iolanthe. Before I left I made telephone calls to Colin Wright and Iolanthe to check that the agreed arrangements were still in place. It was a day I was dreading.

At the hospital I had to cool my heels and wait some time for the doctors to see me. During that period Colin arrived with Iolanthe. I was to receive a tearful greeting from her. She looked wonderful, even though she was wearing her show-biz wig. Kissing her tear stained face revived my spirits.

'Don't forget me,' Colin said eventually. I stepped aside, shook his hand and thanked him for all his help. The arrangement was that he would leave after depositing Iolanthe at the hospital. When he'd gone she sat next to me, held my hand and we talked incessantly about our different ventures over the past few days.

Eventually I was ushered into the doctor's room. Two medics were waiting to see me but there was no sign of Isabel. They were pleased with the healing process of the wound. They changed the dressing and instructed me in more physiotherapy exercises. They said I could try to do without the sling, but to take it with me and if the pain returned to put it back on. I was not to drive however. They wanted to see me again in a weeks time. Once they had finished with me I went upstairs to the ward to search out Isabel. On one of the shopping lists I'd given to my policeman friend, I had included a box of Ferrero Rocher chocolates. I soon found Isabel and handed over the gift, while placing two large kisses on each cheek. We were standing in the middle of the ward with all the other patients looking on. She was clearly embarrassed and could only manage a flustered response.

The arrangement was that the police would come to collect Iolanthe and I from the hospital and take us to the police station. I phoned and they duly arrived in the unmarked people carrier with the tinted windows. The next few hours were painstakingly tiring and very trying.

The two detectives I had seen before saw us together, which I had insisted on. They gave me a brief update on the progress, or more accurately the lack of progress on my case. Then they began to interrogate Iolanthe on her relationship with her family. Again the swarthy policeman took notes. They wanted to know all her family's full names, where they came from in Morocco, the years they had spent together at the circus in Northern Spain and the more recent times on the south coast. At times I felt they went over the top with their probing and said so. They pleaded that they had a job to do. Even after an hour it appeared that there was no consensus as to what they were going to do with her. The main problem of course was that she had no official papers. I asked if she could be given a temporary permit, for say thirty days. They looked doubtful. How did they know she would not abscond, they said.

At that point they took me into another room by myself. '*Señor*,' the bald one said to me. 'In our eyes she is still a potential suspect in your shooting. How can we guarantee your safety if a member of the family we are seeking is living with you?' He had a point, but I didn't admit it. 'We would be failing in our duty,' he added.

'Can't I vouch for her as a guarantor?' I said. 'I think I know her pretty well by now.' Again they both looked at me doubtfully. I explained about her work situation in Marbella, but they remained unimpressed.

I went back to the interview room alone to try and console Iolanthe. Tears were forming in her eyes again. I clasped her hand and tried to comfort her.

'What do you think they'll do with me?' she said.

'I don't know but whatever they do I'll look after you.' I replied and hugged her.

The detectives were gone some time. Another policeman brought us coffee. When the two returned both their faces bore dour expressions.

'We have discussed the matter with our chief,' the swarthy one said. I held my breath. 'He says we will have to keep the señorita in custody for a while.'

'You can't be serious?' I exploded. 'What has she done wrong?'

'Nothing as far as we know,' the bald one said. 'But she is a member of the family, who at the moment, are the major suspects in your shooting. We have to speak with the local prosecutor to seek his advice. And we can not release her until she has proper papers or at least a temporary permit and the prosecutor has to authorise that.' I could see an expression of fear creeping across Iolanthe's face.

'But where will you detain her?' I asked.

'She will have to go to the local women's prison in Malaga. We will need to have her near for interviewing.' By then full tears were running down her cheeks. I moved closer to her and put my arm around her shoulder.

'If I'd known you were going to do this I wouldn't have brought her in,' I said.

'But we would have caught up with her sometime and without your intervention we may have had to keep her in prison for longer.'

'It'll be all right. I promise,' I said to Iolanthe and hugged her tighter. She was dabbing at her tears with a handkerchief. 'Will I be able to visit her,' I asked.

'I should think so,' the policeman replied.

The next half an hour or so were pretty desperate moments. There were times when I thought Iolanthe was going to become hysterical, but with a lot of effort I managed to calm her down. When a policewoman came to take her away, her sobbing began again. I could see she was in a desperate state.

'I will come to see you tomorrow,' I said as she went out through the door. Then there was nothing left for me to do but face the long lonely journey back to my safe haven in the people carrier. Before leaving the police station I had asked if they would take me to the prison next day to see Iolanthe. They said they would see what could be arranged.

I was mad angry with myself. I considered that I had been stupid in allowing matters to happen that way. I also received a noisy disgruntled welcome from Ben about being locked up for such a long time when I got back into the finca. After both our domestic needs and our empty stomachs had been attended to I took him for a walk along one of the mountain tracks. I needed space and air to think. By then nightfall had descended. On our way back I could hear the owl hooting in the trees behind the house. Somehow, without disturbing him we managed to get near to the tree where he was perched. I stood there for some moments and listened to his echoing call. 'I know exactly how you feel mate,' I said before Ben and I retired inside.

That evening I spent some time on the telephone. In the morning Cruzado called in to check on me. He told me that permission had been given for him to take me to the women's jail in Malaga that afternoon. Visiting hours were between three and four o'clock. He said he would be back to pick me up just after two and bring me back to the finca afterwards.

Later in the morning I put in a telephone call to Antonio Silva. He was amused to learn of my current predicament, but he expressed his disappointment about Iolanthe. 'That's why I am calling you really,' I said to him. 'How good a singer is she?' I asked. 'What I want to know is if she's good enough to make a living at it on her own?'

He said he would telephone the manager at the club and get back to me. While I was on the phone I was standing at my lounge window admiring the view. When I'd finished off the call I saw people on the steep part of the track leading up to the house There were four of them, three men and a woman all dressed as hikers. There was no sign of a car. They all had mountain walking sticks. Quickly I moved out of sight, away from the window. I grabbed hold of Ben and pulled him up the stairs to the bedroom, the window there was of normal type, which meant he couldn't see out unless he jumped up on the sill on his back legs. If he didn't see them I hoped he wouldn't bark. I wanted to pretend we weren't in.

I could see the four people getting nearer the house. They were talking animatedly and clearly interested in the finca. When they were nearby they stopped and looked at it intently, pointing out to each other some of the features. From what I could hear of their conversation and mannerisms, I guessed they were Germans, certainly not Moroccan anyway. Then they began to walk up the driveway towards the house. I put my hand over Ben's mouth to stop him barking. He had obviously heard them. I watched them walk around the outside of the house and guessed they were peering in through the windows down below, which I always kept locked as well as all the doors. Their noisy voices confirmed they were German. After five minutes or so they began to move away. I heard lots of '*Ya, Ya,Ya,*' and watched them head further up the track towards the mountain paths.

I knew the pathway outside was a designated footpath to the mountains. There were signs at the bottom of the hardcore track giving the route number. But apart from the policeman those people had been my only visitors since I'd been there and it gave me a strange feeling. For all intents and purposes they looked like normal hill walkers, but it did make me realise how isolated I actually was.

Later on Antonio Silva returned my call. 'My manager thinks this girl of yours is pretty good,' he said. 'It seems that on a few nights she's gone down quite a storm. The men certainly like her anyway, you lucky devil.'

'Huh,' I responded. 'Not much good to me when she's being held in jail.' I went on to say that she might not make this weekend's gigs. He said he would explain the situation to the club's manager, but he didn't think it would stop him from booking her again. I was glad of that at least. For the rest of the day until Cruzado came to collect me I tried to concentrate on my novel. It was, however, hard going. The visitors had disturbed my thoughts and undone the previous contentment I had found in my new home. They didn't come back my way during the rest of the time I was there.

On the drive to the jail I asked Cruzado about the footpath. He said that in the summer it was a well used track, but at that time of year only a few people went that way, because of the length of the walks and the possibility of snow and ice at the mountain tops. He said that the walkers might have not come back past my finca as the whole trip was a circular route to another road on the other side of the mountains.

A different dilemma was waiting for me at Malaga jail. The buildings of the jail are surrounded by a massive, high wire fence, with cameras and floodlights sprouting up at every angle. I was eventually taken to an inmates visitors room. When I met up in there with Iolanthe she was obviously in a fractious state. We had to talk to each other through a wire mesh grill with a solid partition underneath. No way we could even hold hands. There were bags under her eyes as though she had been crying a lot. Her face was devoid of make-up and her hair was tied back in a bun. She kept her head angled downwards a lot of the time.

'Has it been bad?' I asked when we were sat opposite each other.

She lifted her eyes up to meet mine. 'Awful,' she replied. 'The Spanish don't like Moroccans.'

'They're not beating you are they?' I responded vehemently.

'No. Not exactly. It's the abuse, I suppose. It's worse than being beaten. It doesn't help that I can't speak much Spanish I guess.'

'It won't be for long,' I said trying to offer consolation. 'I'm speaking with the consulate.' One of the telephone calls I'd made when I got back to the finca, the previous night, was to the British consulate in Malaga. He'd agreed to meet me at the jail after my meeting with Iolanthe. 'Antonio Silva and the night club manager have both said that your job there is still on hold.' I added.

Those words brought a weak smile to her face. 'I'm glad about that,' she said. 'I have enjoyed doing it so much. One night I got three encores.'

'Great,' I said. 'I'll soon have you back there. You'll be topping the bill by then.'

I'd earned another watery smile. We talked some more about where I was living and the surrounding mountains and about Ben, then all too soon our time was up and a woman warder came in to collect her.

'I hope you're being nice to her,' I called out to the warder in Spanish. 'I do know people in high places,' I added, but I received no response or reply.

Waiting for me in a reception room, outside the prisoners area, was one Gordon Ellis Johnston, the British consulate in Malaga. He was a tall thin man with receding fair hair, wearing a charcoal grey suit, white shirt and blue tie. On the whole he tried to be helpful. To enable him to understand my predicament I had to tell him virtually the whole story, although I attempted to relate it as briskly as possible. In between he nodded and made an occasional brief note on a pad he had with him. At the end of my tale, he emitted a big sigh, then said, 'The problem is that we don't have much say over what the Spanish may do with a Moroccan citizen. At the moment I don't think the relations between the two governments are very good.' He briefly sighed again and re-crossed his legs. 'If we were just dealing with you we would have a fair degree of control over things. In fact our simple advice would be for you to go back to Britain for a while until your attackers are arrested. But I guess your problem is with the woman Iolanthe?'

'Yes,' I said. 'I'm more or less committed to her now.'

He shook his head. 'You see the Spanish may deport her back to her own country. End of the problem as far as they are concerned. At the moment she has no official status in Spain.'

'But I can't leave it like that. Lord knows what would happen to her. If the worst came to the worst I suppose I would have to go back to Morocco with her.'

'Then you might be putting yourself in even more danger than you are here. Here at least the Spanish police will do their best to look after you. Nobody in Morocco would do that.' He sighed again and re-crossed his legs back the other way. 'You'd better leave it with me for a few days. I'll speak to the Spanish Prosecutor and their immigration people, but I can't promise anything will come of it.'

We exchanged telephone numbers, shook hands and ended the meeting. Cruzado then drove me back to the finca.

*****

That evening alone in my bolt hole I had plenty of time to think. On reflection I had to agree that Johnson had been right. At that moment the simplest and safest thing for me to do would be to cut my losses for a while and get on the first plane back to the UK. I had a brother who lived there and for a short while I guessed he would put me up until all this business blew over. Colin Wright would keep an eye on my Spanish property for me. But where did that leave me as far as Iolanthe was concerned? As a result of my most recent actions I had got her into the spot she now found herself in. If I hadn't rescued her from the caravan she would have probably lived out the rest of her life being committed to her family. So I had a responsibility in that respect and like the stupid prat I am, I'd also gone and fallen in love with her.

I therefore went to bed with a disturbed mind. Then, to my horror of horrors, sometime around two in the morning, the alarm bell, sounding like a klaxon horn, woke me up with a jolt. I scrambled out of bed and staggered to the bedroom window. Because of the moonlight and the view of the night time sky I had slept with the curtains open. I could see the outside light was on illuminating the track down the hill. Nothing on it moved. Ben had started barking downstairs in the kitchen. I struggled to put on some trousers and went, as fast as my injuries would allow down the stairs. Firstly I went to Ben to placate him, which was difficult while the alarm still rang. Then, almost instinctively I hurried to the cupboard to fetch the gun Colin Wright had given me. Bullets were already loaded in the shaft. With the gun in my hand and the lights in the house still off, I stood behind the un-drawn curtain at the lounge window. The alarm continued to clang almost deafeningly. However I still couldn't see anybody about. The spotlight shone right down to the olive tree at the bend, but there were no people, and no vehicle to be seen. Ben had his front feet up on the lounge window sill, looking out as well. I wondered if an animal might have set the off the light and the alarm, but the burglar alarm man had assured me that it would take something substantial, like a big deer, to do that.

Mainly because I couldn't stand the noise any more, I went to the switchboard and turned it off. The light had a separate switch and I left that on. From the lounge window I again looked up and down the path both ways, but there was still nothing but emptiness and silence. I went back upstairs, crouched below my bedroom window and looked again around the immediate areas outside property. Still nothing of any consequence could be seen. Back down the stairs I went, with Ben following at a gallop. Almost on tiptoe I crept to the front door and silently opened it. Then, getting down on my hands and knees I peeped out, presenting, I hoped, as small a target as possible.

The light outside was still on. I remained crouched there for some minutes. Still nothing around moved. Remaining on my hands and knees I closed the door, then went to the switchboard and turned off the outside light. Trying not to make any sound I tip-toed back to the door, and painfully, once more got down onto my hands and knees and quietly opened it. I lay out on my front. This time I only opened it by a few inches, just enough for me to see outside properly. I almost had to do a press-up to see anything at all. Holding that position was painful.

Then, just as I was about to give up, a rustle in the scrub shrubbery, across the track caught my attention. It may have been a deer. My shoulder, being held in the brace position was killing me. I had to give in and sank flat out on the floor. One more effort. I heaved myself up again into the press up position. I held it for a brief second, then I spotted a human head, wearing a woolly hat, running down through the undergrowth, to the lower regions of the track. I kept looking for some minutes but I didn't see him again.

For quite some time afterwards I sat in the lounge, with the Luger pistol on the arm of the chair beside me and Ben at my feet. Initially I thought about telephoning the police, but in the end I didn't see the point. Whoever it had been outside, at that stage anyway, had no plans to kill me as he would have made an attempt there and then. If it was my enemies, I guessed it was just a reconnaissance trip to suss out the surroundings. There would be little point in bringing the police all the way up there at that time of night for nothing. I would tell Cruzado in the morning.

What was evidently clear however, was that the finca was, regrettably, no longer a safe haven for me. And even more clearly, no way could I take Iolanthe there. If it had been her family outside, they could quickly be done with me and kidnapped her again.

After an hour or so of constant speculation, having checked all the doors and windows and resetting the alarms, I went back upstairs, with the pistol and the packet of bullets and tried to settle on my bed. I considered it best to leave Ben downstairs in his kitchen basket as he would hear any movement outside and instantly bark. I left the bedroom window open, on the first notch of the catch. To begin with sleep was almost impossible. I heard every creek and groan the timbers of the finca emitted. After some time my pal in the trees behind began to hoot. Eventually his plaintive cry lulled me into some form of disturbed sleep.

* * * * *

I was up at dawn. I let Ben go outside by himself, while I stayed indoors and made breakfast for us both. I wasn't going to risk anybody taking another pot shot at me. By the time Cruzado arrived I had already made a few telephone calls.

He was disturbed by my news. 'You should have called me Señor,' he said to me. I poo-hoed the idea. Straight away he got on the phone to his chiefs. Their instructions were for him to stay with me until the police people carrier arrived. He told me later that it was constructed with bullet proof materials. I was not to be allowed to go outside and I was to pack my things and prepare myself to live somewhere else. My heart sank. I thought the finca would have been ideal, but somehow maybe word had got out about my location.

Sometime later the people carrier arrived with two uniformed policemen on board. This time they wore bullet proof vests and carried automatic rifles. Between them and Cruzado they firstly loaded my goods into the back of the carrier. Ben followed on behind. When I eventually came out, Cruzado stood in front of me all the way to the door of the carrier and the two armed men stood each side of the front door, looking outwards with their rifles cocked for action. Cruzado went back to lock the front door and handed the keys inside the carrier to me. We shook hands. 'Buena suerte señor,' he said to me, then we drove away. I looked back at the finca as we juddered down the track. 'Shame,' I thought to myself. 'I could have been happy there.' I remembered before we reached the olive tree to say a silent 'So long pal,' to the owl. I'd miss him, wherever I was going.

CHAPTER SIXTEEN

I was taken back to Malaga police station and met up with the two detectives again. There was still no further positive progress on my case.

'How could anybody have possibly found me at that place?' I asked them when we were settled and sitting around a table. Ben was at my feet. 'A tracker dog would have a job to find that outpost,' I suggested.

The bald one shrugged his shoulders. 'People gossip. We don't know of course that it was your assailants.'

I described the party of hikers who'd passed early in the day and details of the events in the night.

The bald one replied. 'The man you saw scrambling down the bank may have been another hiker. It's a popular route to the mountains. People do live rough up there for a few days if the weather's good. He may have been looking for shelter around the finca and accidentally set off the alarm. It does happen, but because of your previous experiences we can't take any chances.'

He said there was another house they could take me to. It was in a small town further north and was attached to the police station there. Sometimes it was let out to married police officers and other times let out commercially. At that moment however it was empty.

One of the telephone calls I'd made before leaving the finca was to Gordon Ellis Johnson, the British consul, who agreed to meet up with me at the police station. When he arrived he was ushered into our meeting room. Between the policemen and I, we brought him up to date on the recent events, he spoke good Spanish.

'Oh Lord,' was his initial response to the details of the previous night.

In the long periods of sleeplessness I had experienced during the night I had come up with a sort of plan, which I thought might be temporarily beneficial to us all. Slowly I related my ideas. To be fair to the three men, they listened to me attentively and heard me out.

'The problem as I see it at the moment,' I began, directing my words towards Johnson 'is the presence, in this locality, of me and Iolanthe Moussaoui until the police here,' I said pointing at the two policemen, 'can come to some conclusions about who took a pot shot at me.' The three men nodded their heads in agreement, so I continued. 'We have assumed that Iolanthe's family are the culprits, but we don't know that for sure.' More nodding of heads. 'Having given the matter some extensive thought, I believe it would be better if Iolanthe and I and this mutt,' I pointed down at Ben, 'got away from here for a while.' Those words seem to concentrate their attention. 'I have a brother who lives in the UK,' I continued. 'At a push I suppose he may put us up for a while at his house.' I could see question marks forming on the three men's faces, so I carried on before they could interrupt. 'I guess Ben and I,' I pointed at him again. 'could get there without too many problems, but I wouldn't want to leave here without Iolanthe.' I paused very briefly for breath. 'I'm told that at the moment she has no residential status in Spain, but I'm wondering if we could obtain a temporary visa for her to come with me to Britain?' This time I pointed at Gordon Ellis Johnson. I left the question in the air. I had stunned the three of them temporarily into silence. Then the three of them all spoke at once, in their different languages. Again I butted in. 'Of course we would have to get her agreement first.' That momentarily stunned them again.

There followed an animated and protracted discussion and occasional argument, in both English and Spanish, on the practicalities of what I had suggested. During the discourse, at my feet, with his head on his paws, I heard Ben sigh regularly. After a long period of time it was agreed, by all the parties, that efforts would be made to see what could be achieved. Gordon Johnson said he would have to speak to the Foreign Office and the Spanish prosecutor. The two policemen said they would have to speak to their chief and the prosecutor. I suggested in the meantime that it might be best if I visited Iolanthe at the jail. Perhaps I could do this before I was taken to the new safe house, I ventured. They all left the room to sort out the protocol, leaving Ben and I alone together.

Some time later the two detectives came back to see me again. It had been agreed that the people carrier would take Ben and I to the jail and then onwards to the safe house. I was told that discussions were ongoing between the requisite Spanish and British officials about Iolanthe, but they said it may take a day or so before any firm decision would be reached.

A glum looking Iolanthe was sitting behind the same wire mesh grill, waiting to greet me when I was ushered into the visitors room at the jail. Her face did lighten up a little when she first saw me. Her warder left us alone in the room, saying something about thirty minutes. We still couldn't touch each other or anything like that.

'How are you?' I ventured.

She scrunched up her face and said. 'OK I guess.' She told me that since my last visit the police had been to interview her once and also the Spanish immigration people, but she still hadn't heard anything about the outcome of their visits. She said the language difficulties were a big problem.

'Well, I may have some good news,' I began and went on to relate what had been discussed between myself, the two detectives and the British consul. Her face got brighter with every word I said. 'Of course, if it could be arranged, you would have to agree to it all,' I concluded with. 'Would you agree to that?' I asked.

For the first time a real, wide smile broke out on her face. 'Agree to it! I'd be prepared to die for it. Just get me out of this place, please.'

'Are they still being horrible to you?'

'Not exactly, just not very nice. I've never been to England. Will it be cold there?'

'Colder than here yes. Anyway its not England, it's Wales actually, which is colder and wetter than England.'

She laughed. 'I don't care.'

'We'll have to buy you some woollies once we get there.'

We continued to talk about the possibilities until the woman warder came back into the room and abruptly called out '*Tiempo*'(time). Iolanthe and I managed to touch the tips of our index fingers together through the wire mesh before I left. A smile had remained on her face.

It was about a thirty minute drive from the jail to Lucena a small town with a population of about forty thousand people, so I was told. A popular tourist location surrounded by many nature reserves. A fifteenth century gothic renaissance church, San Mateo, is a dominant feature near the centre of the town. In the police station I was firstly introduced to Captain Gutierres, the officer in charge. He was a tall, dark haired man with a small moustache, who spoke only a little English. He seemed pleasant enough and took me next door to the house, a modern town type dwelling. On two floors, there was plenty of space, with three bedrooms and modern appliances. He checked the electricity and the water, then gave me the keys and arranged for the driver of the vehicle to bring in my goods, while I fetched Ben, who on extensive inspection seemed suitably impressed with the accommodation. Gutierres said he thought it should be safe for me to go about the main streets of the town, but that I was not to venture beyond that without telling him. If I saw or heard anything suspicious I was to tell him or one of the other officers instantly. He asked me to call into the station once a day to prove I was still there. I thanked him and mentioned that my stay might not be a long one. This time I had no Mrs Cruzado to shop for me, so once I had unpacked my few possessions I visited a café across the road and then the nearby shops for provisions.

Afterwards I spent a considerable amount of time on the telephone. Firstly to my brother who lived in the wilds of distant West Wales. Unless they actually followed us there I couldn't imagine any Moroccans or for that matter Spaniards finding that dwelling. Over the previous few years I had received many invites from him to go and stay, which I had never taken up. He had, on odd occasions, come to stay with me in Spain. I'd usually declined his invitations because of the vast distance to his house from any sort of civilisation. Getting there by public transport normally took days. I wasn't expecting any hassle from him regarding the visit, but his tone changed somewhat when I explained I would be accompanied by a dog and a Moroccan woman. 'They're both house trained,' I assured him. However after I had fully explained all the extenuating circumstances he agreed to help out.

I also phoned Colin Wright and Antonio Silva to update them on the current situation. Some time later I got a call from Gordon Johnson. He told me that there was a possibility that Iolanthe may be allowed into the UK on a ninety day permit, on the condition that she remained with me for that period of time. 'You may have to report into a local police station periodically to prove that situation still exists,' he said. 'The problem,' he continued 'is with the Spanish. As I'm sure you know,' he said, 'everything here takes so long. I'm afraid there is nothing we can do about that.' He went on to say that the Spanish may be prepared to release her into British custody, but if they did, it was doubtful if they would allow her back into Spain. Johnson felt it would be best if he went and talked to Iolanthe at the women's jail, to spell out the consequences. I asked if I could be present at that meeting. He said, 'I don't see why not.' Could he send an unmarked car for me I asked? I didn't want to badger the Spanish police any more than I had to. He said he would see what could be arranged.

That news cheered me up immensely. For the next day or so I went about my menial tasks with a little more enthusiasm. I even managed to make good progress on my novel. It was impossible to carry out much of my financial work, but I kept in touch with some of the clients by e-mail. In between I walked and shopped around the main streets of Lucena town with Ben. The thoroughfares were busy enough. The pavements were full of noisy, gossiping Spaniards going about their shopping and the dusty roads busy with revved up, horn honking cars. I also made further telephone calls to Antonio Silva and Colin Wright. I emphasised to Antonio that Iolanthe might not be able to fulfil her immediate forthcoming dates at the nightclub and the reasons why. He told me not to worry. He would speak with the manager, but he was sure that if she went back there he would re-employ her. I advised Colin that I may be away from my villa for some time and my likely destination. He promised to look after it for me. I said I would phone him again before I departed for Wales.

The following morning I received a telephone call from Gordon Johnson. He said he had arranged a visit to see Iolanthe at the Malaga jail that afternoon. Did I want to come along? Naturally I jumped at the opportunity. He said he'd send a car to the police station to pick me up. I advised to park it in the back yard there. I went to see Captain Gutierres who made arrangements for us to take the car inside the Malaga jail compound.

An unmarked consular vehicle took me to Malaga just after lunch. For the first time in weeks I was excited. I felt that at last something positive was being done about our situation. At the prison entrance there was a glass and concrete security office gate. My driver spoke in Spanish to the officer there who looked down at a pad in front of him, which confirmed our access. Inside the modern complex was a court yard. When I got out of the car I was met by a warder, who checked my name with my passport and took me inside to a reception area, where Gordon Johnson was waiting for me. He stood, tall and upright, with a smiling countenance and an outstretched arm, proposing an invitation to shake his hand, which I accepted.

Accompanied by a female warder we walked down what seemed like half a mile of passageway, with many intervening locked gates. This time we were taken to a different reception room, with no metal grill, where Iolanthe was already waiting to greet us. When we walked in she rose from her chair and rushed into my arms. Slightly embarrassed I pulled away and pointed to Johnson, who shook hands with her. She apologised to him, which he deflected with charm. We were all able to sit around a normal table, with a female warder standing at the back of the room throughout.

Succinctly as he could, Johnson explained to Iolanthe the arrangements which would be possible in her case. Occasionally I had to intervene to explain some of the matters she didn't understand. Throughout the meeting her face was filled with enthusiasm and hope. Johnson was keen to emphasise that the whole venture was dependent on the Spanish releasing her from custody. He said. 'If they are not going to press any charges against you I can't see how they can continue to hold you. So that will be the tack we will be adopting. But as you know, or I am sure Adam has told you, things here do take time.' I nodded in agreement.

Johnson then asked her if she would be happy to go along with what he had suggested. 'The decision has to be yours,' he emphasised. 'It may mean that you will never be allowed to come back to Spain, or that you might never see your family again. Do you fully understand?'

She hesitated for a moment, then said. 'I do, yes. I think it is the best in the circumstances. Would I be able to stay permanently in England?' she asked.

'Wales,' I interrupted. She giggled. 'She means the UK,' I said to Johnson.

He thought for a few moments. 'I can't answer that. It would depend on your circumstances at the time. You may have to find work, that sort of thing, but it's a possibility.'

'Let's get you out of here first.' I interrupted. Johnson nodded. He then briefly outlined more of the requirements and arrangements. Iolanthe and I would both have to sign various papers and documents but he didn't think that was worth doing until agreement had been reached with the Spanish. 'Then I think I'll need to see you again, alone,' he said to Iolanthe. 'Just to make sure that you are perfectly clear and happy about what is going to happen. I will also have to see the prison Governor. After that it may be best if we all met up here again.' In all we talked for the best part of an hour. This time the warder didn't interrupt. When we got ready to leave Johnson said, 'I'll leave you two in peace for a few minutes,' and left the room after shaking hands with Iolanthe.

When he'd gone we kissed and embraced, aware of the warder standing by the other door. After a few moments she began to cough, shuffle her feet and move towards us. 'You have been wonderful to me,' Iolanthe said to me. I shrugged my shoulders and we stood apart looking at each other.

Outside the room Johnson was waiting to accompany me back to the cars. We talked briefly in the outside courtyard. He got in his car and I in the one he had provided for me for the journey back to Lucena.

For over a week the days that followed were tiresome and frustrating, mainly because nothing of any consequence happened as far as Iolanthe and our circumstances were concerned. There was also no progress at all with the police on finding her relatives. I made a few telephone calls to the consulate, but the message I got back each time was that they were waiting on the Spanish. I thought about visiting Iolanthe in the prison, but decided against it as I didn't want to impose on Captain Gutierres good nature too often. I also telephoned my brother and Colin Wright a few times regarding my impending visit. Colin was going to bring to the Consulate more items, like warm clothes, that I was going to need for my stay in Wales. By e-mail, I also agreed with him an amount I owed him for all his fetching and carrying. I added fifty euros to the agreed sum and posted him a cheque the next day. In between, all that was left for me to do, with Ben, was mooch around the town of Lucena, on walks and shopping excursions whilst attempting to continue with my novel. There were some spectacular gothic buildings of note around the town centre which did provide some interest.

Then, on what I think was the eighth day of inactivity I received a telephone call from Gordon Johnson. He told me that the Spanish police were prepared to release Iolanthe from jail, into his custody, on the condition that she didn't remain in Spain. Under my breath I whooped and hollered in delight. He said that in Spanish law they are only allowed to keep a prisoner in custody for a certain number of days without bringing a charge. He told me it was a point he'd pressed with the Spanish and as Iolanthe was coming to the end of that period they had agreed to her release on those terms. He went on to say that there was paperwork to organise at his end and that he would need to see Iolanthe again, by himself, at the jail, as had been discussed. Only then would it be appropriate for us all to meet up once more. Accordingly there were more days of frustration for me to contend with.

Eventually I received a message from the consulate confirming a meeting at the jail with Iolanthe and Johnson, on the next afternoon. They would again send a car for me. We all met in the same reception room as before. Again Iolanthe rushed into my arms on our arrival. 'Do you think it is going to be all right?' she whispered to me as we hugged.

'Of course it will be,' I replied.

Johnson went over, for the benefit of both of us, the conditions that would be attached to her asylum in Britain. He needed confirmation from us that we understood all the terms. Iolanthe and I concurred that we did, she with a big pearly toothed smile on her face. We then had to sign various forms which Johnson put in front of us. It was arranged that we would board a flight to Cardiff, with Ben in a flight kennel box, in two days time. Johnson would again meet us at the prison beforehand to ensure her release was acted upon. From there the consulate car would take us to Malaga airport and a member of staff would ensure we got on the flight to Cardiff. The consulate would book the tickets, but I would have to pay for them.

Over the next two days, once I was back in Lucena, I was on the phone constantly making the necessary arrangements. I had to take Ben to the local vet to update his injections, obtain a certificate to that effect and a suitable kennel basket to put him in for the flight. He'd never flown before. I'd bought him as a rescue dog in Spain. Getting him into the basket, as a trial, at the house, necessitated bribery with food. Eventually the day of transfer arrived. By then I was frazzled and worried. I just prayed that everything would go as planned, but there were no certainties regarding any of it. The Spanish could still be difficult.

In the afternoon I made my farewells to Captain Guiterres, then left for Malaga in the consulates car. We all met up inside the jail at the same reception room as before, except for Ben who had to wait in the car. Iolanthe was already in there waiting to greet us, this time accompanied by her travelling bag and the prison governor. Handshakes were exchanged all round. Johnson spoke to the governor in Spanish, while Iolanthe and I embraced. There were more forms to sign, followed by more handshakes when we left the room. I noticed that Iolanthe said nothing to the female warder, who remained standing by the door at the back of the room. In the outside courtyard Iolanthe's emotion overcame her and tears were shed. We both thanked Johnson in our respective ways, then he got into his car and drove out through the metal prison doors. We followed in the other car, the female driver of which was to see us through passport control. Beforehand however, Iolanthe had to endure a boisterous, kissing, licking welcome from Ben. I got in the back with him and held a restraining hand on his collar as we drove to the airport.

Procedures at the flight desk went smoothly. Because of all my goods and chattels I needed two suitcases, which Colin Wright had brought to Malaga for me. Iolanthe had only the travelling bag she'd carried from the prison. Ben, with coaxing from both me and Iolanthe, as well as more bribery with food was eventually persuaded into his basket and taken away by a flight official. Our problems began at the passport control desk. Luckily the consulate lady, Jeanette had stayed with us that far. The uniformed official behind the glass screen accepted my passport with an air of indifference and disinterest. Iolanthe however, only carried the paper documents signed by the various parties concerned, which on inspection, completely baffled the official. He said something in Spanish which neither of us understood. At that moment the consular lady, Jeanette intervened. Speaking good Spanish she engaged him in what sounded to us like a heated argument. He kept pointing to Iolanthe's papers and continually shaking his head. From what little I could translate, one of his points of contention seemed to be that there was no photograph of Iolanthe with the papers. A queue was beginning to form behind us. As Jeanette argued the point he said he would have to speak with his boss. He reached for his phone and I guess spoke to his boss, then asked us to take a seat until he arrived. The rest of the queue began to file through, most of them looking at us with suspicion. I suppose it didn't help with Iolanthe being Moroccan on a British flight. I began to panic as we didn't have much time until departure.

'I wondered if we would have trouble with this,' Jeanette said as she came over to stand by us. 'The problem is that this man has never seen these sort of papers before.' Surely it can't all go wrong at this stage I thought. I could see Iolanthe getting agitated. Gradually the queue that had been behind us all passed through the checkpoint leaving the three of us alone, outside the desk. Jeanette spoke again with the passport man, pointing at her watch and emphasising the passing time. He kept replying that his boss was coming.

It must have been at least quarter of an hour before a short dark haired uniformed man, sporting a gun belt appeared. The man behind the desk showed him Iolanthe's papers. He read through them with due attention, sometimes shaking his head. Jeanette went up to the desk to intervene, continuing to press about the time and the awaiting aircraft. For some minutes the two men continued to ignore her and concentrate on the papers. Then to add to the misery he asked Jeanette for her consulate identification. This, they also took some time to study.

I was becoming really worried about missing the flight. Then, the boss man said, 'Ok,' and handed all the documents back to Jeanette. We both kissed her on each cheek then got moving down the passageway. As we passed the control desk I heard the boss man say to Jeanette 'The Señorita may not be allowed back into Spain with those papers.' I nearly felt like shouting back, 'thank goodness for that,' but there wasn't time. We had to run to get on the plane before they removed the jet-way.

CHAPTER SEVENTEEN

My brother Peter was waiting for us at the arrivals gate at Cardiff airport. There was some slight delay at the passport desk, but nothing like the kerfuffle at Malaga. Firstly Iolanthe had to enter through a gate for non EU travellers, then they took some time reading and assessing her papers. Fortunately there was a supervisor on hand who was able to confirm their authenticity without an enormous fuss. It was a relief therefore to see Peter's smiling face on the other side of the barrier. He had driven up from West Wales. By then I had been to retrieve Ben from the dog compound, where I had been greeted with yelping, tail wagging affection.

By profession, my brother had been a lecturer in economics at Cardiff university. Six years older than me he had taken early retirement having become disillusioned with the British educational system. His real love, hobby, soon to be retirement occupation, was landscape painting. Hence the move to the wilds of West Wales. Some years back he had divorced his first wife, Angela, by whom he had two children, and now lived on a semi permanent basis with another artist named Carol Underwood, who I had yet to meet. From what Peter had told me she was a pencil sketch artist who owned her own property somewhere further up the coast. I gathered that they alternated between his place and hers, until, according to Peter, they got on each others nerves, then for a while they lived separately.

'How are you *brawd* (Welsh for brother)' he said to me when we got to the other side of the arrivals gate.

'Well I guess we are surviving, somehow,' I answered as we shook hands.

'So you've been telling me,' he replied. 'You must enlighten me further. And this is the young lady who the trouble's been about?' he added eyeing Iolanthe up and down. 'I can see now why you were keen to make such an effort.'

She gave him one of her best smiles. I introduced her by her full name, they shook hands.

'Come on,' he said next. 'The car's this way. I'm afraid, Iolanthe, it's going to be a long journey.' In the car park we were guided to his fifteen year old, going rusty, Jaguar, another of his idiosyncrasies. It was roomy inside. I sat up front with him, Ben and Iolanthe sat on the back seat, consoling each other.

The journey west seemed endless. In all it took well over three hours, and was made worse by the fact we were travelling into a dazzling, setting westerly sun. Along the way I brought Peter up to date on the more recent events. He was shocked to learn of all the happenings. Most of the way Iolanthe and Ben either slept or dozed. When we at last got into Pembrokeshire and Ceredigion a more rural aspect prevailed. Once there, through the open car window I began to savour the tang of sea air and awoke Iolanthe to point out the various views. Ben sniffed accordingly when the scents began to drift to the back of the car.

My brother's cottage is eventually reached by driving steeply down a long narrow, wooded lane, dotted with occasional dwellings. The road, which is a dead end finishes facing a sea bay. Off to the right of the bay there is a quarter of a mile long, unmade track which leads to his home. At certain points the track runs along the sea frontage. Iolanthe was impressed and expressed a 'Wow!' and 'What a view!' At the end is a nineteenth century cottage type bungalow, with two dormer windows, situated on a promontory.

The Jag was brought to halt on a hardcore turnaround outside the front door. It was a dull day with a stiff breeze up. Quite normal for West Wales, if it isn't raining. When we alighted from the car the sweet, refreshing nectar of the sea air stung my nostrils. In front of the turnaround was a small lawn, with a few windswept shrubs.

At the end of the garden a low dry stone wall shielded the rocky foreshore that led down to the Irish Sea. The cottage was whitewashed with a slate roof. Peter and I unloaded our belongings from the car, while Iolanthe dealt with Ben. Inside the front door was a tiny narrow hall, which led to a dining room on the right hand side and a lounge on the left. Both were compact with low ceilings. A modern built on lean-to at the back encompassed the kitchen and the bathroom. Two small bedrooms in the roof were reached via a narrow steep staircase. Each had a washbasin, but if you weren't careful you would bump your head on the low ceiling when using them. The front dormer windows provided the most spectacular views out to sea.

'This is the room that Carol sometimes uses,' Peter said as he guided us off the tiny landing into the right hand bedroom. 'She has agreed not to stay whilst you two are here as it will give us more room.'

'Oh dear, I am sorry for all the bother,' I replied.

'Not at all, if you can't help your brother when he's in trouble, who can you help,' he responded. 'If I get desperate I can always go and stay with her for a few days. She's coming to meet you both tonight anyway.' Peter had arranged for us to visit the local pub for a meal later that evening.

After we had unpacked, we all sat in the tiny lounge, being fortified by a couple of strong drinks, while relating more tales of woe to our host. The lounge was cosy, with a small settee and two tiny armchairs. Four of Peter's landscape paintings hung on each of the walls. Both Iolanthe and I remarked on their original style. A log fire roared and spat sparks in the small fireplace. Ben didn't like the sparks but seemed pleased to be discovering new smells as he explored the cottage.

'You two have been through it all right,' Peter said when we had finished unloading on him most of our recent tragedies.' For a lecturer Peter is not a verbally effusive man. Throughout our relationship I had always had difficulty in extracting anything descriptively informative or compassionate from him. Taciturn is perhaps the best description of his personality, which is, I suppose, why we have never actually been bosom pals. Articulate expressiveness on his part was usually channelled through his paintings. 'Where do you two hope to go with it all from here?' he asked next. Instantly I felt under pressure by imposing on his hospitality.

'What we really hope is that whoever took a pot shot at me is soon arrested by the Spanish police and then we can go back to living our lives there,' I said in response and went on to describe Iolanthe's singing exploits. I could see from the expression on his face that he thought he might be lumbered with us for some time.

Later in the evening we travelled in the Jaguar to the local pub, the Swan Inn. Ben accompanied us and again sat in the back with Iolanthe. There was a large car park with much outside lighting. Ben stayed in the car. Inside was comfortable enough, in a stone walled, dark stained timber lined, brass ornamented, studded chair back, sort of way. We ordered some wine and awaited Carol's arrival.

She was late. We discovered later on that she was regularly late. Sometimes, Peter told us, she didn't turn up at all for an arranged meeting. He added that it was part of her artistic eccentricity and he'd just got used to it. He told us that she was quite successful at what she did, with exhibitions of her work featured all over the UK. Before settling to be an artist, she had been a school teacher in and around the county of Ceredigion. She eventually breezed into the bar like a mini tornado, without any apology for her lateness. She had frizzy blonde hair which hung down to her shoulders and an exceptionally slim figure. She wore a floral shirt with the top two buttons undone to reveal a dangling gold chain, faded blue jeans and open sandals and she wore no socks. Peter had informed us beforehand that she was thirty nine years of age, much younger than him. Cheek kisses were exchanged between us.

'So this is the famous author and his runaway,' she said, without any inhibitions.

'More like infamous,' I responded, trying to keep the dialogue humorous. Peter went to the bar to fetch another wine glass for her and the menus while I attempted to relate to Carol an edited version of our troubles. She listened attentively. Out of the corner of my eye I could see Iolanthe watching her suspiciously.

'Well you will go living in those wild and distant places,' she said in an offhand manner, when I'd more or less finished my descriptions. Toasting each others health and deciding on what to eat, filled in the immediate conversation. It soon became obvious that Carol was a self opinionated, liberated woman. Her large blue eyes positively sparkled when she talked. I could tell she was intelligent, and made a mental note not to underestimate her. She described her bungalow and the area where she lived. Once we began to eat I related details of some of Iolanthe's singing activities.

'You can do that here,' Carol interrupted, pointing her fork at Iolanthe. 'These pubs,' she continued, pointing again around the bar with her fork, 'are crying out for entertainers to fill in spots at the weekend. It's so difficult for them get acts to travel down this far west, especially in the winter. Help you earn your keep as well,' she added dogmatically. Iolanthe lifted her head from her food and tried to smile politely.

Our meal and discussions continued in that lively and somewhat provocative manner until it was time for us to leave. Carol invited us to come and visit her bungalow once we had settled. By then Iolanthe and I were both exhausted. It had been a long and stressful day since leaving the prison in Malaga that morning. We were glad to get to bed, where we both slept instantly, without movement or murmur. Through the open dormer window we could hear the sound of the waves crashing in on the seashore in front of the cottage. Ben slept on the carpet at the bottom of the bed.

CHAPTER EIGHTEEN

For the first few days at the cottage we both felt like we were suffering from continuous jetlag. I guess the previous weeks had been so viciously stressful. Short shopping trips or scenic walks across the sea shore left us constantly tired. And we bickered a lot. Something we really hadn't done before. I think Peter sensed the vibrations, so after a couple of days, he announced he was going off to stay with Carol for three or four days.

As he got into his car to leave he pointed in the direction of the cliff top walk. 'From the end of the beach you can walk all the way along the tops to Newquay. Get yourselves out there,' he added, 'whilst the weather holds.'

So once we had kitted out Iolanthe with some suitable clothes from the local shops that's what we did. Peter was right, from the front door of the cottage a footpath traversed up and down the nearby cliffs for miles, providing dramatic vistas before delving into delightful bays. The air was also intoxicatingly invigorating. Gradually, it revitalised our energy and we resumed our normal relationship. My injured limbs became less painful and Ben was in his element.

One lunch time we were dining at the Swan Inn, when I said to Iolanthe. 'How about asking if you can sing for your supper at this place?' I'd seen notices on the adjacent walls advertising folk nights and the like. She looked at me hesitatingly. 'If you can sing in a night club in Marbella for your living, this should be a doddle,' I added.

'But I haven't got my guitar with me.'

'That's not a problem. We can catch the bus to Aberystwyth and get you one there. It's a university town, there's bound to be a music shop.'

When I went to the bar to settle the bill I collared the landlord on the matter.

'Wednesday night is open night,' he replied. 'Anybody who wants to can get up and sing, tell jokes, or play an instrument. It starts at eight o'clock. We do book acts for the weekends, depending on the time of year and how many residential bookings we have, but we'd need to see how she goes on Wednesday first.'

It only took a little persuasion on my part to get Iolanthe to agree, so the following day we embarked on the bus journey to Aberystwyth. A suitable second hand guitar was purchased at a reasonable price and back in the cottage she began to rehearse. During the bus trip I also broached another subject with her.

'If we are going to stay around here for some time I think we need to look for our own place,' I said. 'We can't go imposing on my brother and I think we'd eventually all drive each round the bend if we stayed as we are. What do you think?'

She thought for a moment, the newly purchased guitar was resting on her lap. 'I'll do whatever you want me to do. As long as I'm with you I don't care where it is. All I want is not to have to go back to that prison again, please.'

So we toured the local estate agents in the nearby town of Cardigan. It was also the agreed venue for our reporting in at a police station, so we were able to combine the two matters. A fistful of leaflets relating to various properties to rent accompanied us on the bus journey back.

Then to spoil everything, that night I got a call on my mobile from Colin Wright.

* * * * *

'How is wild West Wales?' was his opening gambit.

'OK, so far,' I replied. 'At least the weather has been reasonable.' Briefly I described how we were and some of the outstanding surrounding scenery.

'Good,' he responded. 'Well I don't want to be a killjoy but I thought I'd better let you know that I saw Iolanthe's people skulking around your villa again last night.' My heart sank on hearing those words. 'I don't think they saw me,' Colin continued. 'It was dark and I was bringing the dogs in from their evening walk. I stayed back down on the beach and watched them till they left. They've changed their van, now it's a grey people carrier thing with tinted back windows. I recognised them though when they stood under the street lamp outside your driveway. Like before they walked around the outside and peered in through your windows, but did nothing much else.'

'What time was this?'

'About eight in the evening. I had to wait until they'd gone before I could get inside my place and phone the police.'

'If they're driving around freely like that, why aren't the police picking them up?' I interjected.

'Beats me,' Colin said. 'Mind you I laid it on the line a bit thick when I did speak to them. I've checked your place over. There's no damage done. I just thought I should let you know that's all.'

We went on to talk a little more about our situation in Wales then rang off. All the time Iolanthe had been listening in on our conversation. She'd stopped strumming the guitar when the phone had rung. 'Your folks,' I said to her.

'So I gather. Thank goodness we're here.'

Before we retired to bed we talked about the matter further. I couldn't believe that the police hadn't apprehended her family by then. It made me wonder that with us out of the way if they had any real intention of actually doing so. By then, partly by being alone together in the cottage and partly due to the healing of my injuries, our love making had returned to its former passion, so that night I was able to sleep reasonably well.

My brother returned to the cottage the following day. I told him about our decision to seek alternative accommodation. 'You don't have to do that,' he responded. 'I do go quite regularly to stay at Carol's place.'

'I'm grateful Peter,' I replied, 'but we may be here for some time. We can't impose on you forever.' I told him about Colin Wright's telephone call.

'Oh Lord,' was his response. I also told him about the estate agent leaflets we had obtained and Iolanthe's decision to revive her singing career locally. 'Great,' he said to that. 'We'll all come and watch you,' he said to her and she hid her face behind her hand. 'You're welcome to use my studio to practise in when I'm not using it,' he added.

Afterwards I was on my phone to the estate agent making appointments to view a selection of properties that were either within walking distance of the Swan Inn or a short bus ride away. In that part of the world there are many dwellings that are holiday homes in the summer and let throughout the rest of the year. Peter had also brought with him an invitation from Carol for us to visit her at her bungalow.

The following morning, a young female estate agent, driving a zippy Ford, called at the cottage to take us on a tour of the four homes we'd chosen to visit. Clare, possessed a full head of tight ringlet, dark hair, down to her shoulders, a tiny, thin figure, skinny shapely legs, barely covered by a mini-skirt and a sharp, penetrating, west Wales accent that almost cut your ears in half when she spoke. She drove us to each of the dwellings as though we were in a motor cross rally. The four properties, three bungalows and one terraced house, were all satisfactorily kitted out for the purpose. Naturally, the one we liked the most, one of the bungalows, was the most expensive and the one which was our least favourite, the terraced house, was the cheapest. We said we'd let her know our choice next day. When we got back to the cottage Peter drove us to Carol's for lunch.

Her nineteen twenties bungalow had a magnificent view overlooking the sea. It was further back from the seafront than his place, adjacent to a normal road. Inside was a ménage of houseplants, cats and her pencil sketches. Furniture of every type, style and age, was assembled in each of the rooms. The whole interior was encompassed on one floor. Very little modernisation had taken place. The kitchen was a nineteen thirties creation with a huge range to cook upon, which also heated the water. The bathroom was pure nineteen fifties. The china bath was enormous and I guess the only way to get it out, if you needed to, would have been to smash it up in situ. All the rooms and cupboard doors were constructed of thin, white painted, planked, timber which creaked and stuck when you tried to open them with an old-fashioned latch. Walking around the bungalow was like stepping back half a century.

In contrast Carol seemed like a young girl who spent half her life at Glastonbury or similar type festivals. She was a creature of the eighties, wearing dangling bracelets and lockets. A femme fatale of wild and extravagant expressiveness. She certainly caught Iolanthe off guard. I wondered how such a staid and undemonstrative character as my brother coped with her.

Our lunch was a concoction of curries with rice, nan bread and red wine, which stimulated the senses. We talked mostly about our troubles in Spain, and we were interested to learn of Carol's past. I still couldn't understand how she fitted in with my brother, but there we are. He is a rock solid socialist, but if I had to categorise Carol I would say she had the traits of a post war anarchist. Everybody agreed they would come to listen to Iolanthe sing on the Wednesday talent night, which embarrassed her somewhat. Afterwards we inspected a selection of the vast quantity of Carol's sketches, the bulk of which were kept in the large second bedroom, that had been decked out as a studio. The sketches were very good; mostly they were desolate, wistful and poignant scenes of landscapes, totally unlike her character. Then she took us out into her much cultivated garden. Shrubs and herbaceous plants, which she claimed were all grown from her own cuttings, filled over a quarter of an acre. She and I inspected the hydrangeas, while Peter and Iolanthe were inside her greenhouse, checking on the cuttings. While were alone Carol said to me. 'Now Adam, if you ever get lonely in that rented cottage you're going to move into, you can always come and visit me here.'

I was too taken aback to reply much, other than 'thanks.'

Later on when we were back at Peter's place and alone together, Iolanthe said. 'I think that woman fancies you'

'Nonsense.' I replied instantaneously.

'I don't think so, I was watching the way her hungry eyes kept looking at you.'

One morning, later on, I was in the bedroom trying to work on my novel, Iolanthe was downstairs practising on her guitar, when my mobile rang. It was Colin Wright. I could tell by the breathless nature of his voice that he was desperate to tell me something exciting.

'I've just had a telephone call from the Guardia,' he began. 'They've arrested the Moroccans!' he continued. 'The Guardia want to know where you are and how to contact you?'

'Where?' I queried. 'Where have they arrested them?'

'At the circus in northern Spain. By all accounts it seems they went back there to work.'

'Good God,' I said.

'They've locked them all up in a town somewhere near where the circus is held,' Colin continued excitedly.

'Thank heavens for that.'

'Do you want me to give the Guardia your number,' he said next.

I thought for a second. 'Yes,' I responded. 'They should have it anyway, together with the details of where I am, but it won't hurt to release it to them again.'

'I think it's good news,' Colin said. 'Perhaps you can get your life back to some normality now.'

At the time that's what I thought, but eventually we were both proved to be wrong. Colin and I talked some more about events in West Wales and matters on the Costa del Sol, then he rang off. Next I was faced with the task of relating the news to Iolanthe. A look of serious concern spread across her face as I spelt out the details. 'Oh Lord I hope they're all right,' was her initial shocked reply. 'I pray they are not torturing them or anything like that.'

'I shouldn't think so,' I said trying to placate her.

'That's the sort of thing they do to our people. Especially if they are thought to be involved with illegal immigrants.'

'What about attempted murder?' I interjected quickly.

We both stood and stared at each other for some moments without saying anything. What I had just said suddenly brought the stark reality of our current domestic arrangement into proportion, which meant our relationship was entering troubled waters.

Some time later in the day I received a phone call from the Guardia. It was one of the detectives I'd met before. He reiterated what Colin Wright had told me. 'They categorically deny attempting to murder you,' he continued referring to the Moroccans. 'They say that they are aware of your relationship with their daughter. They said that they were keeping her at the caravan in the hills, for her own protection as she is so much younger than you. Their visits to your villa were an attempt to trace her whereabouts as they needed to go back to work at the circus. They guessed it was you who'd rescued her from the caravan. Their words are that you abducted her.'

'Well you've met her on her own,' I said. 'If that was the case she would have complained about it to you.' He made no reply. 'What about the illegal immigrant business?' I asked next.

'The three men in question are still in custody and being interrogated,' he said. 'I expect that the situation will remain like that for some days. Then we will either have to press charges or not.'

'What do you want me to do?'

'For the time being I think it best that you stay where you are. If anything positive happens about bringing charges against these men it probably will be necessary for you to come back here,' the detective said. Shortly afterwards we ended the call.

Afterwards, as slowly and quietly as I could, I again spelt out the possibilities of the situation to Iolanthe. A worried frown creased her forehead all the time I spoke. Her dazzling smile was absent throughout.

* * * * *

The following Wednesday we all drove to the Swan Inn to watch Iolanthe's performance. From Cardigan she had acquired a tight fitting second hand, black trouser suit. Her black hair was hanging long and tinted shiny dark, which made her look straight out of a show-biz magazine, certainly a more spectacularly persona than any of the assorted mob in the bar. Each of the entrants drew lots to decide on order of appearance. Iolanthe drew fifth out of a list of ten. Every act was given ten minutes. The lounge wasn't full but it was a lively alcohol induced crowd who gave the place some atmosphere. The first act up was a stand-up comedian who told dirty jokes which eventually drained everybody's patience. The second was a threesome folk group who sang quite well, but couldn't play their instruments. And so it continued, so by the time Iolanthe got up to sing she didn't have a lot of competition to follow.

There wasn't really a stage as such, just a corner of the bar that had been left empty for the acts to perform in. She was greeted with an enthusiastic bout of wolf whistling from the beer swilling men when she took up the spot. In return she issued one of her most glamorous smiles. She sang three songs, all of which were received with enthusiastic applause. On completion of the last one some of the men stood to applaud her. More wolf whistles accompanied her back to her seat next to all of us. Her act had gone down well. We all congratulated her. We had to endure the remaining acts to wait to see who won that nights contest. At its conclusion the landlord called out each of the acts in turn. The winner would be the one who received the most applause. Iolanthe won that by a mile. Before we left we consulted him about further bookings. He informed us that he helped to organise most of the music events in the local pubs and he would do what he could to try and get Iolanthe booked on the circuit. He asked us to call back in a few days to check on the progress. Consequently we all went to our respective homes in good spirits. Throughout the evening though, having been warned about it, I did spot Carol's fiery eyes wandering in my direction.

Economic necessity meant that the terraced house was the only viable option for us to rent. A two up, two down, it was sparsely furnished, but adequate for our purposes with the usual facilities. There was a local bus stop, a hundred yards away, where you could catch a bus into Cardigan. On a storm free night you could also walk to the 'Swan Inn.' When we called in there for a drink a few days later the landlord confirmed that he was arranging for some singing dates for Iolanthe at some of the local pubs, for which she would get paid. 'Not very much though!' he added with a chuckle.

For a week or so my life with her at the terraced house proceeded, if not totally smoothly, at least without any major mishaps. We managed to get on reasonably well together, although the change in climate and living environment did affect her moods.

She was, after all, a girl from North Africa who had also lived in Spain. West Wales was a completely different proposition, but somehow we got by. During those weeks she had secured a couple of folk singing dates which went down well with the respective audiences. Either Peter or Carol would drive us to the venue and attend the gig with the two of us. Carol still continued to give me a lot of attention, much to Iolanthe's angst and I guess jealousy. It was a matter I tried to play down by making jokes about it. The major problem for me, at the time, was money, or more pertinently the lack of it. Because of my repatriation I was unable to earn any new money. Periodically I did receive some small commissions on existing investments, but in my work I only earned any real money on new investments. By using my laptop I was able to keep in touch with most of my clients but that was about as far as it went. Iolanthe's income from her gigs hardly paid for the drinks and petrol we consumed in attending them. I was able to get on with my novel but it was still a long way from completion.

So beneath my placid façade I was a worried man. I knew we would not be able to hold out indefinitely in Ceredigion. My money would quickly run out and I doubted that Iolanthe would cope with the travails of an entire West Wales winter. We both really needed to get back to Spain, but as things stood I also knew that was not a practical proposition. I was still trying to arrange for Iolanthe to be given some sort of temporary visa to stay in Britain. It was however a long and involved process. I kept impressing on the powers that be the possible dangers she would encounter from her family if she was returned to either Spain or Morocco. We were therefore attempting to achieve an asylum protection for her in the UK. Living where we were, a long way from normal civilisation and its bureaucratic requirements didn't help.

One afternoon I took a walk by myself to my brother's cottage. When I arrived he was involved with his painting. 'I'll be ten minutes,' he said. So I sat on the wooden bench on the front patio, marvelling again at the sea view. The sunlight was sparkling on the water. He eventually came outside carrying two cans of beer, sat down on the seat beside me and began removing the paint from his hands with a turpentine soaked rag. At that moment I needed the ear of a third party to run my predicament through. With Peter I knew I would get an unbiased opinion. As brothers we had never held back with criticism of each other. While we sipped from the cans of beer, he listened patiently.

When I'd finished he said, 'To me it appears that the nub of your problems are with Iolanthe. She seems pleasant enough and is a damn attractive woman. That's all very fine, but you still can't be sure of her lifelong commitment to her family. Muslims are usually very family orientated people. Sometimes, particularly women, are not allowed to go against the will of the family.' He paused for breath and sipped on the beer. 'I think that at the moment you are out on a limb with her. You could ditch her, in a reasonable manner, then once it had been sorted out who took a pot shot at you, go back to Spain and continue with your life there as before.' I nodded my head in response. 'However, as I said, you may always continue to have a problem about her total commitment to you if it went against her family's wishes, even if she is in love with you.' I nodded again and took a turn to sup on my beer. Peter continued. 'If it was me I think I would be inclined to make sure she is settled somewhere, then go on living my own life in Spain as before. But only you can decide on that.' He paused for another sip from the can. 'For one thing she is much younger than you. Is she still going to want to look after you when you are in your dotage?' I chuckled. 'And at this moment in time, if any charges are brought against her family, she may not be allowed back into Spain. Where would that leave you? What would happen then? You couldn't leave her here on her own. Her English isn't good enough for her to survive here alone or get a proper job to keep herself, which would mean that you would have to stay here or somewhere else in the UK and keep her financially. Is that what you want? Could you afford that and stay here?'

'I realise all that,' I responded, 'but if she wasn't committed to me would she have left the caravan to run away with me?'

'H'm,' Peter said. 'If I was being kept captive in a hot caravan and had a choice to go off with another man, to live by the seaside, I know which I would choose. Plenty of time afterwards to make it up with the family. And as I've already said she is still a young woman, which means she is susceptible to all sorts of whims.'

I knew that in many respects Peter was right. He was only reiterating what Colin Wright had said to me before. We talked some more, finished off the beers, then I slowly walked back to the terraced house, mulling over all the aspects.

Iolanthe was indoors practising on her guitar when I got in. There was a pub gig that night and she had been trying out two new songs. Before I had chance to say much she wanted to try them out on me. They were both melodic, standard, folk/pop tunes, 'What have they done to rain' and Dylan's 'A Hard Rain is Gonna Fall.' She sang them well.

'Do you think you could make your living doing that here in Wales,' I asked her.

'I doubt it,' she said while fiddling with the tuning of the guitar. 'The fees are so small and the venues are tiny. They don't get enough people in to pay me any more. I couldn't keep myself in food on that let alone anything else.'

'What about back in Spain? Could you make a living at it there?'

'Maybe, but I'd have to go on a wider night club circuit and work most nights of the week. Why do you ask? Are you trying to get rid of me?'

To lighten my response I chuckled before I replied. 'Not exactly, but we have to think of the future. Neither of us can go on living here for ever. In the long run it's just not practical.' She stopped tuning her guitar, put it down on the floor and looked at me. I continued. 'What if your family were proved completely innocent of all the charges. Would you want to go back to the circus and work with them?'

She flicked a strand of her dark hair off her face, looked at me steadfastly, then said, 'Well I suppose that would depend on how much you wanted me.'

For some moments we looked at each other again without saying anything. 'Now you know I didn't mean anything about not wanting you,' I ventured. 'Of course I want you. It's just that we're in a mess and I'm trying to think of the best way out of it for both of us.'

We said no more about it, because we had to organise ourselves for that nights gig, but now when I look back on it I think that conversation was the turning point in our relationship. Carol was driving us to the gig that night. I sat up front with her , Iolanthe was on the back seat with her few stage props and guitar, we left Ben at home. The pub in question was about twenty miles away. It was a much larger venue, with a proper stage and microphone, plus a weekend crowd of about seventy or so boisterous, alcohol affected revellers. Carol and I sat at a table at the back, well away from the stage. Again Iolanthe received a wolf-whistle enhanced ovation when she walked up to the microphone.

Once she began singing I became aware again of Carol's flirtatious attentions. To accompany her bangles, lockets and beads, she was wearing a low fronted, green, tight fitting t-shirt, short white mini skirt, bare legs and open sandals. Her predominantly blonde hair, tinted with other different colours was hanging long in ringlets. 'You are a spoil sport,' she said to me. In front of us, on the table she had a bacardi and coke and to try and save on the money I had half a beer.

I looked at her questioningly and said. 'What do you mean?'

'Well you haven't been round to see me as I asked you to.'

'Yes I have and I'm seeing you now.'

'But you had your lady friend with you when you visited and again now. I mean you to visit me on your own, so we can be alone together.' I felt her hand rest on my knee.

'But you're my brother's girlfriend or whatever. I couldn't do anything like that while you are with him.'

'I'm not with him. That's the point of our current arrangement. It suits us fine as we are both free to do what we like. And I fancy you.' Her hand was still on my knee. On stage Iolanthe was belting out the chorus of her opening song.

I was taken aback. For a few moments I struggled for a reply. 'But at the present time I have Iolanthe,' I ventured eventually.

Iolanthe's opening song had ended. She was receiving rapturous applause.

'But she is so young Adam,' Carol replied when the noise of the applause had died down. 'Surely you're not going to be with her forever. So what does it matter?' She kept pushing back the dangling hair ringlets off her face. Each time she did it the metal bangles on her wrist rattled.

'I don't think I could cope with two women. Not at my age,' I said trying to make a joke of it all.

'Nonsense!' she replied. 'You're in your prime. Live a little!'

I repeated what I had said to Peter, 'that's what got me in the mess I'm in now.'

'Oh well please yourself,' she said curtly.

For the rest of Iolanthe's act we said very little more to each other. The patrons in the pub gave Iolanthe a big ovation at the end of her act. She had to sing an encore. Again to try and save on the money after she had finished and been paid, we made tracks for home. Conversation in the car between everybody was sparse.

When we were outside our terraced house, while Iolanthe was unloading her gear, Carol said to me. 'Now don't forget my invitation.' Regrettably Iolanthe heard the remark and referred to it once we were inside the house. 'That woman's been making a play for you all night,' she said.

'Of course she hasn't,' I said, adding a snigger to my voice.

'Oh yes she has and what's this invitation?'

'She mentioned about us going round to see her again. That's all.'

Iolanthe didn't reply, she just turned away from me and took her things upstairs.

I wouldn't say we actually fell out over the altercation but it was no longer the passionate close love affair it had once been. Our relationship didn't become sexless, but for the most part we concentrated on the business of living together, which was difficult enough in those rather strange surroundings.

*****

Periodically I received telephone calls from Colin Wright and the Guardia in Spain. In between there was a singing gig, which Peter drove us to by himself. I heard nothing further from Carol and kept quiet on the subject in Iolanthe's presence.

Then to my surprise I had a telephone call from the Guardia informing me that they were about to release Iolanthe's family from custody. They told me they couldn't find enough evidence to bring any charges against them. Did I want to come back to Spain, they asked me? What about Iolanthe I questioned? They replied that the family had given her papers to the police and therefore she would be allowed back into the country if that was her wish. If I wanted to return, they said, it had to be my decision, but mentioned caution as they still hadn't proved who had fired the shot at me in the wooded car park.

For some time I thought about the call before saying anything to Iolanthe. In fact before doing so I walked to my brother's cottage again to talk the matter through with him. Like me he was surprised to learn the news. 'Just because they've released them doesn't mean that it wasn't them that took a shot at you,' he said. 'It just means they haven't got any evidence to prove it.'

I mentioned that the Moroccans had been released on bail and were not allowed to leave the area in which they were working. 'I sometimes wonder if the shooting was a case of mistaken identity by somebody else,' I continued. 'Maybe the person or people responsible just shot the wrong bloke?' I said. 'It does happen.'

'M'm,' Peter murmured. 'So do you really want to go back to Spain and risk it happening again.'

'To be honest I don't know,' I said. We were sitting in front of the cottage watching a big westerly sun setting. I had also mentioned to Peter about Iolanthe being allowed back into Spain. 'You see when they first met me her family were quite helpful to me. They even drove me to hospital when I'd badly cut my wrist. That was of course before she moved in with me.'

'Well I repeat what I said before,' Peter said. 'Only you can decide. Couldn't you send Iolanthe back to Spain while you stayed here? She could return to her family or go back to the night club singing in Marbella, till this business with you blows over? It would save you the cost of keeping her here.'

So with those words rolling round in my head I walked back to the terraced house. It looked like a storm was brewing up. Before I got home spots of rain were falling on my head. Inside Iolanthe was practising on her guitar. She put it down as soon as I entered the room. I had the feeling she was getting bored with just doing that and not very much else in that environment. Ben had been sitting at her feet and leapt up to greet me. I sat down on the settee opposite her and immediately told her what the Guardia had related to me. I took some time spelling out all the details.

'Oh,' she responded tetchily. 'So you prefer to tell your brother all that first rather than me?'

Ben came and sat at my feet. 'I went to seek his advice as someone who is impartial on the matter,' I said while stroking Ben's head, he returned the affection with a lick on my hand. 'I want to do what's best for both us and to be honest, at the moment I don't know what is the best thing to do. You and I are both too close to the subject. My brother can look at it from a different viewpoint.'

'And what did he come up with?' she said and flicked some strands of hair off her forehead.

I took a deep breath, then said, 'What do you think about going back to Spain by yourself? You can now either return back there to your family or to Marbella and work at the night club. I could speak to Antonio Silva about it. He'd arrange it. I'm still not sure if it's safe for me to return there. You're not very happy here are you?'

I watched the expression on her face become angry. 'So I was right after all. You do want to get rid of me?'

'Of course I don't want to get rid of you. That's the last thing I want. I'm just trying to decide what's best for both of us.' She didn't look impressed, which forced me into saying something I was trying to avoid. 'However there is also the little matter of my house being burgled and my possessions stolen. Nobody's said anything about that. You tell me you witnessed it all? What am I supposed to do about that? Your family haven't been charged for that?' I paused for breath then added. 'Yet'.

For the rest of that evening we argued over all the matters without reaching any conclusion or agreement. When I took Ben outside for his last visit of the night a real storm was brewing. Not much better out here I thought, as I waited for him to do his business. A gale had got up and rain was slashing sideways into my face.

That night we slept together but there wasn't much affection between us. I didn't sleep well, partly because the problems kept swirling around and around in my head and partly because the gale outside was rattling the gutters and juddering the roof tiles. West Wales faces the full venom of any Atlantic storm. Often the area is the first bit of land the violent, swirling low depression hits and it seems it likes to vent its anger on the inhabitants living below. Throughout the night hail like rain lashed against the bedroom window. It awoke Iolanthe several times and she commented on its velocity.

Except for the welcome daylight the weather had changed very little by early morning. Rather than lie there any longer, doing nothing much but annoy each other, we decided to get up and make some breakfast. Outside the bedroom window I could see trees bending precariously, rubbish flying in all directions and the wheelie bins, on the pavements, waiting for the weekly collection, haring about like demented dodgem cars.

Iolanthe's demeanour remained as truculent as the storm. Getting a pleasant word out of her was difficult. Items for breakfast were passed between us like ships passing in the night, without many words. When I took Ben outside, the force of the gale felt like it was going to take my head off. The storm continued well into the afternoon, when eventually a pale sunshine and calmer weather returned. During the previous night several trees had been uprooted, and there'd been some flash flooding of the rivers in the neighbouring villages.

When I got back inside my reception remained almost as inclement. The phrase about 'wanting to get rid of me' emitted many times from Iolanthe's mouth. During those difficult days I put in some telephone calls to Colin Wright, the Guardia and Antonio

Silva, who confirmed that he would be able get Iolanthe work, again singing, at the night club and re-house her in her previous apartment.

So rapidly I was coming to the conclusion that for us both the best outcome would be for her to go back to Spain by herself until it was safe for me to return there. The Guardia had made no other arrests regarding the shooting incident, although they maintained they were still proceeding with enquiries. Colin Wright had said he would be prepared to meet Iolanthe at Malaga airport and take her on to Marbella. She still hadn't received a temporary visa for the UK, so I had to send many e-mails to the UK consul in Malaga and the social security locally, to arrange for her Spanish papers to be made available for her at Malaga airport.

For me it was a difficult time, not helped by Iolanthe's continuing antagonistic attitude. She was still of the opinion that I was trying to get rid of her. We didn't indulge in any sex again at that house.

I decided eventually to let the matter of the burglary at my villa drop. By then it was history. I'd been fully recompensed by my insurance company for all the goods taken and if I pursued any charges I knew it would only drive another wedge between Iolanthe and me. What was done was done. She knew the truth, I knew the truth, her family knew the truth, but I thought it better to let sleeping dogs lie.

It was at least another week of endless e-mails and expensive telephone calls before I was able to get all the arrangements and documentation in place for her transfer. Some time during that period Iolanthe reluctantly agreed to it all. She ended our argument on the subject by saying, 'that if you're absolutely determined to get rid of me, I suppose that's what I'll have to do.' I continued to try and point out that it wasn't what I really wanted to do, but that our 'present predicament left us with very little choice.' So our final days together, leading up to her flight to Malaga were somewhat fraught. When the weather allowed we did get in some coastal path walks. She played one more gig at a nearby pub. We had a meal out with Peter, during which he tried to spell out to her the benefits and necessity of her going back to Spain by herself. In all that time we didn't see Carol at all. Peter said she was in one of her 'black moods,' and he was keeping well away. He was going to lend me his car to drive Iolanthe to Cardiff airport.

The day of parting was painful for both of us. By then Iolanthe had become quite tearful. We indulged in a lot of hugging but no sex. 'I'm going to miss you,' was a phrase we both repeated a lot. Ben accompanied us for the journey, stretched out on the back seat of the Jag. Iolanthe still had with her the mobile phone I'd got for her in Spain and by then I had instructed her how to operate it properly. There were more tears and long embraces at the departure gate. With a painful and heavy heart I watched her walk away towards the aircraft. Several times she turned around and waved back to me while wiping tears from her eyes.

CHAPTER NINETEEN

I have to confess that for me the days that followed were very lonely and desolate. The West Wales weather was settling into its late autumn mode of endless rain and gales, with dark gloomy skies, which matched my mood. The only consolation was that it left me with little else to do but to get on with my novel. When the weather allowed I was out taking long walks on the coastal path with Ben. Iolanthe had arrived safely in Spain. The same British consul employee, Jeanette, who had seen us off, met her at the arrivals gate at Malaga with her papers and Colin was there to drive her to Marbella. Afterwards I kept in touch with her by phone and also Colin and Antonio Silva by phone and e-mail. She was back in the apartment with the same two girls and after the first week had undertaken two singing dates at the local night club. Down the phone she sounded lonely and unsure of herself. In West Wales, for some companionship, I met up with Peter every couple of days. He tried to persuade me to move back in with him, but having made the break I resisted the temptation. I knew at some stage it was a decision I might have to make as my money was rapidly running out, but in reality all I wanted was to get back to Spain.

Then one day there was a knock on my front door, Carol was standing outside when I opened it. She was wearing a hoop striped, halter top t-shirt under a leather jacket, which exemplified her breasts, tight blue jeans and calf length brown boots. 'If Mohammed won't come to the mountain, I suppose the mountain has to come to Mohammed,' she began. 'You've been ignoring me?'

'Do come in,' I said and held the door open for her. The waft of perfume that caught my nostrils as she walked in front of me was almost overpowering. 'What a pleasant surprise, how nice to see you,' I continued with a slight sarcastic emphasis in my voice.

When we were both standing in the lounge, the posturing of her buttocks and breasts indicated she had clearly called on me with only one intention. Instantly I was on guard. 'Would you like a drink?' I ventured.

'What have you got? Anything strong?'

The best I could muster in that respect was either whisky or red wine. She chose the wine. When I returned from the kitchen with two filled glasses she was seated on the sofa with her elegant long legs seductively crossed.

I handed her one of the glasses and began to move to the safety of an armchair. 'Aren't you going to sit by me, here on the settee?' she said patting the empty space alongside her.

'I think I'll be safer over here,' I replied and sat down where I had chosen. I don't think Ben was too sure of Carol either and he came and sat by the side of my chair.

She took a sip of the wine. It appeared that a liberal amount of red lipstick had been applied that morning as her lips left a stain on the glass. 'So your lady friend has gone?' she said next.

'Yes. In the circumstances we both felt that was the best thing to do. She was never going to settle here, in this climate.'

'No, quite right,' Carol said. 'I couldn't really see that she was your type of woman. How did you become involved with her in the first place?'

'Well we've told you some of the story,' I said. 'What do you think is my sort of woman?'

'Someone of your own culture. Someone like me, I guess. Surely you didn't think you could have a long term relationship with her?' She sipped at some wine, then said, 'So what are you going to do for female companionship while you're here?'

'I don't know if I want any more female companionship while I'm here. I've got to try and finish my novel. Female companionship would only be a distraction.' All the time we were talking her blue eyes were burning holes in my head. 'Then when the novel's finished I hope to go back to my villa in Spain and get on with my financial work, to try and earn some money, before all my clients go off and find somebody else.'

'Ok, but I wouldn't be a distraction while you're here. I would just be available to satisfy your bodily needs and hopefully mine. I wouldn't want to be taken out or anything like that.'

Carol was a desirable and extremely attractive woman. Her body, as it was presented to me that day, was enough to give any man the wanton shivers. And I still remained stirred by the thought of Iolanthe's exotic limbs, and hadn't had sex for weeks. So I was very tempted, but I knew I had to be careful. Not only because of the connection with my brother, but also because of the considerable trouble I'd got myself into over the previous few months, as a result of my dalliance with Iolanthe.

'I've told you before Carol,' I said next, 'there is no way I could do anything with you, even if I wanted to, because of my brother.'

For the next half an hour she tried to persuade me to change my mind, but I kept my cool and remained seated in the single armchair. When we both got up for her to leave she did try to bump into me, but I managed to sidestep her advance. For the rest of the day it was difficult to concentrate on my writing.

Slowly the days ticked by into weeks, but I was at least coming to the end of the work on my novel. When I contacted them the Guardia were unable to report any progress on my case. Speaking to Iolanthe was frustrating as it was difficult for me to detect what her true feelings were. Therefore, in my own mind, I decided to return to Spain as soon as my novel was completed. As far as being shot at again it was something I was just going to have to take a chance on. I didn't want to spend the rest of my life in hiding like a recluse. During that period of time I regularly met up with my brother.

Then, if I remember correctly, it was another damp, wet, miserable day. I was working on my book when my doorbell rang. Because I was in the middle of an awkward piece of text I didn't check through the window first to see who was outside. Then, when I opened the front door, to my surprise and slight horror, Carol was standing outside on the doorstep, looking like a drowned rat. I had no alternative but to invite her in. 'Any port in a storm,' she said as she moved inside. 'I'm sorry to bother you,' she said. 'I was on foot, in the wood behind your road, when the heavens opened. I'd been there trying to find a tree glade I wanted to sketch. I'm sorry I'm soaked through. Can I come in and dry off.'

There was little else I could do but oblige. We moved to the small kitchen. I switched on the kettle then went to fetch a large towel. By the time I had returned with it she'd removed the jacket top she had been wearing and was unbuttoning the white blouse that was underneath, which also looked completely soaked. 'I'm sorry,' she said again, 'you can look the other way if you want, but I'm afraid this is going to have to come off.' Slowly and I guessed almost deliberately she seductively disrobed herself of the blouse. Of course I didn't look away, how could I? Sensuously she began to towel the top her of her body. 'Do you like what you see?' she asked when she could see I was watching her. I certainly did I like what I saw. I remained on a sexual high from my time with Iolanthe and I repeat I hadn't had any sex for weeks.

'Oh yes, I like what I see,' I said and moved towards her. She gave me a coy smile. I reached out for her ample breasts and un-hooked her bra. While my hands roamed she made no protest. Then when our lips met there was an explosion of passion between us. I'm afraid to say we then did it there and then on the kitchen table. I also have to confess it was pretty good.

Afterwards I drove her back to her car, which was parked in the village. We never met up again during the rest of my stay there.

* * * * *

The day after I had downloaded the completed version of my novel to my publishers I went to see my brother and told him of my decision to leave for Spain. He advised caution, but he could appreciate my point of view. I then spent two or three days on the phone and e-mail, contacting Iolanthe, Colin Wright, the Guardia and arranging a flight to Malaga; Colin would pick me up at the airport there. I also had to sort out the estate agent in West Wales about my departure from the terraced house. When Iolanthe and I spoke it was difficult to make out if she was pleased to be seeing me again or not.

On my last evening in West Wales I had a meal with my brother at the Swan Inn. He was going to take me to Cardiff airport next day. Being with him again after so many years had been good, but we were never going to be close pals. There exists too many cultural and age differences between us. I had marvelled at his secluded home, with it's extensive sea views, but it was not the place for me. Carol, I was not too sure about. She didn't appear for our final meal. When I asked about her, Peter said she was still, 'in one of her black moods.' I left it at that. The following morning he drove me and Ben to Cardiff airport and waved me off at the departure gate.

* * * * *

The instant warmth of the air in Malaga brought immediate relief as I walked down the aircraft's gangway at the airport. West Wales had been getting chill and damp and had begun to infiltrate into my injured leg and shoulder. Colin Wright was waiting for me at the arrivals gate. Even Ben appeared more sprightly in the temperate conditions as he trotted alongside us on the way to Colin's BMW. Throughout the journey to my villa Colin kept up a constant chatter. In a slightly cynical way I enjoyed his company and I did owe him a lot for his help over the previous months. He said he'd checked out my villa and everything there was OK. 'No sign of any Moroccans,' he added.

After he'd helped me unload Ben and my few belongings, I said to him 'I owe you, big time.'

'Good,' he replied. 'I'll find a way for you to repay me.' He then made his way home to his villa.

To walk around my sea-fronted home again, after such a long absence, opening all the windows and patio doors, while Ben reacquainted himself with his familiar sniffs, was like entering heaven. I poured myself a large whisky, sat on the front patio in the sunshine and tried to take stock of my current situation. Being back on the Costa del Sol was, for me, a big plus. I had spoken to Iolanthe on the phone and arranged to see her on the following day. I had also organised to meet up with the Guardia. My feelings about my safety was still a major worry. One way or another I was determined to find out the truth. I still had a theory that it was a case of mistaken identity, for I couldn't think of anybody, except Iolanthe's family, who I had crossed swords with enough, to warrant such an action. I also wanted and needed to quickly re-establish my financial business, as for some time to come that was going to be my only likely source of income. My publishers would eventually come back to me with the editorial alterations to my book. We still had to organise a cover and all the other bits and pieces, so it would be some months before the book was going to be out in the shops and earning any money. Originally my publishers had given me a two book advance. This was the second book and it was the remains of that advance that I had lived off while Iolanthe and I were in West Wales.

In the morning I was on the phone to some of my clients, inquiring of their health and their present financial circumstances. In view of the recession many of their investments needed looking at, or changing. Where I could I made appointments to see them. Later on

I drove in the Mercedes to Marbella, with Ben on the back seat. I had arranged to take Iolanthe out to lunch.

He gave her a boisterous welcome when we all met up in her apartment. We exchanged a kiss and a hug but there certainly wasn't the passionate welcome in her lips and arms there had been in the past. My enquiries about her health and how she was getting on were met with 'Ok, I guess.' She told me her singing had gone down well and she'd been welcomed back into the fold at the night club.

We drove to a nearby restaurant for lunch. Her looks still had a powerful hold on me. Over a paella I asked her if she wanted to come and stay with me for the weekend at my villa. The offer was declined. She told me she was doing extra dates at the weekend to try and build up her money fund. 'I have been in touch with my family,' she added. 'I'm hoping to save up enough money to travel up one weekend to see them,' she continued.

'Do you think that's wise?' I asked.

'They are my family!' she replied, slightly cynically.

'I could drive you there if you want.'

'No thank you. I think it is best if I see them alone first.' I nodded my head in response. 'And I've got to start to stand on my own two feet,' she added quickly. 'Whatever happens to us I can't go on living off you for the rest of my life.'

I knew she was right. 'Please promise me that you won't agree to anything quickly,' I replied. 'Whatever you decide I think you should come back here and consider everything first. I am happy to help. And you do still mean a lot to me.' She looked at me closely with her big brown eyes, but said nothing in response.

To be back in her company again had reinvigorated me. I attempted to prolong our luncheon date with lots of questions and talk about our current predicaments. 'And what about us?' I ventured eventually. 'Where do we go from here?'

She hesitated before replying, tucked her long flowing hair behind each of her ears. 'I'm not sure,' she replied. Suddenly I realised I was not looking at the innocent, wide eyed, almost child like girl, I had first spotted under the bougainvillea in town. 'Being on my own has been good for me,' she said. 'Some of it I've hated, but overall it's been good. You see Adam, all my life I've lived with older men. Firstly my father and brothers and then more lately you. I've always been treated a bit like a child and everything's been done for me. But having to do things for myself has been good. I needed to do it.'

'But do you want to go on seeing me?'

'Of course I do,' she replied smiling. 'How could I possibly live without knowing how you are? We've been so close. Closer than anybody else I've ever known. But I have to sort things out with my family first and then decide where I want to go from there.'

Again I advised caution. She agreed. We arranged to meet up for lunch again when she returned from the north. In the meantime, she said she would keep in touch by phone.

'I am so grateful for everything you've done for me,' she said to me when we kissed goodbye in my car outside her apartment. 'I don't know where I'd be now if it hadn't been for you. And I do miss you when you're not with me. Please believe me.'

And so we parted on those terms. I drove home to my villa with a very heavy heart.

* * * * *

After that it was good to get out on the road again and discover that not all of my clients had abandoned me. I also met up with the Guardia which didn't prove as fruitful. The same two detectives I saw before met me in a stuffy, hot interview room in Malaga. During the late autumn and winter the Spanish abandon all use of air conditioning as they consider the air temperature in their winter to be excessively cold. The two men I was speaking to wore long sleeve pullovers, whereas up top, I had on only an open necked shirt. We spent a long time discussing their dealings with Iolanthe's family. The detectives told me that the Moroccan's adamantly denied any involvement with my shooting. Her father had said that he was insulted by such an accusation. He didn't particularly agree with my relationship with his daughter, as any father would, he had added, considering I was so much older than her, but to try to shoot or murder me because of that was preposterous, he maintained. No way would they even think about such a thing, he told the detectives. The detectives admitted that they couldn't find any evidence that would stand up in court to prove otherwise. Nor could they associate them with any illegal immigrants, although they didn't rule that out as a possibility. So reluctantly they said they had to release them from custody. Nothing was mentioned about my burglary so I ignored the subject. The detectives were keen to point out that the Moroccans were still on bail. Their passports were withheld, they had to visit a local police station once a week and were forbidden from travelling out of the region where they worked. They confided to me that their employers at the circus had put up the bail.

As far as any other leads relating to my shooting were concerned there were none. They were both at pains to stress to me that if I continued to live at the villa, as openly as I did, then no way could they guarantee my complete safety. The only way they would undertake to do that was if I went and lived again in a safe haven. Something I had no intention of doing. So, all in all, it wasn't a profitable meeting.

The following day I had an appointment with one of my clients, an aforementioned, Desmond Bloomfield, at his villa home not far from where I lived. I think I may have mentioned that some months before I had invested a large sum of money for him, just over five hundred and fifty thousand pounds in fact. When we re-met, as with all investments at that time its value had dropped sharply because of the fall in the markets and we were considering ways of splitting the money into smaller parcels to see if it would fare any better in more diverse products. At that meeting I had forgotten that the money from his father's estate had been subject to a family dispute about who was entitled to all of it. Then, when Desmond said, 'as long as it keeps it away from that thieving little brother of mine I'm happy,' my ears perked up. Desmond was a man in his early sixties. His brother, I was told was a few years younger. The big hoo-ha had been because his brother maintained that half of the money should have been left to him. When I'd made the investment Desmond had shown me a copy of his father's will and although I couldn't completely verify its authenticity, it clearly showed that the residue of the estate was to go to him. It wasn't my job to get involved in a family dispute. That was for lawyers to sort out. The money was also, at that time, in Desmond's bank account and my task was solely to get the best possible return on it. Up until that moment I had forgotten about the hoo-ha. It was a family matter and nothing to do with me. I had remembered the large half a million pound investment as it had earned me a lot of commission. However, as I was driving home from our meeting I did recall that the brother, whose name I had by then also forgotten, did afterwards send me a particularly nasty e-mail, blaming me for investing the money in a scheme he had no access to. I remember phoning Desmond on the matter, who told me to ignore the mail as his brother was just being stupid. Reading between the lines I guess Desmond had probably used me as an excuse to his brother for putting the money where it was inaccessible to him. However, I never replied to the insinuating e-mail, forgot about the whole incident and never heard from the brother again.

CHAPTER TWENTY

One evening, after dinner, I was out on the beach with Ben and my mind began to turn over those past events. We were making for the old derelict bungalow, where Iolanthe and I had first met. I was missing her very much and thoughts of her and our times together still remained active in my brain. I hadn't been that far on the beach since I had returned to my villa and was interested to see if anything had been done to the bungalow. There hadn't. The place was still empty and boarded up, but on my way back I tried to piece together everything that had happened in my dealings with Desmond and his brother. I recalled that the brother's e-mail to me was a particularly nasty bit of vitriol. At the time I seem to remember taking great exception to it, hence my follow up telephone call to Desmond. When, he told me to ignore it and that his brother was a bit of a nutter anyway that's what I did. I also vaguely remember Desmond saying something about that's why his father didn't leave his brother any of the money, as his dad had been required to bail his brother out of trouble for most of his life. Then I remembered that Colin Wright had given me the lead about Desmond wanting to invest a large sum of money. He was one of Colin's ex-pat cronies.

Next morning I called in on Colin Wright at his villa. Once again a noisy boisterous canine welcome greeted me inside his front door. Colin sent them scurrying into the kitchen with the assistance of his left foot. 'I've come to settle up with you for the excursions on my behalf,' I said as we sat outside in chairs on the patio.

'You don't have to do anything about that,' he replied, making a dismissive wave with his arm.

'Oh yes I do,' I responded. 'The petrol alone must have cost you a small fortune.'

'That was worth it to have Iolanthe sitting alongside me in the front seat. She's got a gorgeous pair of legs,' he responded.

I sniggered, wrote out a cheque for what I considered a suitable amount, then updated him on the latest situation in her respect. I then said. 'Do you remember Desmond Bloomfield? I think you introduced him to me regarding a large investment?'

'I do indeed. I see him quite often at the golf club. The investment was about half a million if I recall. Have you come to pay me some commission on that as well?'

I chuckled but didn't respond. 'What about his brother?' I said, 'do you know anything about him? There was a bit of a hoo-ha about who the money belonged to. The brother reckoned he was entitled to a half share of the money.'

'Terry you mean? Terry's a nutter, always has been. They had to ban him from the golf club. He was always drunk and he molested the women. Rumour was that he was also on drugs, which made him a pain in the arse to be around. Why? Has he been bothering you?'

'Not recently but at the time I made the investment I received a nasty e-mail from him blaming me for him not getting a share of the money. Desmond more or less said what you've just said and told me to ignore it, which I did. I'd forgotten all about it until I met up again with Desmond recently.'

'And?' Colin said questioningly.

'People who have health problems like Terry brood, sometimes on what they consider to be wrong doings to themselves. And they bear grudges, often for a long time. Particularly if things aren't going well for them at that moment.'

'Are you thinking what I'm thinking?' Colin said, while looking at me sternly.

'At the moment it's only a wild guess,' I replied. 'I'm still clutching at straws over this shooting business and the Guardia aren't much help. What more do you know about him?'

Colin went on to describe what background information he knew regarding Terrance Anthony Bloomfield. As Desmond had intimated it appears he had been a tearaway and in trouble for most of his life. As a youngster he had apparently been involved in gangs, fighting and stealing cars. As a result, his father who ran his own successful car business, attempted to curb his son's activities by enrolling him in the army. By all accounts this suited Terry down to the ground, as it enabled him to channel his violent energies into more purposeful ventures. Subsequently, because of his leanings in that respect, he was asked to train for the SAS. He passed all the tests and eventually became a valued member of that squad, serving in Northern Ireland and Iraq. Trouble reared its head again however, when he was dismissed from the service for assaulting an officer. It was rumoured that because of his previous exemplary service record with the unit he was given quite a good pay-off. Back in civi-street, with the money, he tried to set up his own garage business, but from the start it turned out to be a complete failure. He lost most of the money trying to live the high life, before the business had actually made any money. Regularly his father had to bail him out. The final straw came however when Terry was prosecuted for fraudulent dealings with the cars. He was getting hold of cars that had been declared as write-offs, doing them up, then selling them on as legitimate cars. Tampering with mileometers and forging MOT certificates were among the other items that were included on the prosecutions charge sheet. Because of his good record in the army, the defence counsel he employed managed to get Terry off with a light sentence. Fines and a ban from working in the motor trade were his punishment. At that point his father had had enough. Their name association in the motor trade caused his father endless embarrassment, so he told his son to get out of the country and not to come back. Consequently he bought Terry a cheap villa on the Costa del Sol and said he never wanted to see him again.

'Could you ask around about him some more for me please Colin,' I said when he finished telling me the details.

'I'll do that,' he replied. 'The lads at the golf club know everything about everybody. It'll cost you though!' he added with a chuckle.

'Doesn't it always?' I replied.

* * * * *

Over the following few days, as I didn't fancy much being target practice for a nutter, I tried to keep a low profile. I didn't visit any out of the way places or lonely spots. I kept to the main streets in town and my walks with Ben were up and down the beach near my villa. I continued to see my clients, but that was door to door driving in my car.

Then one morning I received a telephone call from Iolanthe. She was back in Marbella and wanted to meet up for lunch. It had been a few weeks since our last meeting. I was pleased to hear from her. I still missed her being around me and of course the luxury of her body. We arranged to meet up for lunch next day.

Her welcome for me when I picked her up at her apartment seemed warm and genuine enough. The glittering smile was back on the pearly white teeth. I drove her to a restaurant we had visited before. Over tapas and red wine she told me her singing engagements were going well. She'd abandoned her wig and reverted to her own hair style and make up style. 'If anything I'm too busy,' she replied when I asked her how it was all going. 'Last week I only had one day off and I have to travel more so I do get very tired.'

'But are you enjoying it?'

'Oh yes,' she replied. 'Because for the first time in my life I'm doing something for myself and earning my own keep. I'll always be grateful for what you did for me. I can never repay you for that.'

'I'm pleased,' I responded.

She continued. 'Last week someone from one of the national agencies came to see my act. I haven't heard anything yet but if anything comes of it I may be able to get on the national cabaret circuit.'

'Great!' I said. 'And what about your family? How did your weekend with them go? What do they think of you singing for your living?'

She brushed some strands of her shiny dark hair off her forehead. She was looking more glamorous than I had ever seen her. I guess the new make-up and the manicured hair helped. 'At first they were horrified,' she said. 'There was a big argument but eventually I got them to see some of the things from my point of view. They are adamant however that they didn't take a shot at you. They said that was an incredible accusation. I think I'm inclined to believe them.'

'Good,' I said. 'I glad about that.' I made no mention about the burglary.

She continued. 'The other point I managed to get through to them was that I've been out of action for such a long time from the trapeze work that my muscles have gone for that sort of thing. I don't think I'd ever get the required power back in them, not for a long time anyway. Which means I would be of no use to them in the act.'

'What did they say to that?'

'Oh, a lot of old fashioned nonsense about the role and duty of a daughter. I told them I was a big girl now and wanted a life of my own. I said, I certainly wasn't going to spend the rest of my life being a housekeeper for them.'

I was impressed. She was no longer the innocent child I'd rescued from the derelict bungalow. 'So how did you leave it with them?' I asked. 'Are you still speaking?'

'Just about. We agreed to give it six months. See how things go. If my singing doesn't work out in that time I will go back up North, to live near them, but get a proper job, where I can earn my own living. But in the meantime I will keep in touch with them by the telephone.'

'You're very brave,' I said.

'I have you to thank for that,' she replied.

'And what about us? Do I fit in with any of this?'

'Yes, if you still want me. I won't go back to living with you as I did before, but if you still want to see me I will come and stay with you at the villa when I have a night off, if that would please you. I repeat you still mean an awful lot to me. And occasionally I might be grateful for a decent lunch out,' she added with a giggle.

So that's what we agreed to do. I would contact her periodically to meet up. Before we completed our lunch I told her about my suspicions regarding Terry Bloomfield.

'Oh Adam,' she responded. 'Please be careful, I don't know what I would do if anything like that happened to you again.'

I tried to console her by emphasising that at the moment it was only suspicions or maybe the imaginations of my over-active mind. We parted as good friends, with a passionate kiss, in my car, outside her apartment. It had been good to be in her company again.

* * * * *

It was a day or two later when Colin Wright came knocking on my front door, bursting with more news regarding Terry Bloomfield. Ben scurried out of the way into the kitchen area as I guided Colin out onto the patio. I offered him a seat then fetched the gin bottle, an ice bucket and some tonic.

'I was wrong,' Colin began as I dealt with the drinks. 'This man Terry Bloomfield is not a nutter,' he said and took a sip of the gin I'd just poured him. I looked at him questioningly. 'He's a complete raving lunatic.' I laughed out loud. He continued. 'By all accounts he is now completely bankrupt. He owes money on his electricity, which I'm told has been cut off. He owes for parking fines and nobody locally will take his credit card as the money usually bounces. The local traders and bars refuse to deal with him unless he pays them in cash. Worse still, when his economic situation began to deteriorate he started taking drugs. That combined with the alcohol, which he already consumed in great quantities, has brought about erratic and sometimes violent behaviour. There have been one or two nasty incidents with his neighbours and even altercations with the Guardia.'

I took a large slug of gin. 'Could he be my assailant?' I said to Colin.

He hesitated before replying. 'After what you told me about the will I think it is a possibility. To make matters worse I also found out that when he first came to live in Spain he was relatively sober and did undertake some work as a mercenary in places like Angola. It's a very well paid profession and his training with the SAS would have made him ideal for the work. Which means he quite probably still has a number of fire arms and guns in his possession.'

I felt a cold shiver tingle down my spine and took a large slug of the gin. 'Did you speak to Desmond, his brother, about it.'

'No, I thought it best to get the word from some independent parties first. Desmond would only give me a biased view, either one way or the other.'

'H'm,' I responded. The news had shaken me. Dealing with Iolanthe's family was one thing, but dealing with a drugged, armed man, who had worked as an assassin, was something completely different.

For a moment I was stumped for a response. 'What the hell do I do now Colin?' I said eventually. 'This thing about bearing a grudge is I'm afraid relevant. I did quite a bit of research on the subject once for one of my novels. From what I read up on it, quite often the fanatic's target has only a vague connection with the facts of the actual grudge. Sometimes the assailant's imagination tends to run away with them, and they blame everybody and anybody for the injustice. Now you tell me this guy also does drugs only makes my theory more plausible.'

We talked some more on the matter. The gin was going down rapidly. 'I agree with you about not mentioning anything to Desmond at this stage,' I said. 'He's bound to be concerned one way or another. He may want to tell Terry about our suspicions or maybe get him out of the area. He is after all his brother, whatever his real feelings about him are.' Colin nodded his head in agreement. 'I think I am going to have to suss this bloke Terry out myself. Do we know where he lives?' I continued.

'Not by yourself you're not,' Colin retorted instantly. 'Yes I do know where he lives, but I'm not letting you go round there alone. You do realise we are dealing with a drugged gunman, who is also probably a psychopath.'

'Do you want to come with me then?'

'Not bloody likely. I value my health too much for that. This is a job for the professionals. I think we need to get Charlie Wolfenden in on the act. This is their sort of work.'

'Couldn't we just go to the police?' I asked. 'Charlie Wolfenden will cost a lot of money.'

'We could go to the police, but at the moment we only have suspicions. On their own they're not going to be much use initially. You can't arrest a guy on just suspicions. He maybe a drunk and damn nuisance but they can't lock him away for long on that alone. We have to build up some sort of positive evidence that Terry Bloomfield is the guy who took a pot shot at you. If I speak to Charlie he won't charge you the earth. But it's up to you. It's your life.'

Before we completely emptied the bottle of gin we agreed that I would sleep on the matter, although that night not much in the way of sound sleep came my way. The machinations going around and around in my head ensured that. Before these latest revelations and now that Iolanthe's family had been more or less eliminated, I had almost convinced myself that the shooting had been a case of mistaken identity. I couldn't think of anybody else who disliked me enough to want to kill me. For the first time I was genuinely frightened. This man, Terry Bloomfield, if it was him who took a shot at me, obviously knew where I lived and at sometime or another had followed me on some of my walks.

In the morning I sent an e-mail to my brother and told him the latest. He was soon back to me. 'You can't tackle this man by yourself,' was his succinct reply. 'He's a known killer and from your description incapable of being responsible for his actions. You'll likely get yourself shot at again if you try and tackle him by yourself and this time you might not be so lucky.'

With his words still revolving in my head I took Ben out for his morning walk. I decided not to tell Iolanthe what Colin had discovered. She'd be worried out of her head if she found out about anything more to do with Terry Bloomfield. On my way back from the walk I knocked on Colin Wright's front door.

When he opened up his dogs leapt out at Ben and began to bark and jump all over him stupidly. While trying to fend them off I said, 'Could you perhaps organise a meeting with Charlie Wolfenden? I'd like to seek his advice before we attempt anything.' Colin agreed to do that and let me know a time and date, then I left quickly. Ben was becoming very agitated, growling and showing signs of aggression towards the other two canine idiots.

A couple of days later Colin was driving me through the pillared gates of Charlie Wolfenden's expensive villa. He greeted me like an old friend outside the large double front doors, then guided us through his immaculately floored tiled interior, to the patio and swimming pool area at the back. Stretched out there on a lounger, wearing only a skimpy bikini, was his glamorous wife Daphne. When she saw us she came to greet us with a full toothed smile then retired back to the sun lounger.

Charlie poured us each a gin then said to me, 'From what Colin tells me you're still having problems?' After taking a sup on the gin I updated him on the latest developments. Colin regularly interrupted, excitedly, with small facts or items that I had left out. I finished by saying, 'At this stage I am just seeking your advice on the best way to proceed. Realistically I want the guy locked up so he can't take any more pot shots at me.'

'Well firstly I agree with Colin,' Wolfenden replied. 'You can't go anywhere near his place by yourself or you're likely to get your head shot off. He obviously knows what you look like, so you'd be a sitting duck.'

From behind us we heard the sound of a large splash from the swimming pool. We looked around and were presented with a view of Daphne's perfect rear entering the water. Few a few moments it was difficult to concentrate on the business in hand.

'I think it best, first, if I send one of my men, on his own, to do some reconnaissance work,' Wolfenden said. 'Let's check this man Bloomfield over, take a good look at his property, follow him around a bit, see if he meets up with anybody interesting, that sort of thing and report back. My men are all trained in that work. Then we'll know exactly what we're dealing with.'

'But how much will that cost me, Charlie?' I asked. 'I'm almost flat broke after all this trouble. And because of all the problems I haven't been able to work properly for months.'

Charlie smiled. 'We'll work out a deal for you. As I said before I'm not going to fleece a friend of Colin. If necessary you can pay me over a period of time if it helps. Let me send one of my men out to take a look first then we can decide what to do.' At that moment Daphne came swimming alongside us in the pool. It was difficult not to look at anything else. 'She's all woman,' Charlie said with a huge grin on his face as she swam past.

So I left it at that. He would report back directly to me in a weeks time on what his man had discovered. We agreed on an initial fee for that work which was almost a months living money as far as my household budget was concerned.

During those weeks I was able get about to see my clients and at last earn some proper money. I was careful to keep a low profile and regularly checked around the outside of my villa before I ventured too far. I also carried the gun Colin Wright had given me wherever I went. I wasn't happy about that but he'd again talked me into carrying it. He also acted as a constant spy on my property and took great pains to convey sightings of anybody who went anywhere near the place. At the time I was receiving downloads from my editor with alterations to my book. Usually I am reluctant to make changes, apart from obvious mistakes, but because of my ongoing condition of penury, I didn't argue much with any of them. I just wanted to get the book out on the shelves as quickly as possible to try and create some income. I kept in touch with Iolanthe by phone. In our conversations I was careful not to mention anything to do with Terry Bloomfield. Up to that point she had made no visit to my villa. By all accounts she was far too busy with her work which was taking her all over the region with many gigs. I was pleased that she sounded happy, so I left it at that.

CHAPTER TWENTY-ONE

It was over a week before Charlie Wolfenden got back to me. 'This man of yours is a bit of a star,' he said to me down the telephone.

'What have you found Charlie?' I replied.

'Well he's into everything. Drugs, petty thieving, most of the time he's heavy on alcohol. In his villa he lives like a down-and-out. As Colin discovered, the electricity has been disconnected. A lot of the time when he's there he's crashed out. It very sad really. He has a beat up old car, but it looks as though it's out of ITV(the Spanish equivalent of the MOT) as there's no current sticker on it. He also seems to get himself into fights. His face and body are covered in cuts and bruises. I guess that probably happens when he's bargaining with drug dealers. That's how it is in that world. In reality the man needs professional help.'

Charlie went on to give me more information. It sounded a sorry tale. He said he'd send me a written report with his bill. I told him that when I'd read it through and digested everything I would get back to him. The report arrived in the post a couple of days later. It was quite detailed and gave a resumé of Bloomfield's comings and goings everyday during the period covered. It told of him meeting up in bars with drug dealers and involved in petty thieving of food from supermarkets. I thought there was enough evidence there alone to have him arrested. Enclosed with the report were a selection of photographs of him taken at various locations around the area where he lived, which was about twenty miles from me. From the photographs he bore no resemblance to his brother Desmond. His face was unshaven and marked with bruises, cuts and scars as Charlie had indicated. It was difficult to discern the true colour of his hair, as it looked matted and was tied at the back in a tight ponytail. His clothes were scruffy and unkempt, in a t-shirt and shorts manner, with sandals and no socks. Amongst the pictures there were also a couple of his beat up Seat car. After I had read through the report twice I took Ben out for a walk on the beach to try and digest all the information.

When I was back inside the villa I put in a telephone call to Charlie Wolfenden. 'Isn't there enough evidence in this report to have the man arrested?' I said to him. 'It seems to me that he goes out and commits four or five crimes of one sort or another every day.'

'There probably is,' Charlie replied. 'But none of it would be enough to put him behind bars for any length of time. He's probably only doing what half the down-and-out's on the Costa del Sol are doing anyway. They'd put him away for about three months and try and get him on a drug programme, but once he was out he'd go back to his old ways. Unfortunately nearly all of them usually do. The police know that, the courts know that. There wouldn't be enough room in the jails to lock them all up for ever.'

I had to concede what Charlie was saying was right. I'd seen enough on my trips to Marbella to realise the severity of the problem. I told him I'd think on the matter further before deciding what to do next.

'Just make sure you are careful in what you're doing and where you go. You never know with these nutters,' he said. 'Keep looking behind you.'

'I'll remember that Charlie. Thanks,' I replied.

My life continued in the same vein for a few days. I consulted Colin on the subject matter a couple of times, showed him the report and the pictures but I still couldn't decide what to do for the best. Then one morning, all my worst fears were realised. I was out on the beach with Ben. We were heading away from my villa towards the old derelict bungalow when suddenly, from somewhere behind me, I heard a lot of shouting. I turned around to look and saw, coming out of the sand dunes, the figure of a man running towards me and waving his arms frantically in an agitated way. Instantly I recognised him as the man I had seen in the photographs. It was Terry Bloomfield. He was coming straight at me, still shouting and waving. I froze with fear. His actions caused Ben to bark and rise up on his back legs. My feet remained glued, motionless to the sand. Then, as he got closer, I could see a pistol in Bloomfield's right hand. Ben continued to bark aggressively, while standing up on his back legs. Without any warning Bloomfield started to fire bullets in my direction. Instinctively I ducked and crouched down on my haunches. None of them hit me but I could feel and hear the swish of them as they passed over my head. He was getting nearer. I could see his face was covered in a lather of sweat and he looked evil.

Then to my horror of horror's, Ben escaped from the grasp I had on his lead. He could obviously sense the danger approaching us. By then, I guess Bloomfield was about forty yards away. Before I could think Ben was off hurtling towards him, barking and bearing his teeth. 'Ben!' I shouted at the top of my voice. 'Come here.' He ignored me and kept on going for Bloomfield. I hardly dared to look. Then the wretched man fired the pistol at him. It only took one shot. The dog crashed to the sand instantly, some twenty yards away from him, never to move again. Instantly I remembered the pistol I had in my pocket. I was always hopeless with it, but somehow I managed to get the damn thing out of my pocket while Bloomfield was standing, staring down at the dog. Don't ask me how, but I managed to move the safety lock, then began firing pot shots at Bloomfield. My aim remained hopeless. Regretfully I missed him with every shot, but it did force him to turn and flee back in the direction of the sand dunes. At that point I gave up on the pistol and ran to Ben, who I could see was motionless. When I reached him there was no breath in him, nothing. I knelt by his side and stroked his head. At that moment I didn't care about anything but Ben, but I could see Bloomfield still running for the dunes.

Colin Wright had heard all the commotion and gunshots on the beach. I guess he also thought it might be something to do with me, so the next thing I saw was him running towards us, carrying a shotgun, from which he was firing bullets in Bloomfields direction. None of them hit and made it to the sanctity of the dunes. Colin also had with him his mobile and before he even reached us I could hear him on the phone to the Guardia, summoning help.

When he reached us I was still hunched over Ben's body, stroking him. For many moments all Colin could do was stand and stare. Then he bent down to him and tried to feel Ben for a pulse or a heart beat. 'I'm afraid he's gone mate,' he said to me. I could feel the tears welling up in my eyes. Between us we carried his limp body back to my villa. In the background I could hear the sirens of the police cars heading in our direction.

* * * * *

Their arrival at my villa coincided with us reaching my front gate. Without having to say a lot they could see what had happened. We all went inside and after resting Ben's body in the spare bedroom I went and fetched Charlie Wolfenden's report and the pictures of Bloomfield and his car. While I spoke my whole body continued to shake violently. Tears still choked most of my words, so Colin took over. Immediately one of the policemen was on his mobile arranging for their cars to be out on the main road looking for Bloomfield. They had the details and the registration number from the photos. They also copied Bloomfield's home address off the report. I found out later that they caught up with him somewhere on the main road, half way to his home. Even then I'm told, it required a frantic car chase to apprehend him. They had to force his car into a wall to stop him continuing. When they got him out of the vehicle they found him to be high on drugs and alcohol.

The Guardia men weren't long at my villa. I told them about the two detectives at Malaga who had all the details of my case. They took a statement from me about what had happened on the beach. Because of my continued incoherence, Colin had to interpret for me and then they took a brief statement from him and left. As soon as they had gone Colin took me across the road to his villa and poured me the largest brandy I had ever drunk. While I sipped at it, I blubbered on about Ben's death being my fault. To this day I still blame myself. During those dark moments Colin was already on the phone to the local vet arranging to take Ben there for cremation; something we'd agreed upon during my blubbering. He eventually accompanied me back to my villa and after lots of strokes and one last pat farewell we put him into a black plastic bag and carried him out to Colin's car, for transmission to the vet.

When they'd gone I was morose with grief, pain and anger. Over and over I kept blaming myself. I wanted to strangle that bloody man Bloomfield. Eventually as a result of Colin's brandy and several more I had inflicted on myself, I must have crashed out asleep.

What time it was, I haven't a clue, but many hours later I was awoken by a noise coming from the front door. I looked up, outside it was dark. For a few moments I thought it had all been a bad dream, a nightmare. I was lying out on the settee. I half expected Ben to come padding over to me and lick my ear, as he often did in that situation. Reality soon hit me. However, moments later, walking into my lounge were Colin and Iolanthe. Unknown to me he had telephoned her and instantly she'd cancelled that night's gig, claiming a bereavement in the family. After taking Ben to the vet Colin had gone to Marbella to fetch her.

Her presence that night, I think saved me from total despair. On my own I don't know what I may have done. I fell into her arms when I got up from the sofa. Colin soon left us. She stayed the night and most of the next day. We slept together, but there was no sex. As soon as my head hit the pillow, I relaxed into her embrace and partly due to the volume of alcohol still in my system fell instantly asleep

CHAPTER TWENTY-TWO

Her company the following day was irreplaceable. She stayed with me until the early evening, then I drove her back to her apartment, where she changed for that nights gig. I took her to the venue and then sat through her performance. I still felt totally lousy, but she went down a storm. Afterwards I returned her to her apartment then drove home in the early hours. I hadn't touched a drop of liquor since the day before.

The days after that I brooded and continued to feel lousy. The two detectives from Malaga came to visit me. They confirmed that Terrance Bloomfield was safely behind bars. A long list of charges were being prepared against him. Visiting his villa they found an arms cache which would have been comparable to a whole gang of terrorists. A random selection of drugs and purloined items from various shops and supermarkets were also scattered about his home they told me. They said there would have to be a trial, which I would be expected to attend and give evidence, as well as Colin. I dreaded the thought of it but I knew I had to do it for Ben's sake, if nothing else.

The weeks that followed were desperate. I made attempts to see my clients and sporadically on her days off Iolanthe would come to stay with me. I would pick her up in Marbella, she would stay the night, we'd indulge in some sex, then I'd drive her back the next day. Colin called in regularly and I'd walk with him on the beach, accompanied by his monster dogs. I knew it was a superfluous precaution, but I was still reluctant to venture too far afield on my own. Somehow, I half believed that Terry Bloomfield would somewhere creep up behind me and take another pot shot at me. By then I had Ben's ashes in an urn at the villa.

One of the hardest tasks I had to do was to contact Desmond Bloomfield. I didn't particularly want to lose him as a client. 'I wondered if I might hear from you,' he said when I called him on the phone.

'This was none of my doing,' I replied. 'I have never met Terry in person,' I said to Desmond.

'I know,' he responded. 'That lad's been a complete idiot from the start. I think the trouble was that he was spoiled by his mother. He was her blue eyed boy from the day he was born. She brought him up to think he could walk on water. I assure you it won't affect our relationship,' he added and I was pleased about that.

Gradually over the following weeks the pain of seeing Ben shot that way began to lessen. It never completely disappeared, I suppose it never will. Constantly, except when Iolanthe was there, my villa felt lonely and empty. There was nothing around my feet anymore for me to bump into. Getting stuck into my work as a financial adviser helped. Meeting different people and trying to sort out their financial problems kept my mind off other matters. At last I was starting to get out again and earn some reasonable money. My novel was eventually published and out in the shops. In time, from those royalties, I will be able to settle my bill with Charlie Wolfenden. Then a few months later Colin and I had to face the prospect of Terry Bloomfield's trial. The judiciary system in Spain is long and tortuous. Before the real trial there has to be what's called an investigation trial, in an instruction court, to validate that there is a sufficient case to be brought before the oral trial can proceed. No witnesses are required at the instruction court. Usually it's just the defence and prosecuting counsel who present their respective cases to a panel of judges. The prosecution don't always have to reveal all their case at that juncture.

* * * * *

In the weeks leading up to the oral trial Colin and I had various meetings with the two detectives and we needed to go to Malaga for a session with the chief prosecutor, who spoke good English. He attempted to prime us both on the type of questions the defending counsel would throw at us. I was dreading the day of the trial, but I was determined to see it through and look Bloomfield in the eye.

I remember it was a cold February morning when Colin and I set off for the court at Malaga. Over the previous few days a brisk north westerly wind had set in. February is usually our coldest month. He drove us there in his BMW sports car.

On arrival at the court house the prosecutor spoke with us briefly in one of the reception areas. Then we had to sit around half the day waiting to be called. Both Colin and I were wearing what you might call our most respectable clothes. In my case flannel trousers, a black blazer, white shirt and blue tie. Colin had on a pair of corduroy trousers, a tweed sports jacket, check shirt and cravat. He could have passed off as a country squire. He was called to give his evidence before me. The court room was half empty. The principal judge of three, was a dark haired, middle aged Spanish lady, who wore pince-nez glasses perched at the end of her nose, through which she had a tendency to look down on everybody she spoke to. Desmond Bloomfield was also called as one of the witnesses. There was a jury of twelve Spanish people, eight men and four women.

Colin wasn't long on the stand. Briefly he was asked and gave evidence about what he had seen on the beach that fateful morning. The defending counsel didn't pursue him much on any of it. Because the defendant and some of the witnesses were British, the two counsel spoke in fluent English, as did the lady judge, except when they were speaking to the Spanish witnesses. For the evidence that was heard and spoken in English, the jury were provided with headphones, through which they received a translation into Spanish. Similarly, for those parts that were conducted in Spanish, the principal witnesses, which included me, Colin and Desmond, as well as Terry were provided with a similar facility in English. Each time that was about to happen the lady judge forewarned everybody in advance. During the course of the day various police officers, including one of the two detectives I'd met, plus a forensic expert and a psychologist also took the stand. The forensic expert confirmed that the bullet found at the car park could have been fired by one of the guns they found at Terry's villa. He added that the bullet could also have been bought at any gun shop and would fit most standard guns of that nature. The psychologist stated that on examination, he found Terry to be suffering from depression and psychopathic symptoms, probably aggravated by excess amounts of alcohol and drugs.

I was the last of the witnesses to be called. I guess because of my direct involvement, I was the prime witness. The prosecutor questioned me in detail about the shooting incident at the car park near the wood. He made me go over the extent of my injuries, the bullet that the police had found, previously identified by the forensic expert and how close I had come to being murdered. Recalling it all in a court surroundings was difficult. I was also required to outline the time I had spent at the safe houses and my period abroad in Wales. Then, he made me go over the events on the beach when Ben was shot, which for me was even more trying.

'And who was the man who shot your dog?' the prosecutor asked me after I had described the early part of that skirmish.

I looked across the court at Bloomfield. They had cleaned him up a bit for the trial. He was wearing a coloured shirt and fawn slacks His face was still an unshaven mess, but he had received some sort of haircut, however, he still looked a sick man. Sobered up he almost looked remorseful as I stared straight into his eyes and pointed directly at him. 'That man there,' I said forcefully while still pointing, 'Terrance Bloomfield,' I added. For a moment he held my stare then looked down at his feet.

The prosecutor had finished questioning me. The defence counsel though wasn't as sparing with me as he'd been with Colin. He first referred back to the shooting incident at the car park.

'From your evidence,' he began, 'I gather you have never been able to identify the person who took a shot at you there?'

'That's correct,' I said. 'Fortunately or maybe unfortunately for me, I had my back to the assailant. All I really remember is coming round with the paramedics attending to me.'

'So you are not able to identify Terry Bloomfield as your assailant at that incident?' the defence man continued. He was short in build ,with grey short hair, a round face, wearing check court trousers and a dark jacket.

'No I can't,' I said.

'And can I remind the court,' he continued, 'that neither the police or their forensic department can produce any evidence to link my client with that incident.' He looked down at the notes he was holding in his hands. 'Now mister Sherwood,' he said next. 'Is it true that in your capacity as a financial advisor you invested a substantial amount of money, over five hundred thousand pounds in fact, for my client's brother in April of last year.' Earlier when Desmond had stood up to give evidence he had to relate about the disputed money and the fractious argument it had caused between him and his brother. He was also made to confirm that he was aware of the state of penury that Terry had got himself into.

'That is correct,' I said in response to the defence counsel's question to me about investing the money.

'And were you aware of the dispute there was between the two brothers over the money?'

'I was vaguely aware,' I replied. 'At the time it was only mentioned by mister Desmond as an addendum to our discussions. When we first met, the money was in mister Desmond's bank account and he had shown me a copy of the will which clearly stated that the balance of the money was due to him. My job was to advise on the best way to earn income on the money, which is what I did. It was not my business to enter into a family dispute.'

'But you were aware of the money being a contentious issue between the two brothers?'

'Yes, as I said, I was vaguely aware, but I repeat I didn't consider it my job to enter into that dispute.'

During that period of the trial I was gradually becoming aware that Terry's defence counsel were attempting to build up a case for him of diminished responsibilities. 'Ok,' the defence counsel continued. 'Let us now come to the incident on the beach when your dog was shot.' I felt a lump come into my throat. 'Did any of the bullets it's claimed my client fired at you, actually hit you?' He asked.

'No,' I replied feeling my voice quiver with the emotion of it all. 'But they flew all around my head.'

'But none of them actually hit you,' the counsel restated.

'No,' I said, 'or I wouldn't be here today.'

'How many shots were fired?'

'I couldn't say exactly. I was too frightened to think properly. Two or three probably. If I remember that was the number of spent cartridges the police found on the beach.'

'And how far away from you was my client at the time?'

I hesitated before replying. 'About forty or fifty metres I guess. Again I can't be accurate because as I said at that moment I was fearful for my life.'

'Forty or fifty metres,' the counsel repeated. I nodded my head in response. 'Are you aware that my client is highly trained in the use of firearms. In fact he used to be a member of what in England, you call the SAS regiment, which specialises in the use of guns of all descriptions in war zones.'

'I have been made aware of this recently,' I responded, 'but at the time that did not enter my head as if it had I would have been even more fearful for my life.'

'Quite,' the counsel said. Suddenly I could see where this was all leading. 'The point I'm trying to make is that would a man who is specialised at shooting and killing people, as part of his work, be likely to miss a standing target like you at a range of forty or fifty metres if he was really trying to hit you.' The court room fell deathly silent waiting for my reply.

'He probably missed me because of the drunken and drugged state he was in, which the police later confirmed, when they arrested him a very short time after the incident,' I said.

'Ok, but did your dog not run at my client in an aggressive manner, as though he was about to attack him.'

I could feel more lumps forming in my throat as I attempted to visualise the situation. 'Yes, but that was only after Bloomfield had fired the two or three shots in my direction. My dog was only doing what came naturally him, which was to try and protect me in a violent situation.' My voice continued to shake with emotion.

'We perfectly understand and accept that,' the counsel said. 'We don't dispute either that when he was on the beach with you that day my client was in a drunken and drugged state, brought about mainly by the depression he was suffering from. A depression I'm given to understand was as a result of the desperate financial situation he found himself in.' The counsel paused and looked again at his notes, then continued. 'Now, when my client takes the stand later he will claim that he felt, mistakenly or not, that you were responsible for his financial plight and having spotted you on the beach, he was chasing after you to remonstrate with you about the matter. When he approached you, admittedly in his confused and drugged state, he genuinely believed that your dog was going to attack him. He will testify that is why he fired the two or three bullets in your direction, hoping that you might call off the dog. You have already confirmed to us that your dog did race at him in a threatening manner. We now know that my client did regrettably shoot the dog, for which he is sorry. He will testify on oath that in his dilapidated mental condition he genuinely believed he shot at the dog for his own protection.'

'That's not how I saw it.' I replied. 'I can't accept that for one moment.'

The defence counsel and I both looked each other squarely in the eye, then he continued. 'And isn't it true that both you and mister Colin Wright, a previous witness, then both fired shots from different guns at my client as he tried to make his escape from you both?'

'That is true, yes,' I replied. 'But we only fired those shots to try and frighten off that man, Terrance Bloomfield,' I said pointing at him again, 'who had approached me in a threatening and lethal manner, touting a pistol, having already shot my dog dead. What would you have done in the same situation?' I said.

'I have no further questions for this witness,' the defence counsel said and then sat down.

After asking the lady judge's permission the prosecutor got out of his seat and walked towards me to ask me 'some supplementary questions.' 'Can I ask you,' he said to me, 'that before the incident on the beach, had you ever met or seen the accused in person.'

'No,' I replied, 'although I had by then seen a photograph of him. That's how I recognised him on the beach. And after investing the money for his brother I did receive a rather nasty and virulent e-mail from him, blaming me for him not being able to get his hands on any of the money.'

'What did you do about it?' the prosecutor asked.

'I spoke to mister Desmond, who told me to ignore it, which I did, then I completely forgot about it.'

'And you never had any further contact with the accused until the incident on the beach.'

'No I did not,' I replied.

Then I was asked to sit down. When I took my seat amongst the other witnesses I felt I had let our side down. It seemed to me that I was suddenly the one on trial and that my testimony was being disputed. I was gradually beginning to realise that the defence counsel was a very clever man. At the start of the trial Bloomfield had been charged with attempted murder on two counts, being in possession, at his villa, of a substantial cache of unlicensed armaments and illegal drugs, as well as various items stolen from local shops and supermarkets. In addition, resisting arrest and driving without insurance or tax, in a drunken and drugged state, while being well over the legal limit, were also included on the charge sheet. Bloomfield had already pleaded guilty to all those charges, except the two attempts of murder. His counsel, I guess, had realised that he was going to be sentenced to a prison sentence whatever. If he was found guilty of attempted murder he would probably be sentenced to life or what remained of his useful life anyway. However, if he could get him off those two charges and claim diminished responsibility because of his health problems, he would get a much lighter sentence, possibly at a psychiatric prison, where he could receive treatment for that complaint. Those thoughts rattled through my addled brain as Bloomfield took the stand.

Accompanied by two warders he shuffled uncomfortably from the dock to the witness stand. Whether he was putting on an act or not I don't know but he did look a sick man. He stumbled as he got onto the stand and the warders had to help him. He read out the oath in a shaky, croaky voice. The lady judge asked him to speak more clearly. He gave out a hoarse, cigarette infected cough to clear his throat, then his counsel approached him. Firstly he got him to confirm once more that he was pleading guilty to all the secondary charges. Again in a croaky voice, he replied, 'Yes I am. I regret all of them and particularly the shooting of the dog.' He looked across at me when he said that.

His counsel then went on to question him about the charges of attempted murder. He got him to say that he had never in his life visited the car park near the wood where that shooting had taken place. Various times the lady judge had to intervene to ask him to speak up. 'I can't hear a word you're saying,' she abruptly said once. There was more coughing and clearing of the throat by Bloomfield. 'I apologise ma-am,' he even replied on one occasion. 'It's me lungs I'm afraid,' he added in his cockney accent. I remember thinking at the time that it was a lovely bit of acting.

There followed a re-telling of the incident on the beach, this time in his words. With his counsel's prompting he made out that he considered I was responsible for him not getting his share of his father's estate. As a result he had enquired through the financial services registry and discovered the address of my villa. He said he wanted to remonstrate with me on the matter. He admitted that by then his health was in a poor state because of his financial situation and the drugs and alcohol he was consuming were making it worse. With hindsight he said he knew he shouldn't have attempted to approach me in that condition.

As his counsel continued to prompt, he spat out, through more coughing and croaking, his version of the events of that day. Repeatedly the lady judge asked him to speak more clearly. Under questioning he said that when he reached my villa he spotted me on the beach with the dog and ran down from the sand dunes to catch up with me. He claimed that as soon as he got near the dog started to bark at him and jump up on his back legs in a threatening manner. To try and warn the dog off, he said, he began to fire shots from the pistol he was carrying. He maintained that none of them were meant to hit me. Then, when the dog was released and ran directly at him, baring his teeth and barking ferociously, he said he shot at him to protect himself. He told the court that afterwards he bitterly regretted doing it, but added that his actions were partly a result of the mental and depressed state he was in at the time.

At that moment I thought Terrance Bloomfield was entitled to an Oscar for his brilliant acting performance. His counsel then made a real meal of Bloomfield's recollections of me and Colin firing shots at him on the beach. Bloomfield claimed that he had to run for his life to escape from us and our bullets. There were more questions about events that followed which he continued to answer in a contrite, and inarticulate manner.

Afterwards for a good forty minutes or more the chief prosecutor harangued him with questions about his history of debts, the number of armaments he kept at his villa, the amount of drugs and alcohol he was in the habit of regularly consuming and his training and experience as part of the SAS regiment and his later work as a mercenary in Angola and elsewhere. Throughout, in between more bouts of coughing, Bloomfield stuck to his line of not denying any of it. Sobered up, even in his decrepit state, I had to admit that he was no fool. He said he couldn't come up with any alibi for the day I was shot at in the car park. He added that it was so long ago and in the state he was in at the time, with drugs and alcohol, he could hardly remember what happened from one day to the next. He reiterated though that he had never visited that car park in his life and wouldn't know how to find it if he had to.

The prosecutor then said, 'I put it to you that on two occasions, because of your theory that you were cheated out of a share of your father's will, that you tried to extract revenge for that on Mister Sherwood by attempting to kill him.'

'I categorically deny that,' Bloomfield retorted instantly. The prosecutor then sat down.

It was getting towards the end of a long day. The lady judge decided that summing up and the verdict would have to wait until the following morning. Colin and I were left to travel home in moody contemplation of what had taken place. I wasn't happy at all. I felt the defence counsel had turned the whole case on its head and that I was the one whose evidence was up for question. Later on when I was in my villa, Iolanthe telephoned me wanting to know about everything that had happened. It was another sleepless night.

* * * * *

Next day I drove us both to the court house in my old Mercedes. During the journey I expressed my reservations about the outcome of the trial. Colin was of like mind. Before the proceedings began there was a quick conversation with the prosecuting counsel. I took the opportunity to express to him my doubts about the verdict. His reply was that you never knew in these sorts of cases. It depended, very much, he said on how the jury viewed all the evidence. That didn't make me happy at all. The last thing I wanted was Terry Bloomfield free and active and able to take another pot shot at me.

Colin and I settled down in the court room and listened as the two counsels delivered their final presentations. Each of them took about thirty minutes. They both basically reiterated the evidence they had already produced. The prosecution emphasised the state of Terry's mental health and his total disbelief at being left out of his father's will, together with his agitated feelings of revenge, which he had stated that he wanted to take out on me. His defence counsel, when he rose to speak, repeated that his client was pleading guilty to all the secondary charges and was full of remorse about them. He asked the jury to remember that on each occasion of the shootings I had not actually been shot dead, something which his client was more than capable of doing if that had been his intention. He finished by looking directly at the jury and saying, 'I put it to you that there is more than reasonable doubt in this case that my client ever attempted to murder Mister Sherwood and on that basis you should acquit him of the charges of attempted murder.'

Then the lady judge began her summing up which took about twenty minutes. She also mentioned the elements of doubts in the case. At that moment I didn't feel that things were going our way. She then asked the jury to retire and consider their verdict.

Colin and I sought the refuge of a canteen which was situated in the courthouse. When the jury returned in less than two hours I feared the worse. The lady judge asked the foreman if they had reached a unanimous verdict. He confirmed they had. 'And what is that verdict,' she asked him in Spanish. *'No culpable*(Not guilty),' he responded. A noisy murmur spread around the court. Colin and I just looked at each other and said nothing, I shook my head in disbelief. Terry Bloomfield who was already standing, pumped his right arm above his head and shook his fist in celebration. The lady judge said the three judges would then have to retire to consider their verdict on the charges he had pleaded guilty to.

Afterwards we spoke to the chief prosecutor who participated in much shoulder shrugging. Colin and I again retired to the courthouse canteen. We stayed on as I still wanted to know of Terry Bloomfield's fate. I was far from happy at the thought of him being on the loose.

It was another forty minutes before the judges returned. The lady judge read out all the relevant charges and then declared that the defendant would be sent down for five years, initially to a prison that specialised in psychiatric treatment. I let out a sigh of relief. Terry Bloomfield didn't look so pleased. He was taken away muttering to himself.

For Colin and I, it was a tiring drive home. It had been two long, stressful days and I was glad to be able to recourse to the whisky bottle when I eventually got into my villa.

EPILOGUE

For these past few months I have slowly been able to revert to the life I had before all this began, albeit without Ben. I still however seem to carry the mental scars of it all, particularly his death. Maybe they'll never go away. I have buried his ashes in a small plot of earth alongside the beach, near the spot where he discovered the abandoned boat. The plot is marked with a tiny wooden cross, about eight inches in height. On my morning and evening walks down there I say 'morning Ben' and 'good night old pal,' plus a lot of other stupid things as I walk past. Knowing Terry Bloomfield will not be around for at least five years has enabled me to relax somewhat, although a tiny doubt still remains in my head about who actually took a pot shot at me at the car park near the wood. Needless to say I have never been back there since.

Iolanthe continues to visit me for a night, or a weekend, depending on how busy her work schedule is. Our relationship is never going to be like it was at the start. I sometimes wonder how long it will actually last. She is now an independent woman, living off her own income. She has appeared a few times on national television, headlined big cabaret venues and concerts in Madrid, Barcelona and other cities. Recently she acquired her own apartment in Marbella and drives a swish Porsche sports car. A manager now looks after all her bookings and business matters. I gather that Toni Silva still gets ten per cent of his fee. Some things never change, you know. On her last few visits she has tried to persuade me to go to the local animal rescue centre to get another dog. On her next visit she threatens to take me there herself, so I will probably end up doing it.

Colin Wright and I have reverted to the love-hate relationship we had before, but I know I can never repay him for the care and help I received from him during my troubles. Fortunately the financial markets have picked up and I'm earning some decent money again at that. My book is also selling well in the shops in the UK and the USA.

Then out of the blue last week I received an e-mail from Carol Underwood, my brother's girl friend. In it she said she was shortly coming to Spain on a holiday trip and wanted to meet up with me. Instantly I e-mailed Peter to see what the latest situation was between them. By return, amongst other gossip, he related that they had split up a few months back.

Sitting in the lounge of my villa, with the sun blazing through the patio windows, looking at my brother's reply on my laptop screen, I wondered what on earth was next in store for me.

THE END

Richard was born in North Wales. He has also lived in the highlands of Scotland, the Wye Valley, Spain and Majorca. All his page turning novels are set in places where he has had a home.

Milton Keynes UK
Ingram Content Group UK Ltd.
UKHW042034031224
452078UK00001B/118